AFTER THE STORM

A Project Artemis Novel

K.M. SCOTT
ANINA COLLINS

Books by K.M. Scott and Anina Collins
In The Darkness (Project Artemis #1)
After The Storm (Project Artemis #2)

Books by K.M. Scott

Hard Work (Standalone)

If I Dream (Corrupted Love #1)
If You Fight (Corrupted Love #2)
If We Fall (Corrupted Love #3)

Crash Into Me (Heart of Stone #1)
Fall Into Me (Heart of Stone #2)
Give In To Me (Heart of Stone #3)
Heart of Stone Volume One Box Set
Ever After (Heart of Stone #4)
A Heart of Stone Christmas (Heart of Stone #5)
Return To Me (Heart of Stone #6)
Forever With Me (Heart of Stone #7)
Heart of Stone Volume Two Box Set

Temptation (Club X #1)
Surrender (Club X #2)
Possession (Club X #3)
Satisfaction (Club X #4)
Acceptance (Club X #5)

Crave (Addicted To You #1)
Adore (Addicted To You #2)

Shatter (Addicted To You #3)

Claim (Addicted To You #4)

Books by K.M. Scott writing as Gabrielle Bisset

Blood Avenged (Sons of Navarus #1)

Blood Betrayed (Sons of Navarus #2)

Longing (A Sons of Navarus Short Story)

Blood Spirit (Sons of Navarus #3)

The Deepest Cut (A Sons of Navarus Short Story)

Blood Prophecy (Sons of Navarus #4)

Blood Craving (Sons of Navarus #5)

Blood Eclipse (Sons of Navarus #6)

Stolen Destiny (Destined Ones Duology #1)

Destiny Redeemed (Destined Ones Duology #2)

Love's Master

Masquerade

The Victorian Erotic Romance Trilogy

Books by Anina Collins

The Eleventh Hour (Poppy McGuire Mysteries #1)

After Hours (Poppy McGuire Mysteries #2)

Top of the Hour (Poppy McGuire Mysteries #3)

The Darkest Hour (Poppy McGuire Mysteries #4)

Happy Hour (Poppy McGuire Mysteries #5)

The Witching Hour (Poppy McGuire Mysteries #6)

The Finest Hour (Poppy McGuire Mysteries #7)

After the Storm

Kate Sheridan thought she had a handle on life. She had a good job as a legal assistant, great friends, and a life in New Orleans she enjoyed. Until her life became a mess. Now her boss is dead, murdered along with one of his clients, and Kate is on the run from the police who think she's a prime suspect.

And things are going to get worse before they get better because what her boss stumbled on to involves far more than just some case in the Big Easy.

Roman Gregory is proud of his work with Project Artemis. After spending years as an Army Ranger, he's committed to helping women in danger. He's one of the members Nick and Persephone can always rely on to solve a case and get the client's life back to normalcy because he never lets anyone get in his way of handling a problem. And he never lets anyone get close.

Then he's given the assignment in New Orleans and everything changes. But will protecting Kate be something he can do without letting her in?

CHAPTER ONE

IN THE DISTANCE, the raucous sounds of revelers celebrating Mardi Gras in the French Quarter filled the air as Kate Sheridan paced across the old wood floor of her living room waiting for more information to come, terrified by what the first text she received minutes before said.

Something is wrong. Jonas isn't answering his door but I know he's still in his office. I'm calling the police.

Over and over, Kate checked her phone for another message from her co-worker Minnie Donner but saw nothing except the first dreadful text. Jonas Flynn, her employer, was a lawyer and often kept strange and awkward hours when he was deep in working on a case. She didn't want to overreact to his not answering his door when Minnie knocked. Jonas routinely got lost in work and didn't hear the phone ring right next to him, much less a knock on the door a few yards away.

Minnie was just being silly. He probably answered the door right after she called the police and now she's standing there with New Orleans finest having to explain why she bothered them needlessly on one of the busiest nights of the year. Minnie just didn't know how Jonas operated since her boss made sure he never worked past six.

Everything was fine.

Kate stopped and looked down at her phone once again. Nothing.

She wondered if maybe she should call her. Now that she thought about it, she should have done that right off. If she had, she could have stopped Minnie from making such a fool of herself over nothing.

I should call her. Just to put my mind at ease. God, I really don't need this kind of craziness on Fat Tuesday, of all nights. Didn't she remember me telling her I had plans to go out with Eve and her cousin tonight?

As she scrolled through her list of contacts, her phone vibrated against her palm, sending a shiver of fear through her. Quickly, she swiped to her message screen and saw another text from Minnie. Her heart slamming against her chest, she read it, her eyes racing over the words.

Jonas is dead. Found murdered in his office. Two shots to the head. The police

say one of his clients was found dead about an hour ago in his home in Slidell. Why would someone want to kill them? I'll call you when I'm done with the police.

Staring down at her phone, Kate tried to form a complete thought but one word repeated on a horrible loop over and over. Murdered. And she knew just who the client was too.

The walls began to feel like they were closing in on her. She needed to get out of that tiny apartment. But everything had changed now.

Jonas's warnings to her about his case raced through her mind, and fear began to take her over. Was she in danger now too?

This case is huge, Kate. This is bigger than anything I've ever done, but it's more dangerous too, so I don't want you to speak a word about this to anyone. Understand?

She'd nodded her understanding when he made those cryptic statements to her, never giving them much thought as she continued to prepare the brief he needed for later that day for another far less interesting case. She hadn't even thought he was serious when he claimed it was dangerous. Jonas Flynn handled basic, everyday lawsuits. Everyone knew that. What could be so dangerous about suing someone for workplace injuries?

Whatever he'd been doing with that client, it

had gotten him killed, and now Kate wondered if it would get her killed too. She'd been his only legal assistant, so anyone who wanted to get rid of all the people who knew about that case would assume she knew all that he'd been up to.

The truth was, though, that Jonas had kept virtually every detail of this case to himself. Unlike usual, he hadn't made her do much of the work for this client he at first called Mr. X. He wouldn't even tell her the foundations of the case. It had taken him months for him to finally even let her know the man's name.

Not that it would matter now.

She threw a t-shirt, a pair of shorts, a pair of underwear, and her toothbrush in her bag and hurried out of her apartment. Running down the stairs from the second floor of the house she lived in, she ran out to the road and prayed the streetcar would arrive in the next few minutes. As she stood waiting for it, she looked around and worried whoever had killed Jonas and his client could be nearby waiting to kill her.

Stop it! You're being paranoid. Nobody wants to kill you.

Kate looked off in the distance and saw the streetcar slowly making its way toward where she waited. Damnit, why were they always so slow? Never before had she wished New Orleans had a much faster form of transportation.

Like a bullet train.

She rummaged through her purse to find her pass just as the streetcar stopped in front of her, and she hurried on and found a seat close to the driver, somehow thinking that might help her. One look at the thin older man guiding them toward the French Quarter told her if something happened she'd likely have to protect him instead of vice versa. The strongest thing about him was the dayglow green safety vest he wore.

A group of drunk tourists in town for Mardi Gras talked loudly at the back of the street car about which stop to use to get back to their hotel, distracting her for a moment from the awful events of the night. When they piled out onto Canal Street, she followed them in the hope of getting lost in the crowd.

The mob of partygoers in the French Quarter provided her with the anonymity she needed, and soon she arrived at Lafayette's, the bar Eve had said she and her cousin would be at all night. The typical Bourbon Street party spot, it possessed little charm and far too much neon lighting, not to mention the loudest band they could squeeze into the space.

A stunning brunette, Eve towered in four inch heels that made her legs seem like they went on forever in a dress that looked like a metallic gold prom gown that had been cut in half. She stood out from the crowd instantly as she hung out near the end of the bar with a much shorter and plainer woman Kate suspected was her cousin. Not that meeting her and enjoying the festivities mattered much now.

Eve saw her coming toward them and opened her arms wide, a drink in each hand. "Where have you been? We're at least four drinks ahead of you, honey!" she yelled as she enveloped Kate in a drunken embrace that resulted in at least half of the drink in her right hand spilling down Kate's back.

Quickly extracting herself from the hug, Kate waved her toward a corner of the bar where she hoped it would be quiet enough to explain what happened. Eve's cousin stood drunk and confused looking at her, but there was no time to explain or apologize for being rude.

Eve's heels tripped her as they walked toward the corner, causing more of her drink to spill out of the glass as she grabbed onto the back of Kate's shirt. "Damn! I'm not going to have anything to share with you at this rate, honey," she said in her usual chipper voice.

Away from the crowd, Kate could finally hear herself think for the first time since she walked into Lafayette's. Now all she had to do was explain to Eve all that had happened and figure out what she was going to do.

"You know, my cousin Cherise has been dying to meet you. Why did you drag me all the way over here, for God's sake? She's going to think you're a bitch, Kate," Eve said as she sat down hard in a wooden chair she took from a nearby table.

Leaning down close to her friend's face, Kate said, "I need you to listen very carefully to me. Something has happened."

"You didn't wear the dress you said you'd wear. What's going on?" Eve said, completely missing the serious tone in Kate's voice.

She had to be more obvious and let her worry show. All the better. Hiding it was making her more stressed out.

Kate forcefully held her friend by the shoulders so she had to focus on her. "Pay attention, Eve. Something terrible has happened. I think I'm in real danger. I need you to understand. Do you understand me?"

For a moment, she wondered if Eve understood anything she was saying, but then her friend nodded. "I'm a little buzzed, Kate. I'm not stupid. What's got you all tied up in knots?"

Looking around, she checked to see if anyone around them was listening and saw not a single person cared one iota about what they were doing in the corner. She leaned in close near the side of Eve's head, and as the band began blasting some song, she said loudly in her ear, "Someone murdered Jonas tonight. He was found dead in his office."

Eve leaned away and stared at her in horror. "Jesus Christ! Are you serious? Who would want to kill Jonas Flynn, for God's sake? He's a two-bit lawyer who doesn't pay his employees enough and works twenty-four-seven, but none of that is a reason to kill him. Well, other than his being a lawyer."

Stunned at her friend's bad timing for lawyer jokes, Kate's mouth dropped open for a moment before she said, "Now you think is a good time to crack jokes? I'm in real trouble here."

"Why? I mean, it's terrible that someone killed Jonas, but what does that have to do with you? You were just his legal assistant."

"Someone killed one of his clients tonight too. On a case he said could be dangerous. Something's very wrong, Eve. What if whoever killed them thinks I know something? I was his assistant, after all. His only assistant."

Eve stood up and began marching toward the door. "Come on! We need to get you to the police."

"No! I don't want to go to the cops," Kate said, tugging on her friend's arm to stop her. "Plus, you can't leave your cousin all alone here."

That made her stop and she turned around

and nodded. "Right. Let me get her and then we'll all go find a cop. Hang on."

Before she could stop her, Eve had stumbled over to the bar to get Cherise. Kate had a sense as she watched them talk that her cousin didn't want to leave, especially since she seemed to like the good looking guy to her left hanging all over her. All the better. Three would be a crowd anyway.

A few moments later, Eve returned to where she stood and announced her cousin had a good reason to stay. "I think she and that guy are going to get together, so she wants to stay. Let's go find the cops for you."

Kate shook her head, terrified at the prospect of talking to the police about this. "No way. I don't know much about this case, but Jonas told me it had something to do with the police. I don't trust them on this."

"Then what do you want to do?"

"I don't know," Kate said, unsure where to go to find safety. "Maybe if I can just find a place to hunker down for the night I'll be thinking clearer in the morning. Can you stay with me tonight?"

"Sure. Where do you want to go?" Eve asked as they walked outside into the street still full of partiers celebrating the final few hours of Mardi Gras.

Her mind raced with possibilities, each one quickly dismissed as too easy to figure out for anyone looking for her. The noise from a group of drunk guys singing some song next to them made thinking next to impossible. Fucking tourists!

Finally, she remembered that hotel they stayed in that night in high school after the prom. It wasn't exactly The Ritz, but at least it would give her one night to get her head straight and figure out what to do.

"The Bayou Motel. Let's go."

The shock of hearing that name registered on Eve's face, and her eyes flew open wide. "The Bayou? That place is a dive. Only cheating spouses and high school kids who can't afford anything nicer go there. Can't we find somewhere a little posher to go?"

Kate pushed her down the street through the crowd. "There's no time to argue about this. One night in The Bayou Motel won't kill you."

"Honey, that place is an advertisement for tetanus and probably for at least a half dozen STDs."

Grabbing hold of her friend's arm, Kate trudged forward. "I don't have time for this, Eve. Don't argue with me tonight. Just move faster."

Behind her, Eve whined, "Faster where? The Bayou? I don't want to go there, honey. Let's just slow down and think about where we could hang out for the night. How about Keaton's? He's always happy to let us hang when we need to."

Kate listened to her but had no plans to go to their friend Keaton's house. His wife and three kids made that idea impossible. She didn't want to endanger anyone she didn't have to. Dragging Eve into this was bad enough.

"Or what about Pigeon? I know we haven't seen her much since we all graduated high school, but I accepted a friend request from her the other day, so she might be interested in catching up on old times tonight. I can message her right now and we can be hanging out with her in no time."

Tired of Eve's complaining, Kate stopped dead in the street and spun around to face her dear friend, who at the moment she wanted to shake to get some sense into her. "We don't have time for this nonsense. What about that don't you understand? My boss is dead, and his biggest client is too. That's not a coincidence, Eve, so just stop trying to think of someplace else to go and move!"

The people around them stopped for a moment at Kate's yelling, and suddenly she became frightened. Any one of them could be there to find her. She needed to get the hell out of the Quarter now.

Scanning the crowd, she saw a man who looked far too interested in the scene playing out between Eve and her. Was he looking for her? Who was he? Quickly, she tried to think if she'd ever met him, but he looked like every other person in the Quarter that night.

She leaned in close to Eve and said in her ear, "There's a man about fifty yards behind us. Calmly turn around and look at about two o'clock."

Eve did as she instructed her to, and the man began walking toward where they stood. Panicked, Kate yanked on her friend's hand to get her moving again.

"Let's go! Did you see him? Did you see that man with the blond hair and black t-shirt looking at us? He started walking in our direction as soon as we looked back at him."

"I think you're suffering from a little paranoia, honey. I didn't see anyone who even cared what we were doing. He's just one of thousands of people in the Quarter tonight. It is Mardi Gras, you know," Eve said in a breathless voice, struggling to keep up with Kate.

After a few more feet, she became too much of a drag on her, and she had to stop again. Spinning around, she scanned the street for that man but didn't see him anywhere. Had he ducked into a doorway somewhere and was watching them at that very moment?

"What about talking to that cop over there?" Eve asked, pointing down the street.

Kate swiveled her head to look and saw a man

in a police uniform standing on the corner next to a lamppost. She couldn't tell him what was going on, though. She couldn't trust anyone, not even a cop.

"No. I can't. We just have to get out of here and we'll be okay. Come on!"

They hurried down the street for another three blocks until the crowd finally thinned out. Kate took a deep breath and let it out slowly, hoping to give Eve a moment of rest before they continued.

"We need to get a cab. Do you see one?" Kate asked as she looked up and down Canal Street.

"No," she said, shaking her head. "Are you still stuck on that idea of hiding out at that flea bag motel tonight?"

Then, out of the corner of her eye, Kate saw that man in the black t-shirt again walking slowly down Chartres Street toward them. Why did he continue to follow them?

Her body settled into flight mode, and she quickly said to Eve, "He's coming for us. We need to run!"

Jumping off the curb, she nearly got hit by a car, so she hurried back onto the sidewalk, but Eve couldn't go any further. Tearing her hand from Kate's hold, she pleaded with her to just talk to the cop a few blocks back.

"That's what he's there for, honey. He'll help

us."

Panic raced through Kate. "No. I don't know who he is. I don't know if he can be trusted."

Eve opened her bag and took out her phone to dial 9-1-1. "The police can help you, honey. They'll be here in just a few minutes and then you'll be safe."

She couldn't keep doing this with her. As much as she didn't want to go alone to the Bayou Motel, she didn't have a choice. Eve would only continue to slow her down, and with that man slowly coming toward them step after step, she didn't have any more time to waste.

"I can't! I'm sorry, but I have to go. I'll call you when I'm safe," she said as she broke into a full run down Canal Street, unsure where she was going but just knowing she had to get the hell out of there.

A police car sped past her toward where Eve stood, and the last thing she saw before she raced across Canal Street toward the Garden District was a cop getting out of the car to talk to her.

For now, Kate believed she was safe, but the sooner she got to that motel and into hiding, the better she'd be able to figure out her next step. She didn't know who had killed her boss, but she suspected she knew why.

And they'd be coming for her next.

Chapter Two

TOO MANY PEOPLE in one house, even in a house the size of a small country like the Blackmore Estate, meant even when Roman closed the door to his bedroom to find some peace and quiet, he didn't get what he wanted. If it wasn't one of the other guys who lived there knocking on his door to ask him something, it was the construction crew working on the addition he kept hearing would make things much better.

Highly unlikely. It hadn't happened when they put on the last addition, so why would this time be any different?

He'd spent time in close quarters with other men in his lifetime. His years in the military had meant living around dozens of other soldiers, so it wasn't like he didn't know what it would be like when he signed on to Project Artemis. He also knew how lucky he'd been to be recruited first, which meant he got his own bedroom. At least he could count his blessings for that. If he'd had to share with someone like Julian or Xavier, either they or he would have been dead by now.

But something about being out there at the estate they all lived on had begun to make him stir crazy in the past few weeks. He hadn't been out on an assignment in nearly a month. They went in rotation or based on ability, and since being an expert shot hadn't been required, he wasn't next in line.

Not that he necessarily relished the idea of having to go out and work a case.

No, that wasn't it. He just needed to get away from the people he saw far too much of every day. No matter what time he ate meals, it seemed he couldn't find time alone. If he ate breakfast before dawn, someone appeared in the kitchen with him. If he waited and didn't eat until mid-morning, somehow at least one other man showed up to eat at the same time. It had gotten to the point that he almost accepted the fact that he'd never eat alone again.

Added to that, the sound of hammers and saws from morning to night made him feel like if he didn't get the hell away from that place sometime soon, he'd go mad.

Closing his eyes, he laid his head on the pillow at the top of his bed and tried to push out the sounds of the house around him. He felt like a stranger in his own body. Never before had noise bothered him. He'd done two tours in Afghanistan, so he'd lived through the noise of war, for Christ's sake. As he lay there wanting to be anywhere else in the world than that bedroom at the end of the house, he wondered why any of this was bothering him now.

Maybe he just needed to keep himself busy. A few hours out at the shooting range might do him a world of good. With any luck, none of the others would be there too.

Roman sat up and swung his legs off the bed. Sitting on the edge of the mattress, he looked around the room for his gun. He and Marius had gone to the range last week, and he thought he'd left it on his dresser.

Nope. Not there.

Had Xavier borrowed it again like the last time he noticed it missing?

Standing, he marched over to the dresser and moved his comb and after shave for no good reason since the gun clearly wasn't there.

Damnit! This was another reason he'd grown to hate being around all of them.

Roman stormed over to his bedroom door and nearly tore it off the hinges when he flung it open. It slammed off the wall as he headed into the hallway to go find Xavier and his gun. That he had to do this at all pissed him off.

By the time he reached the game room, he

wanted to punch something. Or someone. As usual, Xavier and Gideon sat in the leather recliners watching some game. No matter what the season, those two had a sport they watched religiously. It grated on his nerves now for some reason he couldn't exactly put his finger on as he stood in the doorway looking at the two of them lounged out like two frat boys blowing off class.

The Indians and some other team played on the big screen TV, large enough to make you feel like you were there at the ballpark. He said Xavier's name loud enough that both men could hear him, but neither one responded.

So he said it even louder a second time. Same response.

"Xavier, where the fuck is my gun?" he bellowed from the doorway.

Both men turned their heads, their expressions showing their shock that someone had dared to interrupt their lounging around. When Xavier recovered from his surprise, he muted the TV and returned the leather recliner to its usual position, letting his feet fall to the floor.

"What? Can't you see we're trying to watch the game? What's with coming in here and scaring the hell out of us like that?" he asked, irritated but nowhere close to how pissed Roman felt.

Taking a step into the room, he stopped and

asked his original question again. "Where the fuck is my gun?"

Xavier looked up toward the ceiling to think about it for a moment and then shrugged. "How the hell would I know?"

Roman took another step closer to where he sat. "Because you were the last person around it, other than me, and it's not in my room. Did you borrow it again?"

The word borrow was the nice way of describing how Xavier had a habit of taking things he liked and not returning them. It made Roman want to beat the hell out of the guy. Often.

Once again, he looked up toward the ceiling, like someone had written the answer up there. Nodding, he looked over at Roman. "Oh yeah. Remember I asked you to borrow it because I wanted to decide if I should get a Ruger and wanted to get a feel for it?"

Sometimes this guy made him want to lose his shit. As if a grown man needed to try on a gun like some shirt or pants he wanted to buy.

"Whatever. Where is it? I want to go to the range, so just go get it."

Xavier threw him a disgusted look to tell him he felt put out by his demand and stormed out past him. A few moments later, he reappeared and stuck the gun into his hands. "Here."

Roman looked down at his gun and tightened

his fingers around the grip as Xavier sat back down in the recliner and turned the sound back up on the baseball game. Gideon looked over at him one last time before focusing his attention back on the TV.

Disgusted, Roman turned on his heels and walked out, fed up with those two and their frat boy bullshit. He made it two steps into the hallway before Tess nearly ran into him. Persephone and Nick's very attractive assistant, she was a welcome change to the constant stream of men who seemed to fill his days.

"Roman, Nick wants to see you," she said, catching her breath from rushing down the hall.

He eyed up the beautiful woman who seemed more a gopher than anything else for Nick and Persephone, the two leaders of Project Artemis. Petite with big green eyes and short brown hair, Tess never failed to brighten up the place with her warm smile, and Roman appreciated the interjection of a female in the overwhelming sausagefest the estate had become.

"Any idea what he wants?" he asked as they began to walk down the hallway toward the other side of the main house.

She flashed him that gorgeous smile of hers and shook her head. "You know I'm not privy to those kinds of things. I'm merely an assistant."

The way she said that told him she knew full

well what Nick wanted him for and knew everything that went on at the estate. Merely an assistant. Right.

"Okay, if that's the way you want to play it," he said with a chuckle.

They walked along in silence, neither one of them having anything to say. He didn't mind, though. Never much of a talker, he preferred quiet more often than not anyway.

As they began walking up the stairs to the main level of the house, she finally broke the silence. "It might be nice if he gave you an assignment, though. You've been stuck here for a few weeks now, haven't you? He's given the last five cases to Marius and Dax. Those guys have been out nearly constantly for almost a month."

Looking down at her, he smiled. "For being merely an assistant, you seem to know a lot about all of us and our comings and goings."

Tess stopped on the second to last stair and screwed her face into a grimace. "You have a bad effect on me, Roman. Do you know that? You say so little that I end up filling the space with things I shouldn't be saying."

He looked back at her but kept walking into the main entryway. "Don't blame me. I was just walking along and you started talking."

She stepped up into the foyer and huffed at him. "You strong silent types are the worst. Now I hope he keeps you here and forces you to spend all your time with Xavier and Gideon. How's that sound?"

Turning to look at her in horror at the very idea of being confined with those two sports obsessed frat boys, he shook his head. "You went too far with that, Tess. I'm going to blame you if that happens."

Giggling, she nudged him in the side with her elbow as they continued toward Nick and Persephone's office. "I was just kidding. Don't freak out. Nick wouldn't do that to you. He likes you. Plus, I think he promised Persephone when they started this that he wouldn't do anything to cause anyone's death in the house, and I'm pretty sure you or one of those two would end up dead if he stuck you together."

"You should assume it would be one of them. They'd be easy targets since they never leave that damn game room," he said, not trying to hide his disgust for the two men.

Tess didn't respond and remained silent until just before they reached the office. She touched him on the forearm, and he looked down to see her frowning.

"You might be happier here if you spent some time with any of the other men, Roman. They're really not bad guys once you get to know them."

"Don't worry. I'm not unhappy, Tess. I just

like to keep to myself. Doesn't mean that I'm miserable."

She shook her head and sighed. "Nobody uses the word miserable unless they are, Roman. Give someone here a chance."

"Uh-huh," he said, wishing for more of the silence from a few moments ago.

"You might find out you like them," she said quietly before giving him one of her sweet smiles.

As she walked away to go to her desk, he thought about what she said and immediately pushed the idea out of his mind. He didn't want to spend time with anyone at the estate. Letting people get close only ended up hurting everyone involved. He'd had enough of that in his lifetime to know things were better if he kept to himself.

Pushing open the office door, he walked in to see Persephone sitting at her desk on the left side of the room talking on the phone and Nick sitting on the other side at his desk looking at his laptop. Focused on something, he didn't see him until he tapped on the edge of his desk.

Nick looked up, surprised, and smiled. Extending his arm, he said, "Roman, good to see you. Take a seat. I want to talk to you about an assignment."

As he sat down, he wondered why he always said that when he had a case for him, even though it wasn't like any of them could turn down an assignment. Unless they were on death's doorstep with some kind of disease, each of them was expected to do their job. But Nick always made it sound like they'd discuss the possibility and then decide if he wanted to go.

Roman sat down and waited to hear what his next case would be. The last one had involved a schoolteacher being terrorized by some rich teenager's parents. It wasn't exactly full of danger for him, but that mother and father had been pretty nasty to that poor teacher. All she'd done was given the kid detention for mooning her. She hadn't deserved to have her brake lines cut or to be stalked like prey just because his parents worried he'd be shunned by a good school for the blemish on his high school record. Roman had been happy to see them taken away in handcuffs at the end of things.

Leaning back in his office chair, Nick folded his arms across his chest. "So that woman you helped out in Ohio couldn't say enough nice things about how you handled her case. I guess those parents were a little crazy."

"I'd say they passed crazy going about one hundred and ten miles an hour. They tried to kill her, for God's sake. And over what? One detention because their punk ass kid likes to show his ass to schoolteachers."

The leader of the Project Artemis team

chuckled at his remark. "Yeah. I guess that's the definition of overzealous. Well, this one I have for you today is a little different. No teenage boys showing their asses on this case."

Since his last three cases hadn't exactly challenged him much, Roman sat up straighter in his chair, immediately interested in this new assignment that sounded far more like something he could sink his teeth into. "Oh yeah? I'm all ears."

Nick leaned forward and began tapping on his keyboard. "You're going to be heading to The Big Easy. I don't have many details, but let me bring up what we know."

New Orleans? He had never had a chance to see the city, although he'd served with someone from there who had claimed it was the greatest city on the planet. Even better than New York and Paris, according to him.

He'd always thought that to be a pretty dubious claim since he'd spent time in a lot of great cities around the world and none topped those two. Now he'd see if Butcher had been telling the truth or just bullshitting like usual.

Once he found what he'd been looking for, Nick began to give him the information he'd need to start the case. "The client's name is Kate Sheridan. She's a legal assistant to an attorney named Jonas Flynn. Mr. Flynn was found murdered a few hours ago, along with one of his clients. This woman believes she's in danger and can't go to the police."

"Then how did we find out about her?" Roman asked, confused how Project Artemis was sniffing out these assignments if not by the usual way of through the cops.

Looking up from reading the information on his laptop screen, Nick answered his question. "Her friend told the police down there what I just told you. One of them called Persephone about twenty minutes ago. From what he said, she might be in real danger because they're considering the possibility that her boss's and his client's deaths as mob hits."

"Mob hits," Roman repeated. "That's definitely not some teenager flashing his teacher."

A slow smile spread across Nick's face. "No, it's not. You might be walking into something pretty serious and not overzealous parents bad either."

"I'll start with the friend, so I'm going to need her name and where I can find her."

"Gotcha covered. Her name is Eve Devereux and I'll text you her address," Nick said, nodding as he grabbed his phone.

"Anything else I need to know?" Roman asked, his mind already working on what the cops down in New Orleans thought about the lawyer's death.

"Other than it's a possible mob hit and it's in New Orleans? That's pretty much all the officer told Persephone. He got the feeling this Kate Sheridan's friend knew where she's hiding out, but she wouldn't tell the cops. All she said was Kate didn't trust anyone but her."

"Any chance there's an estranged husband or an ex involved?" Roman wondered aloud.

Something about this case smacked of someone close to her being part of it.

Nick shook his head. "I don't know. I don't have any information about her boss being anything other than that, her boss. No romantic entanglement mentioned."

"And the client? Any idea what kind of case he and the lawyer were working on? I'm thinking maybe he's well-known for mob cases since the cops down there are pinning this on the mob not twenty-four hours in."

Once again, Nick turned back to his laptop and began typing away. "I don't know. Let's see what kind of law Attorney Jonas Flynn practiced."

As he searched for that information online, Roman thought about how good it would be to get away from the estate. Even if just for a few days until the New Orleans police could find Flynn and his client's killer, it would be just what the doctor ordered. Tess may have thought getting chummy with the sports lovers would help, but he knew better.

Time away and work were what would make him happy. The more he had to focus on a case, the better off he'd be.

Still looking at his computer, Nick read what he'd found out about Flynn. "He was just a regular lawyer who handled a lot of basic personal injury cases. You're average, run-of-the-mill legal eagle. Nothing special. He has no reputation for any special kind of cases which would make him a mob lawyer or anyone associated with the mob."

He turned to face Roman and said exactly what was running through his mind at that moment. "I wonder why the New Orleans police tagged this as a possible mob hit."

"Must be because of the way the two victims were killed. I'm guessing something pretty damn violent if they're going with the mob as being behind this. The mob likes to make sure killing someone gets the point across. Never really ones for subtlety."

Nick rifled through a small stack of papers on the other side of his desk and picked one out of the pile. After scanning it for a moment, he shook his head.

"No. They were both found shot in the head, but there's nothing to even hint at a mob hit. The client, Samuel Darnell, was a carpenter. Why the hell would the mob give a damn about someone like him?"

Roman had no answers for him. All he had were more questions. "So what was this carpenter's case Flynn was working on? Maybe that's what got them killed? That might explain why the legal assistant thinks her life is in danger."

A few more seconds of reading through notes and then Nick shrugged. "Weird. We have nothing on what the case was. I wonder why the cops didn't bother to share that information."

"Maybe they didn't think it was related?" Roman suggested, knowing how ridiculous that sounded.

"A guy and his lawyer are killed on the same day and cops don't think the case that connects them is related to their murders? This isn't some backwater small town we're talking about, Roman. This is New Orleans. Let me ask Persephone."

Nick yelled over to the other person who ran Project Artemis, and she held up a single finger to tell him to hold on while she talked on the phone. A few seconds later, the woman who founded the group Roman worked for walked over to join them at Nick's desk.

"Sorry, I was on the phone. Nick, I think I have a case for Julian, so let him know when you're done here. He'll have to leave as soon as possible."

"Okay, but first, Roman and I are trying to figure out why we don't know what case this Flynn guy was working on with the client who was also murdered in the New Orleans assignment with this Sheridan woman. Seems like an important detail we should have, doesn't it?"

For a moment, Persephone stared at Nick and then looked over at Roman, her dark eyes narrowing as she thought about what she'd just heard. "Hmmm. I don't know. The officer who called me told me they didn't have a lot of details on what was going on, but they thought it might be a mob hit. We're not going with her being in danger of being the next victim?"

Nick shrugged. "No, that's not it. She very well might be a target of the person who killed her boss and his client since she probably knew about the case, but it seems strange we don't know what that case was about."

"I can call him back, but I think this Kate Sheridan is in real danger, gentleman. Why don't we start working this case, and when I find out the details about this legal case, I'll send it to Roman."

The two men agreed, and as she began walking to her desk, she looked back at Roman. "The plane is waiting for you. Tess can have the helicopter ready to go when you are, but I don't think we should wait much longer to get going."

Roman had worked for Persephone long enough to know when she was truly worried about a client. She didn't show it on the outside, remaining cool and collected like always, but concern hung off every word. She had a sixth sense about this kind of thing, and he couldn't explain it other than the fact that she herself had gone through something hellish that made her start the group to help women in danger. Whatever it was, he didn't doubt her gut feeling on things like this.

It dawned on Roman that he had no idea what this Kate Sheridan looked like. "I need to see a picture of our client and then I'll be on my way."

Nick spun his laptop screen around to show him a picture of a woman with brown shoulder length hair and blue eyes. Next to it, he read her vitals. Twenty-eight years old, single, five foot seven. He found himself staring at her image because something about her screamed smart and confident even with her girl next door looks.

He had to admit he liked the combination.

Standing to leave, Nick stopped him with a serious glance. "Watch yourself down there, Roman. Mob hit or not, something sounds wrong with this case."

"Don't worry. You know me. I take care of

business and then I leave. I'll probably be finished before the weekend and then I'll be back to dealing with going stir crazy in this house again."

Roman hoped that wouldn't be how it went down, though. He craved some excitement in his life. The last thing he wanted was another schoolteacher case he could wrap up in a couple days.

At the very least, he hoped this Kate Sheridan would turn out as interesting as he'd decided she was from her picture.

CHAPTER THREE

HER EYES FLUTTERED open, and Kate saw the reality of the room around her hadn't all been just some horrible nightmare. The bedspread with its bizarre red and brown geometric print and triangles that looked like they would stab a person in their sleep still lay underneath her. She'd pulled it back when she got to the room and there in front of her eyes were dingy white sheets with stains she didn't even want to think about or guess where they came from.

Or who they came from.

Eve hadn't been wrong. The Bayou Motel could best be described as a dive. The idea that cheating spouses came to this place to have their sexy rendezvous made Kate's stomach turn. She'd had to talk herself into sleeping on top of the bedspread. No amount of convincing, even if it was from the sexiest man on the planet, would ever get her beneath those sheets.

Rolling over, she looked down at the floor and the worn green carpet that matched nothing else in the room. Green floor, strange red and brown pointy triangle bedspread, and draperies that had been white at some point in their existence but now appeared like what she thought the color white would look like if all the other colors in the spectrum had ganged up on it, beating white senseless and leaving nasty streaks of their colors on it after their brawl.

The entire feel of Room 12 at the Bayou Motel made her sick to her stomach.

Inhaling, she couldn't say the smell helped either. The room had a putrid odor to it, but she couldn't place the scent. Possibilities ran through her mind, each one worse than the one before. Did dried blood smell like that? She thought she caught a whiff of vomit in the mixture that threatened to make her add to the horrible smell around her.

The thought of putting her feet down on that carpet caused her to cringe, so she'd slept with her shoes on. The only other choice would have been to recreate the game of lava floor she and her sister had played when they were kids. The problem with that was there was nothing to climb on to avoid touching that ugly carpet with God only knew what stains on it. Even the pillows at the top of the bed looked disgusting with their dingy off-white color, so she couldn't use them to create a pathway around the room either.

Staring up at the ceiling with its brown water stains, she mumbled, "I can't believe this is what my life has become."

The truth of it was her life would now be her on the run until she figured out what to do. With Jonas dead, she had no job, but even worse, whoever killed him and his client would likely be looking for her too because they'd guess she knew the details of the case as well as Jonas.

Even if she didn't.

That fact made everything that had happened so much worse. Jonas had kept her in the dark about much of the Darnell case. She'd asked him over and over about it because each time he gave her something to do regarding it, she had nothing to work with. Being in the dark about the details, she constantly had to ask him for help. But each time, he refused to give her anything more than the sparsest details she needed to do what he wanted.

Even thinking about it now, she still had no clear idea what Mr. Darnell had come to Jonas for. A carpenter from Slidell, he hadn't been in an accident of any kind. Those were usually the kinds of cases Jonas represented, but Samuel Darnell wasn't disabled from a car crash or industrial mishap. In fact, she'd only seen this mysterious client once and he'd looked perfectly average and healthy to her.

A white man in his early fifties or so, he didn't walk with a cane and appeared fit. So why had he hired Jonas Flynn, a lawyer who spent much of his career on what many would consider ambulance chasing? Whatever personal injury his client had suffered, Kate had never been able to ascertain exactly what it was and how it affected him.

Or why he'd need an attorney.

Jonas had kept her so much in the dark that she didn't even do his filings for that case. Her job had been relegated to looking up old newspaper articles about Hurricane Katrina and the aftermath in Lafayette. And when she'd ask him why, he simply nodded his head before returning to whatever work he was busy with.

Except for two nights ago. Then, she asked why he needed all this information, and his eyes grew wide. Never before had she seen Jonas look afraid, but that night in his office, the terror she saw in his eyes told her something or someone had scared the hell out of him. And then he said the words she'd never forget until the day she died.

"This case is going to cause an earthquake in this state, Kate. I'm doing everything I can to protect you, but if I fail, trust no one, especially the police and the government."

He refused to say anything more, and she was

left with two statements that made little sense and even less when put together. His words rang in her ears now as she sat in that horrible motel room near the river, sending a chill down her spine like they had when he'd first said them.

Kate had no idea what her boss had tried to protect her from or who, but he'd failed and in that he'd lost his own life. Tears welled in her eyes at the thought of Jonas gone. In the four years she'd worked for him, never once had she heard even the hint of a complaint from a single soul about him. Sure, he wasn't a crack attorney who'd ever take a case to the Supreme Court, and his cases were often more about people trying to get money for injuries that really didn't change their lives much than addressing real and tragic harm done to his clients.

But in the big scheme of things in a city full of corruption, Jonas Flynn had helped some people along the way and made a few bucks for himself and her, his only assistant. He never got rich, and even though he had an office in a building with other lawyers, they never associated with him socially. He simply wasn't big enough or important enough.

Until now. Something had changed to make Jonas Flynn and his client, Samuel Darnell, very important to someone. Important enough to kill them.

Kate took a deep breath of fetid motel room air into her lungs and let it out slowly as a single thought filled her brain. She had to figure out who had killed Jonas and his client and why. But to do that, she needed first to find a safe place to hide that didn't make her skin crawl.

She'd paid for the night under a name that was a combination of her first name and her mother's maiden name. Not that Landrieu as a last name would help her stay under the radar, but she hoped it at least made it slightly harder for someone to find her than her own name.

Fuck. She wasn't good at this cloak and dagger stuff. She kept on the right side of the law at all times. She paid her taxes like she should, and whenever she got behind the wheel of her friend's cars, she made sure to wear a seatbelt and not drive over the speed limit. Damnit, she'd done everything right and look where it had gotten her.

Hiding out in a shithole motel room that smelled like a mixture of blood and vomit.

"I can't meet my end here," she mumbled as she rolled off the bed and set her feet on the floor. "I won't. If they're going to kill me, I'm going to at least die in a decent place."

As Kate walked across the room to the nastiest bathroom ever, she thought about that little bout of bravado she'd just showed. Pretty ballsy for someone who had no way to escape the city, little money to pay for anything, and no one to help her.

She flipped the switch on the wall that made the fluorescent light flicker on above the medicine cabinet that doubled as a mirror and stared at her reflection in front of her. A crack in the mirror ran diagonally through her face, giving her a nice funhouse look with the top half of her head shifted left and the bottom half shifted right.

"You've had bad mornings before, Kate, but this takes the prize. No hangover beats this look you've got going on now," she said to herself, punctuating her comment with a sardonic chuckle.

For all the partying she'd done in her late teens and early twenties, none of those mornings after had ever looked this bad. Her mascara sat underneath her blue eyes, accentuating the dark circles there from a poor night's sleep. Yesterday's youthful and attractive look had given way to today's mess, and since she didn't have any makeup with her in her purse, she'd have to go through the day looking like this.

Even worse, her dark hair looked like those bedspread triangles had come to life during the night and gone to war with one side of her head. Tangled and frizzy, that half looked only marginally worse than the other half that sat pressed to her scalp.

"You're the personification of this motel room," she groaned to her reflection.

Behind her, the old shower curtain hung in a clump at the end of the rod to show off the black and mildewed grout lines between grimy green tiles. As she tried not to focus on the millions of microbes that must be living on that shower wall, she wondered if the tiles were supposed to match the carpet.

"No shower for me today, it seems," she said as she forced herself not to look at the disgusting shower.

She didn't even want to imagine how bad the tub looked. One glance at that and she might really throw up. Keeping her eyes on the mirror in front of her, she turned the hot water faucet handle with her left hand and heard the pipes make a terrifying groan, as if she'd awoken some horrible creature that lived inside them. Quickly, her gaze dropped to the sink to see what would come out, but after a few more angry groans, nothing happened. She turned the hot water handle completely off and prayed for better luck with the cold water.

Hopefully, the monster that controlled that temperature would be friendlier.

Cautiously, she turned the handle with a C on it and watched in surprise as water actually flowed into the sink. A smell like low tide hit her nostrils, turning her stomach for a moment, but she'd take the slightly murky cold water over nothing at all.

Wetting her hands, she scrubbed her face and wiped the area underneath her eyes until she no longer resembled some goth or punk rocker chick. Once more under the water to get her hands wet again and then she dragged her fingers through her hair to fluff the one side and untangle and calm the other.

When she finished, Kate looked into the mirror again and saw not much improvement. She looked about as good as she felt, which considering what she'd been through in the past twelve hours and where she'd spent the night was pretty damn bad.

If only her biggest problem was how she looked.

Clean and as ready for the day as she possibly could be, Kate next had to tackle finding out what information the police had released on the murders. Someone had stolen all the knobs from the old TV that sat on top of the dresser, so finding out that way wouldn't be happening. She'd seen a newspaper machine on the sidewalk about half a block away from the motel when she arrived the night before, so hopefully the paper had something to help her.

Opening the motel room door, she poked her

head out and looked around at the world outside. She saw no one in the parking lot, and looking down the sidewalk toward where guests checked in, she saw no one working the desk. Clearly, the Bayou Motel didn't expect many cheating spouses or high school partiers at five-thirty in the morning.

She felt her back pocket for the key she'd gotten when she paid for her room and found it still there, so she stepped outside onto the sidewalk in front of the motel. A handful of cars sat parked in front of other rooms. Looking out toward the road and the sidewalk that ran next to it, she saw the newspaper machine chained to a telephone pole.

Kate ran as fast as she could to it before realizing she might not have enough change to get a paper. Stopping in front of the navy blue newspaper vending machine covered with stickers from local bands and people's pet causes, she rummaged through her pockets but only found a quarter, two dimes, and a penny.

"Who the hell carries change anymore?" she asked before cursing out the newspaper business. "No wonder these damn things are going the way of the landline."

As she considered trying to break into the machine by kicking her foot through the glass front, she saw the entire front page of that day's newspaper edition displayed for her. Crouching down, she read the headline at the top and the sentence beneath it that stunned her.

LOCAL LAWYER FOUND DEAD
Police looking into possible love triangle

Kate sat back on her heels in amazement. Possible love triangle? That was the line they were spinning? A love triangle between a forty-five year old lawyer who was married to his work and hadn't dated in ages, a man in his fifties, and who?

A horrible thought rushed into her mind. Did they think she was the third in that love triangle and she'd killed both men? Was she a suspect in the two murders?

The very thought made her blood run cold.

Suddenly, she felt utterly vulnerable out there in the open, so she rushed back to the room and slammed the door shut. She pressed her back against the door and tried to catch her breath as her heart raced.

Maybe she was overreacting. She had to be, right? No one in their right mind would think she, Jonas, and Samuel Darnell were involved in a love triangle. They'd never been in a room together for more than a minute. Anyone in the offices or in the building where Jonas had his law office could attest to that. Why the hell were the police floating the idea of a love triangle no one could possibly say they had any evidence of?

This couldn't be happening. All she was guilty of was going to work every weekday and doing her job. She couldn't believe anyone would ever think she could kill anyone, least of all her boss she liked or a man she didn't even know.

Her mind raced with what to do next. She couldn't go to her family. That would only put them in danger. They didn't deserve that, even if they could help her.

She ran through the names of her friends, deciding after each one popped into her mind that she couldn't go to them either. That she had dragged Eve into this whole mess even as much as she had filled her with regret.

Then the memory of that man following them through the French Quarter came rushing back to her, bringing tears to her eyes. In her haste to get away, she'd left her best friend alone with him just a block behind.

Kate covered her face with her hands and began to cry. "How could I have done that to her? What if he got to her before the police showed up?"

She had to find a way to see if she was okay. God, what had she done?

Her eyes flew open at the sound of someone

outside the door, pushing thoughts of Eve out of her head. Was she going mad? Had she heard anything or was her mind playing tricks on her?

She strained to listen for the sound again but heard nothing. Good God! At this rate, she'd be out of her mind by day's end.

Then she heard that sound again. Closing her eyes, she listened and thought she heard breathing. Someone stood on the other side of the door. What could they be doing there? What did they want?

She silently prayed to God the person outside was that pimply-faced check-in clerk she'd met last night. Maybe he'd stepped away from his desk for breakfast and now wanted to offer her fresh towels or something like that.

Or maybe the person on the other side of the door stood ready to blow her away the moment she opened it to see who it was. She spun around to check the peephole to see who stood out there and found no peephole in the door.

Christ! How could such a seedy place not have peepholes? What kind of people just opened the door to strangers who could be ax murderers?

Clearly, the people who stayed at the Bayou Motel.

Terrified the person outside would try to get in, she tried to lock the door, but her fingers fumbled with the doorknob, causing it to make a sound whoever was outside had to hear. Then, her heart skipped a beat as the knob began to turn against her hand.

They were coming in!

She backed up into the center of the room and looked around for anything she could use to defend herself. The TV was from sometime in the mid-eighties and stuck out from the wall like two feet, so it would be too heavy to pick up. Her head swiveled over toward the nightstand and the hideous oversized frosted glass lamp. That could work.

Running over to it, she gripped the base and yanked hard, but the thing wouldn't budge! This place didn't worry about letting guests see who was outside their doors, but they worried about people stealing ugly lamps so much they screwed them to the nightstands?

She was about to die in the worst motel in the world run by people with no sense of priorities.

Frozen in place, she watched as the door slowly opened. Her heart pounded so hard she wondered if it would explode out of her chest. Whoever this person was who planned on coming into her room, they better be ready for a fight. She didn't have anything to defend herself with, but she could kick and bite as if her life depended on it.

As she planned her attack, a man walked in,

and she felt like all the oxygen had been sucked out of the room. He closed the door behind him and stopped, leveling his gaze on her. It felt like he was looking into her soul.

This man stood perfectly still, and for a moment, she wondered if he'd changed his mind about killing her. She didn't see a gun, but that didn't matter. Someone his size could easily snap her in half with his bare hands.

His short hair made him look like a soldier. Was he some kind of mercenary hired to kill her now that he'd killed Jonas and Samuel? What had her boss gotten himself into that made someone like this come after him?

"I'm not going to let you kill me," she said as a second surge of bravado came over her that morning.

The very large, very muscular man took a step toward her and shook his head. She waited for him to say it wouldn't matter what she did because he had orders or whatever hit men said right before they killed their targets, but he said nothing.

She paused for a moment and then her flight or fight instinct kicked in. Her desire for self-preservation chose fight, so she lunged at him, ready to defend herself to the death.

CHAPTER FOUR

ROMAN HAD ONLY a few seconds to size up the woman in front of him before she came at him like a madwoman. As beautiful as he thought she would be from her picture, Kate Sheridan also appeared to be out of her mind.

Her arms flailed in front of her as she lunged at him, doing nothing to a man his size. Even though her face looked menacing, well sort of, the way she tried to attack him made him want to laugh.

Pushing her back, he held his arm out to keep her far enough away so he could say something to let her know she didn't need to act like this. As he moved to calm her, she caught his jaw with her nails and scratched him clear to his neck.

Stunned, he picked her up and pinned her to the bed. She looked up at him not with rage in her eyes but fear that bothered him.

"If you promise not to take another swing at me, I'll let you up," he said in a sincere voice he hoped would convince her to calm down.

It had the opposite effect, though. With a nasty scowl she tried to get free, kicking her legs out at him and pushing on his hands that still held her down by the shoulders.

"I'm not going to just let you kill me, you bastard!"

He leaned down close to her face and quietly said, "I'm not here to kill you, Kate. I'm here to help you."

For a moment, she stilled and seemed to consider what he said, but then she shook her head and returned to trying to kick her way free. "You're holding me down. Why would someone who wants to help me do that?"

Done with being calm, he raised his voice and barked, "Because you're acting like a banshee. Now promise me you'll behave yourself and I'll let you up."

Her eyes flashed pure anger. "Behave myself? Don't talk to me like I'm a child. You don't even know me. Let me up!"

Roman found this woman infuriating. Twice her size, he could crush her like a bug with no effort whatsoever, but still she fought with everything she had. He couldn't help but be impressed by her courage, though.

He let go of her and backed up a step, hoping to show her that he wasn't there to harm her. It didn't work. She bolted toward the door, so he stepped in front of her.

Holding her by her wrists, he shook his head. "Kate, I'm not letting you leave, so you might as well stop trying."

Even that didn't work. Clearly still on the defensive, she refused to listen to what he said. No matter. He had a job to do, and he had no intentions of budging from that spot until she calmed down and listened to him.

She looked up at him, visibly confused. "Why? Who are you? If you're not here to kill me, how did you find me?"

Roman raised his right hand and smiled. "I swear on my honor I'm not here to hurt you. We really don't have time for me to explain who I am. I just need you to trust me."

She stopped fighting him and for a brief moment, Kate stared up at him in a way that made her look vulnerable. Something about it triggered a reaction in him he hadn't felt in forever. Bothered by it, he let go of her hands as he looked away.

As he fought back an emotion he'd sworn he'd never feel again, she sat down on the bed. "So I'm supposed to trust you, a perfect stranger? Maybe I should know your name then."

Turning to face her, he watched as she rubbed her wrists from where he'd tightly held her. "Roman. My name is Roman."

"Roman what?" she asked like he just said something odd.

"Just Roman. Get your stuff. We need to get out of here."

She scowled again and mumbled "Just Roman" but she didn't move.

Frustrated, he said sternly, "We have to go."

Stubbornly, she crossed her arms and stared up into his eyes. "I know nothing about you, so why would I just up and leave with you, just Roman? Like, here's a good question. How did you find me? No one knows I'm here. Well, except the people who may be trying to kill me. So how did you find me if you're not here to kill me?"

Roman took a deep breath and let it out in a heavy sigh. He understood her being skeptical, but wasn't it obvious he didn't plan on killing her since he hadn't done it yet? He could have at any point since he walked through the door.

Pinching his nose, he groaned. "Your friend Eve told the police you'd probably come here to hide out. Someone in the New Orleans Police Department let my firm know you needed help, and I was the lucky soul who got assigned to the mission. When you went out to get the paper, I spied you from across the street. So now that I've brought you up to speed, let's go."

Kate didn't seem happy with his explanation,

though. Holding her head, she began to pace back and forth in front of him across the room.

"God, Eve! Why would you tell the cops, of all people? Do you want to see them kill me?"

On one of her passes, he grabbed her, spun her around to face him, and held her in place by the shoulders. They didn't have time for this. This woman needed to get her damn head together.

"Did you not understand me? We need to get out of here before the people who want to kill you get here."

"I know full well what you said, but since Eve told the very people who would like to see me dead, it's probably too late."

"Who do you think wants to kill you?" he asked as she turned out of his hold and began pacing again.

Kate stopped and glared at him in exasperation. "The police! Aren't you listening to me?"

"Why do you think the New Orleans police want to kill you? Nothing I was told makes that sound even remotely the case."

She shook her head and huffed her disgust at what he said. Throwing up her hands, she snapped, "And just what were you told? Because if the cops were the ones doing the telling, that explains why you're stalling and trying to keep me here."

Roman felt his mouth drop open as he looked at her in shock. He was the one stalling and keeping her there? This woman was certifiable.

"Rewind a minute and you'll see how wrong you are. I'm the one who was just trying to get you to leave here with me."

Kate jabbed her finger toward him. "Ah-ha! See? You keep getting me to argue with you so I won't leave. You're trying to keep me here. Why? Is your partner running late and you need to waste time until they get here? Is that it?"

He didn't give a damn how beautiful this woman was. She clearly had lost her mind. Roman didn't have the patience or interest in finding out what had sent her around the bend, though. He just needed to get her the hell out of there before whoever had killed her boss and his client showed up looking for her.

Taking a step toward her, he reached out to grab her by the arm. She anticipated his movement, though, and spun away out of his hold once more. Jesus, was this woman a ballerina in her spare time?

"We don't have time for this craziness. I don't know what your problem is, but we have to go. I'm not going to hurt you. I'm here to help you. You need help, whether you know it or not, Kate. I'm that help, so let's get moving."

She held up her hands in front of her as if to

signal her surrender, and for a split second, Roman felt they were making some progress. But then she began talking again, and any progress he had hoped for evaporated into thin air.

"Whoa! You don't make the decisions here, pal. I don't even know who you are, just Roman. So until you give me some more details about who you are and why you're here, I'm not going anywhere with you."

At that moment, he had to admit he missed the teenage mooner and his psycho parents. While they had been borderline insane, he at least could figure out what their motives were and Karen, the schoolteacher, had been a true delight compared to this woman.

He tried to keep his calm and quietly asked, "What do you need me to tell you to convince you I don't want to hurt you since it's obviously not enough evidence that I haven't done anything yet and I've been standing in this motel room for the last five minutes? You do realize you're like half my size. I could have snapped you in half easier than a twig two seconds after I walked in here."

A look of disgust came over her face, and as her right hip shot out, she set her hand on it in defiance. "No, you couldn't have. I know how to defend myself, just Roman."

The chuckle that erupted from his throat

couldn't be stifled, even if he wanted to stop it. She thought she was tough when she was anything but.

"No, you don't. You know how to flail around like a fish on the end of a line. Anyone looking to hurt you could have had you down on that bed and under their complete control in a matter of seconds."

Instead of frightening her, his words only made her angrier. She took a step toward him and stopped about a foot away, craning her neck to look up at him.

"I don't know who you think I am, but no one has complete control over me, buddy. And as for me being down on that bed—"

Roman cut her off before she got too far into her rant. "Enough. If I tell you all I can about me, will you at least try to think logically so we can get the hell out of here?"

Kate opened her mouth to protest, probably hating the part where he more than insinuated that she wasn't acting sane, but after a few moments finally said, "Fine."

"As I told you half a dozen times already, my name is Roman. Your friend told the police that she thought you were in trouble, and someone from the New Orleans Police Department called the firm I work for, Project Artemis."

While he spoke, Kate relaxed and seemed to

listen. Roman expected her to lash out at any time, though, so he kept his guard up as he continued to explain how and why he'd come to help her.

"My entire job is to safeguard you from danger. I promise you I mean you no harm."

Kate's shoulders sagged and she let out a huge sigh. "Okay, just Roman. What exactly is this Project Artemis anyway? I've never heard of it. Are you guys like the X-Men or something?"

She didn't mean to be cute, but he couldn't help but smile at her question. "No, we're not like the X-Men. We're just men who work for two people who've decided to dedicate their lives to protecting women like you, women in danger. Nothing supernatural or special about that. Just good people trying to do good things for women who need our help."

"Just men? Aren't there any women who do your job?" she asked, narrowing her eyes to slits.

Roman had never put any real thought into why there were no women who worked alongside them, other than Persephone. Now that Kate had asked the question, he tried to find an answer that wouldn't elicit another argument with her.

"Not that I know of yet, but I'm not in charge. I just go out on the assignments as I receive them."

Slowly, Kate lowered herself to the bed and

sat down. "So who is in charge? Another guy like you?"

The hint of contempt in her tone bothered him, so he quickly explained how Project Artemis had come to be. "No. A woman named Persephone started Project Artemis after she was kidnapped. She and the man who helped her escape her captors run the group and the focus is on helping women like she was helped."

Looking up at him, she forced a tiny smile. "Oh. Well, it's hard to say anything bad about that, I guess. So you and the others who work in this Project Artemis put yourselves in harm's way for women like me who you've never met for what reason? Do you have a death wish or something?"

Whatever else Kate Sheridan was, she definitely had a way of making him laugh. Chuckling at her question about them having a death wish, he thought about Xavier and Gideon and considered the possibility that one of them might. Marius definitely seemed to like the job more than most of them, so maybe he did too.

But he definitely did not have a death wish.

He shook his head. "No death wish. It's just my job to help you. That's it. If I can do it without getting hurt, all the better, but I know my duty being part of Project Artemis. Your safety is my top priority."

Kate looked at him with a strangeness in her eyes. "And your other priorities? What about them?"

Confused, Roman shook his head again, not understanding her questions. "What do you mean other priorities? My job is to protect you."

"That's it? Who's paying for you to do this for me?" she asked, her suspicion clear.

She still didn't believe he was there to help her.

"Nobody pays us to protect anyone. Project Artemis is self-funded," he answered proudly.

"So you do this for free? Are you independently wealthy? Did your family invent shoelaces or something, so you don't have to work a regular job?"

Roman had to admit this woman had a way of making him want to laugh one minute and walk away from her the next. He'd never met anyone so unwilling to trust in his life.

"No, my family is just like most people's. No shoelace empire here. Project Artemis pays me to do this. Now, have I answered enough of your questions so we can get out of here?"

She stood from the bed and put her hands on her hips. Clearly, he wouldn't be spared more questioning, so he waited for the rest of her interrogation. He just hoped all this question and answer business wouldn't put them in danger. He honestly had no idea who might be after her, and he had a gut feeling it would only be a matter of time before whoever they were found out where she was hiding.

"I have about a hundred more questions, but at the very least, you need to answer one more."

"Fine. What do you want to know?" he asked, relieved she only wanted to know the answer to one more question.

Kate stared up at him for a long moment and asked the only question he didn't want to answer for her. "What is your last name, just Roman?"

And there it was, the one piece of information he never shared with clients. Most of them didn't ask, strangely enough. They were too busy hoping to live and doing whatever it took to make that their priority to care what his name was. To every one of them, he'd been Roman. It gave him a way to keep them at arm's length so he could do his job more effectively. He didn't want to ever get close enough to any client to share that part of him.

Letting a client in like that could endanger both of them. He never wanted to risk that again.

"You can just call me Roman, okay? Let's go."

He turned to walk toward the door, but Kate stopped him by grabbing his arm. Looking back, he saw she didn't plan to give up on this.

"How am I supposed to trust a person who

won't even tell me his last name? You know who I am and things about me I'd rather you not know, for God's sake. Do you think I enjoy having a near perfect stranger knowing someone out there might want to kill me and thinking I can't take care of myself? I'm not asking for your blood type or how many people you've slept with. I just want to know your last name."

"A and less than ten. Can we go?" he answered, pulling her toward the door.

"Damnit, Roman! You expect me to trust a man who comes waltzing into my motel room who won't even tell me his whole name? No way. I'll take my chances on my own. I'm not trusting someone who refuses to tell me something so simple."

He closed his eyes and tried to remember he needed to be patient with her. That her world had been turned upside down in the past day and she'd lost someone she cared for. But the truth was, what she asked wasn't simple. Telling her his full name meant sharing with her something he'd never shared with any other client.

It meant letting her in just a little more than he'd ever let anyone else in since…

"Kate, let's go. My job is to protect you, and that's what I intend on doing. If that means having to carry you out of this place over my shoulder, I'll do it. I'd prefer not to go that route, but I will do it."

Before she could argue anymore, a loud banging on the door a few rooms away stunned the two of them. A voice bellowed out, "Kate Sheridan! This is the New Orleans police! Open up!"

Roman reached back to pull out his gun from his pants and turned back to look at Kate. He saw all the defiance she'd displayed since he arrived disappear. Terror filled her eyes at the sound of the police officer outside.

But were the cops really the people she should be afraid of? He had a hard time believing they had any part in her boss's death or that of his client's.

Kate grabbed hold of his hand, her blue eyes full of fear, and pleaded, "I swear to you if they find me, they'll make me disappear. They think I know everything about the case. I don't, but it won't matter. I can tell you're a law and order kind of guy, maybe even a former cop yourself, so you instinctively think the cops are good, but they're not. Not in this case. You can't let them take me."

Roman wondered if Persephone and Nicholas had been wrong about this woman. Was she in danger, or was she the one who'd killed her boss and his client? The papers were already claiming a love triangle lay at the bottom of this case. Were they right? Going against the cops felt wrong to him, but something about Kate made him want to help her.

Even more than want. He needed to help her, even though he couldn't understand it since up until the cops arrived, she'd fought him every step of the way so far.

The pounding started on the door next to the room where they stood, and she begged, "Please just get me out of here and then you can go back to your happy life and forget all about me. Please, Roman."

How wrong she was when she described his life as happy. When he returned to the estate, he'd go back to being alone, even in a house filled with people, and he'd crave the time when he received his next assignment just so he could fill his days with work.

The cop outside began barking orders to open the door, and Roman knew they didn't have much time to escape. Taking her by the hand, he pulled her toward the bathroom as she grabbed her bag.

"We'll go out through here," he said as he threw up the window and looked out to see a short drop to the concrete pad below. "You first."

She hesitated, unsure about escaping this way. "I don't know if I can do this."

"You can. I'm right here. You'll be fine. It's

just a few feet to the ground."

After she tossed her bag out, he lifted her up to ease her out the tiny exit barely big enough for her to fit through and watched her land safely on the concrete. Stuffing his gun back in his pants, he began to squeeze through the window, careful of the small backpack he carried on his back. Just then, the police banged on the motel room door just feet away from him and he knew they'd run out of time.

"Kate Sheridan! We know you're in there! Open up!" the cop bellowed just as Roman got his shoulders and chest out the window.

While the pounding continued on the motel room door, he wriggled his body to fit through the narrow space. Suddenly, he felt a searing pain in his side! Looking down, he saw a hole torn in his shirt and blood where a nail on the windowsill had cut him. But he didn't have time to worry about how bad it was.

As pain streaked down his side, he made it out and down to the ground below where Kate waited. He grabbed her hand and they ran as fast they could from the Bayou Motel and the cops who wanted to speak to her.

Roman didn't know if he'd just saved a woman in danger or helped a murderer escape. All he knew was he had to help her.

Even if he didn't know why.

Chapter Five

ROMAN TUGGED HER arm, practically dragging her down the street as they headed toward the French Quarter. Kate had no intention of going back there where that suspicious man had followed her and Eve the night before, so she pulled away and stepped into a doorway to hide.

"Nope. Whatever you're thinking, we're not going back to the Quarter. No way."

He narrowed his eyes to angry slits and stared down at her in disbelief. "What? Why? We need to get to a nicer place than that fleabag motel you were hiding out at. I need somewhere I can start to work on this case in peace and quiet where the cops aren't going to be threatening to bust down the door."

"I don't care. The first place they'll look is in the Quarter."

"At six o'clock in the morning? I doubt it. The cops probably think you have no money or very little to be spending on places to hide out.

They're not going to suspect you of being at a five star hotel."

She hated to admit it, but what Roman said made sense. Plus, the idea of a five star hotel with a bathtub where she could wash off the grime of the past twelve hours and a bed she didn't have to worry would have something waiting to crawl on her sounded incredible.

Looking up and down the street, she saw people beginning to head to work. If they wasted any more time discussing his plan, the sun would be up and the cops might see her. They needed to get to the hotel right now.

"Fine. I hope you have money because I can't afford much more than The Bayou."

He wrapped his hand around her forearm and gently pulled her out onto the sidewalk. "Don't worry. I've got it covered. Let's go. I don't want to be out once the sun comes up."

They hurried down the street with Kate keeping her head down and Roman guiding her, his hand holding her steady. With every step, she wondered if they'd actually be able to escape being noticed by the police, but then she reminded herself where she lived.

New Orleans had its fair share of bizarre people, so a woman walking down the road with her head bowed while a man held her tightly to him likely wouldn't arouse any suspicion whatsoever. Now if they were half-naked and wearing feathers on the half of their bodies that were covered maybe, but dressed as they were in ordinary casual clothes, they wouldn't even be noticed by most people who passed them by.

That feeling of anonymity had always been one of the greatest things her city offered. To others, it might make them feel lost and meaningless, but not to her. The mixture of eccentric and bizarre lived right at home with the ordinary in New Orleans, and she loved that.

Roman hurried toward Canal Street in silence, making Kate feel like she needed to fill the silence between them with something. She wasn't used to being this close to someone and not talking. It made her nervous.

"Is this your first time in New Orleans? If it is, you should definitely check out the Quarter at night. Also, I'm told those cemetery tours are interesting for people visiting the city," she said, instantly feeling foolish.

She wanted to fill the space, not sound like some pushy tour guide.

He turned his head and looked at her like she was an idiot. Now she felt uncomfortable and irritated. This guy had quite an effect on her, and most of it couldn't be worse. At least he was attractive. She couldn't deny that.

Focusing on that as they walked toward the

major chain hotel down near the waterfront, she took her first good look at the man who said his job was to protect her but refused to give her his last name. Tall, with short hair that made him look like a cop or some kind of military guy, he definitely had a pure Alpha male thing going. Looking down at where his hand sat wrapped around her forearm, she liked what she saw.

Strong and powerful, his hand held her just tight enough to keep her next to him.

He had a protective nature to him Kate had to admit she liked too. She suspected all the men he worked with had that same way about them since they'd signed up to willingly put themselves in danger to help women in need.

Kate thought about that and how honorable it sounded. As they walked toward the main entrance to the hotel, she asked, "Are all the men who work for this Project Artemis like you?"

He shook his head. "Yes and no."

She wondered if he worked at being intriguing like that or if it came naturally, but before she could ask him which it was, he pushed her away from the building and began walking much faster. She tried to keep up, but he made it difficult by nearly running down the sidewalk.

"Why aren't we going in there?" she asked, suddenly worried that the man she'd set her hopes on helping her wasn't there to protect her but instead to do exactly what she'd believed he would when he walked into her motel room nearly an hour before.

Roman didn't answer but kept walking so fast she felt like at any minute her feet would leave the ground and she'd take flight like a kite behind him. His hold on her arm began to hurt, but when she tried to pull away, he clamped down tighter, squeezing her skin.

"You're hurting me! Slow down! I can't keep up," she cried out, hoping he'd do as she'd demanded.

Not that she expected it. Alpha males rarely listened to others, a trait she distinctly disliked in them.

When he didn't slow down even a little, she tugged as hard as she could and yanked her arm from his hold. Tiny shoots of pain radiated up toward her elbow, so she stopped and rubbed her skin.

Roman stopped a few feet ahead on the sidewalk and glared back at her, but she saw fear in his eyes too. What had happened back there in front of that hotel?

"What's going on? Why couldn't we go in? Where are you taking me?" she asked, each question rattled off in succession as her own fear grew by the second that Roman wasn't the honorable protector he'd claimed to be.

He took a single step toward her and stopped without saying a word to answer anything she'd asked. Glancing around, he took another step until he stood less than a foot away, still glaring but now so close she could practically feel his emotions coming off him.

But were they borne of fear or anger? She couldn't tell and he didn't seem to be willing to even speak to her now.

"Why have you suddenly gone mute? Can you please tell me what's going on?"

Roman grimaced like he was in pain and looked over her head back toward the hotel they'd just run away from. "We couldn't go into that hotel because there were two cops standing at the check-in desk. I'm trying to figure out where we can go now, so that's why I'm not answering the thousand and one questions you feel the need to throw at me."

So he believed her about the cops. Maybe he was on her side and trying to protect her after all.

Kate's mind raced with ideas about what other hotel they could go to. There were dozens in the area within walking, or in their case, running distance, but which would get them out of view quickly? Then she remembered Jonas telling her about a lawyer get-together he'd gone to last Christmas at the Allton Hotel located just a block away from where they stood.

Now she grabbed Roman's arm, her hand getting nowhere close to making it all the way around it, and tugged him down the street. "Come on. I have someplace I think can work. It's a beautiful hotel. Even better than that one back there. It's just on St. Louis Street right down here."

He resisted her taking the lead for a few moments but then relented and caught up with her. "Let's just hope the cops aren't there too."

She hoped that too. After the night she'd had, she needed somewhere nice to rest and clean the grime from that awful place off. A mint on her pillow would be a nice touch too.

They turned onto St. Louis Street, and Kate saw the Allton Hotels sign above the main entrance. "There! My boss attended a party there once and told me it was gorgeous."

"I don't need gorgeous so much as Wi-Fi, something to eat, and a place to start working," Roman answered as they walked toward the grey building with black wrought iron railings so typical to the French Quarter.

"I'm sure they'll have all that and more. You said five star, and this is it."

She just hoped when they walked in that they wouldn't be met by New Orleans finest and be forced to run for their lives through the Quarter. She also hoped that all the Mardi Gras partiers had left town already and they even had a room to give them. But she didn't mention that to Roman since he already looked stressed out.

They exchanged a quick glance, and Kate took a deep breath as Roman guided her through the front doors. One look at the white marble floors and enormous glass chandelier above their heads as they stepped into the lobby told her this place was no Bayou Motel. Her eyes darted left and right looking for any sign of the police, but she saw no one other than the single man at the check-in desk and a bell man standing in a lounge area watching a TV.

"I think we're good," Roman said quietly. "All we need to do is check in and we'll be fine."

She let him go attend to getting them a room as she took in the opulent surroundings of the Allton Hotel. No wonder Jonas had raved about it. The furniture in the waiting area alone convinced her she loved this place. Plush burgundy couches and chairs arranged around a large circular mahogany coffee table made her want to sit down and relax, but the less time they spent in the lobby out in the open the better.

As she avoided the bell man's gaze, she turned to look at Roman and saw blood on the side of his tan shirt. Had he been hurt helping her get out of that horrible motel room?

Then on a TV in the waiting area, she heard

the beginning of a news report about her boss's murder. She spun around to see her picture from her driver's license right there on the screen as the reporter said, "New Orleans police are looking for Kate Sheridan, the victim's legal assistant. Anyone who's seen her is asked to call 9-1-1."

Horrified, she prayed to God the bellman hadn't been paying attention and hurried over to where Roman stood speaking to the desk clerk. Burying her face in his shoulder, she asked, "Done yet, honey?"

He looked down at her, confused by her sudden coziness with him, and arched one eyebrow. "Almost, honey."

The front desk clerk, a handsome young man with slicked back hair and bright blue eyes, smiled and handed him the room key and his ID. "Thank you for staying with us, Mr. Madson. You're in room 243. Just take the lobby elevator to the second floor and turn left as you get out. Our restaurant, Bon Temps, is open late tonight, and if you want a drink, Roxanne's is available starting in a few hours. They're both located just down there here on the first floor. If you need anything, please don't hesitate to call down to us here at the front desk."

Kate eagerly tugged on Roman's arm, desperate to get away before the desk clerk paid any attention to her. "Come on, honey. I'm tired after our trip."

Instead of just smiling and walking away, Roman said, "Women. They can be so demanding, but what can you do, right?"

His brand new friend behind the desk chuckled knowingly. "Have a wonderful stay, you two."

Hysterical. Just what she needed at that moment—male bonding over how demanding women were. What she wanted to do was slug him in the arm and remind him how she'd found that place, not him, but she didn't do anything but grimace as they walked toward the elevators.

Another hotel guest waited there already, so Kate once again buried her face in Roman's shoulder and hoped they wouldn't be riding up to the same floor. She didn't mind hiding, and his shirt smelled pretty damn incredible from either the sexiest laundry detergent or cologne that made her want to close her eyes and take a deep breath in. But it was hard to be angry with him while she had her face pressed to his body.

Thankfully, the woman seemed lost in her own world and didn't say a word to them as they rode up to the second floor. They got out, leaving her alone in the elevator, and began walking to their room at the far end of the hall.

Alone in the very elegantly designed hallway that resembled the downstairs lobby but had deep burgundy and gold carpeting on the floor, Roman said to her, "I'm not sure what you were going for with all that, but it didn't make you any less conspicuous. Just so you know."

Not that he helped one bit with that whole making her less conspicuous. Furious at him, she walked through the door as he opened it and found herself standing in a gorgeous hotel room decorated in what she assumed were the hotel's colors of deep gold and burgundy. If only she could enjoy all this opulence.

All at once, the vision of her face right there next to the news anchor's head rushed back into her mind. She began to pace again as she had at the Bayou Motel, flailing her arms.

"My face is all over the news. The cops put my face on the news, for God's sake! That's why I kept trying to hide my face."

"Don't worry. Assuming that woman didn't wonder why you were acting like a bitch in heat, I think you're fine," he said as he sat down in a chair near the window.

The way he referred to her made her fall speechless for a moment before she snapped, "I'm sure she did wonder since you were such a cold fish! She probably felt bad for me stuck in the gorgeous hotel with such a cold fish of a man."

He looked up at her blankly but didn't react to her attack, so she stormed toward the bathroom. "I'm taking a bath to wash off the layer of skeeze from that motel room. Unless someone shows up to kill me, don't come in."

Slamming the door behind her, she stormed over to the tub and turned both the hot and cold water fully on. Kate looked around at the toiletries the hotel supplied and found a tiny bottle of bubble bath, so she poured the entire thing into the water before laying the white bath mat down on the floor.

She needed this bath. Of all the things she needed in life at that moment, if this bath was the only one she could have, she'd be happy. All she wanted to do was recline in the water up to her neck and hope the bubbles took away the stress of the past day. She didn't want to think about Jonas, Samuel Darnell, or how their killer might very well be out there looking for her right at that moment, wanting to kill her for what they thought she knew.

Which she didn't.

No, she wanted to let her mind go blank and not think of a thing. Not even the sexy man who had appeared in her life an hour ago and now sat just outside the door in the hotel room they shared.

Definitely not him. But at least she now knew his last name. Madson. Roman Madson. It had a strong, masculine sound to it. It matched him well.

But she didn't want to think about that right now. All she wanted to do was get lost in that bubble bath behind her.

Kate stripped out of her clothes and tossed them on the vanity before sticking her toe into the bathwater. Perfect. Not too hot and not too cold. As the bubbles multiplied and grew higher, she stepped in and sat down in the tub.

Sliding down into the bubbly water until every part of her but her head was submerged, she reveled in the feel of her muscles slowly pushing the tension and stress out of her body. With every moment, the hot water and bubbles cleaned her of the grime from that awful Bayou Motel. She'd have to tell Eve she was right about that place.

As thoughts of Eve rolled through her mind, she began to think about Jonas and his client. When Samuel Darnell came to the office that first time, he'd been so jittery and seemed terrified of everything he wanted to talk to Jonas about. She'd thought he'd been overreacting to whatever it was that scared him, but now she felt stupid for minimizing his concerns in her mind. God, she and Jonas had joked about how nervous he'd seemed that first day. How cocky they'd been.

And now the two of them were dead, murdered by some unknown killer who likely thought as his assistant Kate knew all about the case too. For all her bravado in front of Roman, she knew the truth. She was terrified. Hiding her face in her hands, she tried to understand how her life became such a mess.

Just as misery threatened to take her over, the bathroom door opened and Roman walked in, startling her. She hurried to cover herself with bubbles as he took a good long look into the tub.

"Take a picture. It'll last longer," she snapped, still trying to cover her body with bubbles that seemed to dissipate as soon as she moved them.

Then she suddenly remembered what she said earlier about only coming in if someone was there to kill her. "What's wrong? Is someone here?"

"No," he said, still looking down at her as she lay in the tub.

"Well, then why are you standing over me, gawking at my body?"

He remained silent for a long moment before he said, "I'm going down to the restaurant, so I thought I'd ask you if you want something to eat."

She pointed at the door as bubbles dripped off her arm onto the floor next to the tub. "Get out!"

He didn't leave, and she realized his gaze had moved from her face down to her chest. She looked down to see her breast only half covered with bubbles. Quickly, she covered her chest with her arms and barked, "Just go and leave me alone!"

He turned to leave, but then she stopped him. "Wait. Get me a cheeseburger and fries. Please."

"I'm not sure they'll have that since it's breakfast time. Do you have a second choice?"

Kate thought for a moment. God, she just wanted something to fill her stomach. Why did this man have to make her life so difficult?

"French toast."

Roman smiled and nodded before leaving the bathroom. "I'll lock the door, but lock this one behind me too."

He closed the door behind him, leaving her there with her nerves on their last edge. Her world had come crashing down around her, somebody might very well want to kill her like they had done to her boss and his client, and this man who'd been sent to protect her made her even more uneasy.

In the middle of everything, she didn't want to think about incredibly sexy Roman was with his dark eyes that seemed to always be watching her and his muscular body she'd only felt through his clothes but knew must look fantastic without them. He did have a way of moving like a predator that she couldn't help find intriguing and sexy.

Swift, decisive, and lethal. That's what he looked like when he approached her. It made her wonder what he was like when he wasn't on a case.

"If only I'd met him before I became a woman on the run. He probably thinks I'm wrapped up in all of this anyway," she mumbled, disgusted that it took her life falling apart for a man like him to finally show up.

She let herself slide under the water and wished she could forget everything outside that tub.

Chapter Six

ROMAN CLOSED HIS eyes and tried to push the image of Kate lying there in that tub barely covered by bubbles out of his mind. He didn't want to think of her like that. Christ, the last thing he needed was to start thinking of her as anything but just another client.

This is just another job, Roman. Nothing more. All you have to do is find out who's behind her boss and his client's murders and make sure they aren't after her and then you'll be done with this assignment. Just focus on the case.

That he needed to talk himself into what he should already know signaled how far he'd let himself go with her. He couldn't even explain it either. Kate Sheridan had given him nothing but grief from the moment he met her. Her insistence on arguing every point and asking a million questions had made this case more difficult than it had to be from the beginning.

For all those reasons and his cardinal rule never to let himself feel anything for clients, he shouldn't be thinking about how sexy she looked lying there in that bubble bath. Or how much he wanted to stay in that bathroom and run his hands over every inch of her soapy body.

Shaking his head, he hoped to get rid of all those thoughts and get back to what he should be focusing on. The job. Protecting her from whoever was out there and may want to hurt her. Fulfilling his duty as a member of Project Artemis charged with this woman's safety.

He took a deep breath and headed out of the hotel room, happy to put some space between Kate and himself. The problem was he couldn't stay away from her for long and still do his job.

This was why he didn't let himself get too close to any client or any other person, for that matter. Keeping people at arm's length had served him well for years. True, it ensured he was always alone, but he'd grown used to that.

Better to be alone than to let himself care about another person. He knew what could happen if he let that happen.

The bar downstairs didn't seem to adhere to the hours the desk clerk had claimed, so after ordering their food at the restaurant, Roman sat down and ordered himself a whisky. He didn't make it a habit to drink for breakfast, but he wanted something to take the edge off. As he sat there staring at the bottles behind the bar and letting the drink warm his insides, a blonde wearing a red dress and dozens of sets of beads around her neck sat down on a barstool near him and ordered a gin and tonic.

Out of the corner of his eye, he saw her looking at him and smiled. Not normally someone who needed or wanted to talk to strangers in a bar, Roman felt the desire to strike up a conversation with her. Maybe it would take his mind off Kate upstairs naked and half covered in bubbles.

"Were you in town for Mardi Gras?" she asked, leaning over toward him so her plunging V-neck dress showed nearly all her breasts and causing the beads to tap against the bar.

He preferred when a woman left a little to the imagination, to be honest, though he had to admit that she had a great body to show off. The breasts may have been bought and paid for, but he didn't really care. It's not like they would be spending the rest of their lives together.

Turning toward her, he smiled. "No. I'm in town for work."

A man trying to get her into his bed would have bothered to ask what she was doing in town, but Roman didn't bother. All he wanted he could get right there in that bar.

"What kind of work do you do?" the blonde asked before taking a sip of her drink.

"Security. I protect people," he answered, okay with that half-truth he'd just told her.

Technically, that's what he did. One of the most important parts of working for Project Artemis was not talking about it. Sort of like Fight Club but without all testosterone flying around all over the place.

Roman's mind went back to the estate full of men and Xavier and Gideon watching sports twenty-four-seven in the game room. Okay, maybe it was like Fight Club with the testosterone but without all the bashing in of people's heads.

Lost in thought about back home, he didn't hear the blonde ask him a question about who he protected and didn't notice her move so she could sit next to him. When he stopped daydreaming, he saw his casual conversation had moved to a different level with her, if the way she was looking at him and licking her lips was any indication.

Some women you had no problem figuring out what they wanted. This one practically wore a neon sign around her neck. She wanted to be fucked.

"What's your name?" she asked in a voice that had almost a purring quality to it.

He imagined being talked to like that on a regular basis could sound nice. Even better when she was naked and underneath him.

"Roman," he said before drinking a mouthful

of whisky. "Yours?"

"Cheri," she answered with a smile as she fingered one of the sets of beads hanging between her breasts.

For a moment, he wondered if Cheri was more than just a good looking woman sitting at a bar at seven o'clock in the morning. Any big city had its fair share of prostitutes, although she didn't look like she had enough miles on her to be a hooker.

Curious to see if he was correct, he asked, "Were you in New Orleans for Mardi Gras, Cheri?"

She nodded and giggled as she lifted the beads up as evidence. "Yeah. My friends and I come every year from D.C. for the party. They all decided to turn in early, but I wasn't tired, so I came down here instead of sitting around the hotel room. We're here for another two days, so I'll have time to sleep then."

"What do you do for a living?" he asked, truly curious now that he'd decided she wasn't trying to sell herself to him.

Not for money anyway.

Cheri smiled and lifted her glass to take another sip of her gin and tonic, never taking her eyes off him. "You wouldn't believe me if I told you."

Roman couldn't help but be intrigued. More

than once, he'd wanted to say that in response to the question of what he did for a living. Who was this Cheri woman?

He leaned over until his mouth brushed against her long hair and whispered, "Try me."

She licked her lips and answered, "I work for the Government Accounting Office in D.C. A very boring desk job that makes trips like this one a must so I don't go out of my mind."

"I can't believe someone who looks like you do works a boring desk job," he said, intentionally flattering her. He honestly hadn't pegged her for a pencil pusher, so it wasn't a complete lie.

It's just that he didn't care as much as he made it seem.

Cheri took another sip of her drink and put the glass down on the bar. When she lowered her arm, she grazed his chest before letting her hand land gently on his thigh. He had to give her credit. She didn't leave any doubt as to what she wanted.

And if he didn't have a job to do that involved protecting a much different and far more argumentative woman, he may have taken Cheri up on her unspoken but definitely clear offer. It had been a long time since he'd been with anyone, and parts of him liked where she wanted to go with this little thing they had going between them there in the bar.

Especially the parts between his legs, which had already decided the whole idea was a go and enthusiastically waited for the rest of him to join in.

But his brain and heart weren't in it. He'd always been a man who had to care about someone enough to stick around after sleeping with them, which explained why he rarely had a woman in his bed. He just couldn't promise he'd ever be there after they finished making love.

"So are you here alone, Roman?" she asked in that purring voice he had to admit he liked.

He shook his head and saw the bartender hold up the bag of food he'd ordered from the restaurant next door. "No, and I have to head back up to the room to get back to work."

Cheri's hand slid up his thigh toward his crotch to stop him from leaving. "So soon? I won't have anyone to keep me company once you're gone."

Standing, he angled his hips away from her and grabbed the bag from the bartender. "Sorry. Wish I could stay, but duty calls."

Roman tossed two twenties on the bar and turned to leave, but Cheri touched his arm to stop him. "Wait."

He turned and saw her push a napkin toward him as she smiled. Taking it, he glanced at it and saw her name and her room number 515. He couldn't say Cheri didn't make the effort until the bitter end.

"See you later, Cheri."

"I hope so, Roman."

As he walked back through the lobby toward the elevator, he silently thanked her for helping him take his mind off the woman who waited upstairs. Cheri had successfully distracted him at least for a little while and helped him remember that he needed to push down whatever he was beginning to feel for Kate and forget it.

Forever.

It was the only thing he could do. She didn't need any more problems in her life. She had enough to deal with right now, and he couldn't offer her or any other woman what she deserved.

When he reached the second floor, he checked out the exits on each end of the hallway and the stairwell just in case they needed to get the hell out of there in a hurry. No one odd or suspicious looking lurked near their hotel room. In fact, he saw no one at all after leaving the bar.

Satisfied they hadn't been found out yet, he returned to the room to find Kate sound asleep on the queen size bed wearing the white robe he'd seen hanging on the back of the bathroom door when he went in there. She lay on her side with her left leg peeking out from under the robe, the tan skin a stark contrast to the pristine whiteness of the fabric. Just seeing her wearing it brought back the memory of how sexy she'd looked in that tub with too few bubbles to cover her.

Christ, he didn't want to think about how her body looked all wet and slick as she lay there.

Staring at her as she slept, he tried to think of anything but how much he'd wanted her. He needed something to distract him or he'd spend the rest of the day thinking about Kate and how much he now wanted to climb into bed with her and run his hands over her body to see if what he'd thought as he looked at her in the tub had been true.

Focus, man. This is a job. Not to mention that the woman is a huge hassle. She argues with you constantly. Who needs that shit in their life? Think about Cheri. She wouldn't argue. She'd never argue. Cheri is all about giving men what they want. Think about her and eat your damn food. Forget about that woman in the bed right there.

This was the second time he'd had to give himself a talking to about Kate. He sat down in the chair and pulled the coffee table toward him to make a table so he could eat his hamburger and fries. Anything to keep focused on the job at hand.

Looking over toward her, he thought about waking her so she could eat her cheeseburger but decided against it. She needed sleep more than she needed a greasy burger at that moment.

And he needed to stay away from her and focus on his job.

He kept telling himself that as he turned on the TV and tried to get into some basketball game he found on ESPN College. He hated basketball, so it didn't exactly help to keep his mind off the woman who lay fast asleep just a few feet away.

The hamburger and fries tasted like something that Bayou Motel might serve up for its guests, surprisingly. Roman ate his meal because it had been nearly a day since he had any food, but for the amount they charged, he'd expected better than a greasy beef patty on a stale bun and soggy fries.

When he finished, he tossed the wrappers in the bag and tried to busy himself with flipping through the channels to find something—anything—interesting to watch. He watched some early morning television with its shows created to amuse and dull the senses, but this morning, it wasn't accomplishing either goal.

He'd gotten some sleep on the plane to New Orleans, so he wasn't tired yet, and until Kate awoke and they could talk about who she thought would want to kill her boss and his client, he couldn't even start on the case.

That left sitting there in that chair next to the bed and doing everything humanly possible not to let his gaze drift over toward Kate as she slept.

As he started to give himself the third pep talk since they got to the hotel room, Kate began thrashing around, kicking her feet and flailing her arms at the air like she had when she first saw him back at the other motel. He watched as her face grew dark, and then she sat up and began to scream in a way that made his blood run cold.

He hurried over to her side and sat down next to her on the bed. Wrapping his arms around her shoulders, he tried to calm her. "Kate, it's okay. You're okay. I'm right here."

She turned to look at him, her eyes wide with pure fear. "Where am I? What happened?"

"We're at the Allton in the French Quarter. We came here after we left the motel you were at. You're okay. You just had a nightmare."

Kate took a deep breath and looked around the hotel room. "The Allton? And you're Roman Madson, the guy who's supposed to protect me, right?"

He smiled at her mistake with his last name. Of course she would have assumed that was his real name since he'd used it to pay for the room. Just one of his aliases he used on the job.

"Yes, I'm Roman. You don't have to be afraid. I'm here and you're safe."

She stared up at him for a long moment and then nodded. "You went to go get food, right? My cheeseburger? How long have I been asleep?"

"Not long. I just got back from getting the food. Your cheeseburger and fries are over there on the table."

Looking around him toward where he pointed, she searched for the burger and then covered her face with her hands. "This is all a mess. Someone wants me dead. I know it. They killed my boss and his client, and now they're out there wanting to kill me. Jonas told me to not trust the cops, so all I have is you to keep me safe, and I don't even know you. If it wasn't for the desk clerk saying your last name, I wouldn't even know that since you wouldn't tell me."

The way she said that sounded so sad that he couldn't lie to her about his name anymore, even though it shouldn't have meant anything to her and he would be breaking one of his cardinal rules telling her his real last name. None of that mattered as he listened to her sound so unhappy.

"I gave the desk clerk an alias. Madson isn't my real last name."

Kate dropped her hands into her lap and turned to face him. Frowning, she asked, "Will you tell me what it is, at least to make me feel like I know something about the person who just showed up at the Bayou Motel claiming to want to help me?"

Something about seeing her frown after

hearing her sound so dejected made his chest hurt. For as difficult as she'd been from practically the minute they met, Kate Sheridan wasn't a bad person. She wasn't even that difficult, if he was being honest.

She was just a person forced into the middle of something she had no business being involved in. Roman couldn't even say for sure he believed someone wanted to kill her, but he wanted to protect her, nonetheless.

So even though it broke the number one rule he lived by, he told her the truth about his last name. "Gregory. My name is Roman Gregory."

Her eyes grew wide, like the very fact that he'd told her surprised her. "Is that the truth? Or are you lying to me just to shut me up?"

Chuckling, he had a feeling more than one person in her life had lied just to shut her up or at least to stop her from asking so many questions. Something about her need to be so inquisitive began to charm him, though.

"No, I'm not lying, and I doubt it would make you shut up anyway. My name is Roman Gregory."

The smile he received in return for telling her his real name lit up her beautiful face. "Okay. Well, thank you."

"You're welcome."

The happiness quickly faded from her

expression, and she frowned again. "You know, I'm trying to be tough and strong, but I can't pretend not to be terrified that someone may be out there who wants to kill me like they killed Jonas and Samuel," she said sadly. "I don't know what to do. I'm just a legal assistant, or at least I was. Now I'm wanted by the police, who I can't trust, and I might have a target on my back. God, my life's a mess."

"Don't think about that now. I'm here, and I won't let anyone hurt you. I promise, Kate."

She tried to force a smile, but she couldn't. He understood. He knew what being afraid felt like, and he didn't blame her for not being able to pretend to be happy.

"I hope you aren't making promises you can't keep."

With a sigh, she lay back down onto the bed and curled up next to him. He knew he should move back to the chair. Better to let her just be.

But he didn't.

He sat back against the padded headboard and didn't push her away when she rolled over and rested her head on his chest. Then he watched as she fell back to sleep all curled up against him. He couldn't help think that beneath all that sharpness she showed, behind the endless stream of questions and bravado she put on, she was as sweet as she was beautiful.

For Roman, his job with Project Artemis forced him to come to terms with his desire to use the skills he'd learned in the Army for something other than fighting. He'd always leaned toward protecting those who needed help, but he'd made sure to keep the women he helped at arm's length, never letting them in as he did his job. He knew himself well enough to know that decision ensured no one got hurt because of him losing focus.

People died when you lost focus. He knew that better than most.

But Kate roused a protectiveness in him he thought he'd pushed so far down inside that he'd never feel it again. He'd never looked at a client like he looked at her. She made him want more than just to help her.

Shaking his head, he looked down at where her head lay on his chest and thought he didn't know if he could let himself feel that again. He didn't know if he could let himself feel anything for a woman again.

Whatever happened, he'd keep his promise, though. He wouldn't let anyone hurt her if he had anything to say about it.

CHAPTER SEVEN

OPENING HER EYES, Kate looked around the dimly lit room for any sign of Roman but didn't see him there with her. She stretched the sleep from her limbs and worked on waking up. As she slowly came around from what felt like the deepest nap she'd ever taken, she remembered bits and pieces of the last time she saw him.

He'd been next to her on the bed. Or at least she thought so. Had she been dreaming?

It didn't feel like a dream, but she couldn't tell. Hell, she couldn't be sure of anything at that moment other than she felt more rested than she had in years and the white robe she wore was very possibly the most comfortable thing she'd had against her skin in her entire life.

She ran her hands down the front of the robe as she tried to make out whether she'd been dreaming or not when she thought Roman had held her as she fell asleep. The more she thought about it, the more it seemed she'd dreamed the whole thing.

Damn.

It had been months since she fell asleep in a man's arms. She missed that feeling of being held by a strong man as she drifted off with nothing to worry about because she knew he was there by her side.

Now all she had were worries. And even worse, she didn't even have anyone to hold her, except in her dreams.

Her mind drifted back to the feeling of Roman next to her and she remembered him saying he would protect her. The guy really had that protector thing down pat. Not that she didn't like it. She did. Kate had never met a man like him. He walked into her life out of nowhere and in less than a day she'd come to find that she wanted him around.

Maybe it was just because her life had turned into a shitstorm. She'd never been the type of woman who needed a man. It just wasn't who she was. She'd been single for long enough that a man didn't really figure into her life.

That's why this feeling of wanting Roman around confused her. He certainly didn't fit the mold most of the men she'd been with fit into. Sure, he had that whole Alpha male vibe she loved. Any man who couldn't hold his own in the world turned her off instantly.

Even more, any man who couldn't handle her

immediately became someone she didn't want to be with. Kate had often been called difficult. She wore that insult like a badge of honor. For her entire life, people had bemoaned how eager she seemed to fight every point tooth and nail. It wasn't that she loved to fight everyone. She never wanted it to be her against the world. It just always turned out like that.

If they could see inside her heart, they'd learn that she wanted nothing more than to find someone to lean on who would be her knight in shining armor. That she'd love to have someone standing beside her who could make the fight even the tiniest bit easier.

Or even better, someone who would fight for her so she didn't have to do it alone all the time.

Shaking her head, she let that fantasy recede to the back of her mind where it belonged. Roman was merely a man doing his job. While that may have been honorable, it didn't mean he could ever be that man she dreamed of one day finding and settling down with for a happily ever after.

Then she remembered how right before she fell asleep in his arms he told her his last name. Such a tiny detail but it meant so much to her that he'd finally relented and given her that.

An honorable Alpha male who cared about making her happy. Maybe it hadn't all been a dream after all.

Whatever Roman Gregory was, she needed to figure out what to do now that the police were after her. Kate grabbed the remote from the nightstand and flipped through the channels as a tiny voice in her brain told her not to. But the inquisitive side of her overruled everything else and she continued to search for the local station to see if they'd found Jonas's killer.

She knew the likelihood of that came in somewhere around impossible, but hope sprang eternal with her in moments like this. Unfortunately, or maybe fortunately, none of the local stations had any news on.

Maybe it was for the best. She'd probably just freak out again when she saw her face positioned next to some perky newswoman's head.

The sound of the door opening made her freeze in place, but then Roman walked in and her entire body relaxed. He stopped at the dresser and slid his large gold watch off his wrist before placing it and all the change in his pockets next to the TV. Reaching into his pocket, he pulled out a folded napkin and gave it a quick glance before he crumpled it up into a ball and tossed it into the small wastebasket next to him. Finally, he pulled his backpack off and set it down on the floor.

"Feeling better?"

"Yeah. I don't think I've felt this rested in

years. How long was I asleep?"

With a chuckle, he said, "A while. You must have been tired."

"What time is it?"

"Three in the morning."

Stunned that she'd slept for so long, she swung her feet off the bed and adjusted her robe so she didn't flash him as she stood up. "Three? Oh my God! I slept for nearly twenty-four hours. Why did you let me sleep for so long?"

A slow smile inched up the corners of his mouth and made him far too sexy for someone she had just been fantasizing about. "I didn't see any reason to wake you up. You looked so content there, so I let you go."

God. How could she be angry at a man who let her sleep uninterrupted for nearly a whole day? Then she realized that meant that the cops hadn't found them yet either.

"Any news on the manhunt for me?" she asked, choosing to be flippant to hide how terrified being wanted by the police made her.

Roman shook his head. "Nothing yet."

Why had he returned to saying little again? Kate had thought they had a sort of breakthrough once he told her his last name. Now she wondered if it had only meant something to her.

"Did you get that cheeseburger from the restaurant?" she asked, feeling awkward suddenly.

He pointed toward the coffee table where a white bag with grease stains sat. "I got you a cheeseburger and fries, but they must be ice cold and hard as rocks by now. Do you want me to go down to the restaurant and get you something hot?"

"No, that's okay. I bet they're not too bad. I'm not really hungry anyway."

The truth was she didn't want to be alone in that hotel room anymore.

"Okay. Let me know if you change your mind. I'm going to grab a shower, and then I want to sit down with you and talk about what needs to happen next."

Then he turned and walked into the bathroom without giving her a chance to ask about exactly what he meant. What were the choices as to what should happen next? Did one of them involve finding a way to make the police understand she had nothing to do with her boss's murder and his client's while at the same time protecting her from those very same police?

Because if not, she didn't know what they'd be talking about because those were the only things she worried about.

The sound of her stomach grumbling reminded her that she really did want something to eat, so she padded across the floor and grabbed the bag of food. Reaching in, she touched the

French fries and cringed.

Ice cold, just as he'd said. Well, beggars couldn't be choosers, and how bad could cold, greasy French fries be?

Two bites into one and she knew the answer. Very bad. Disgusting bad.

Had he brought her a drink? She scanned the hotel room but saw no cans of soda.

Maybe the room had a little refrigerator with some water. She walked over to the dresser that held the TV and opened the doors on the bottom. Inside, she found a refrigerator.

"Please let there be even a single bottle of water. Just one will do the job," she said as she pulled open the door.

Before her eyes, she saw two bottles on the center shelf. Never before had she been so thrilled at the sight of a bottle of water. She grabbed one and quickly twisted off the top before drinking nearly the entire thing.

"Thank God for water."

Her need for a drink satisfied, she tossed the bag of gross food in the garbage and picked up Roman's watch. Heavy in the palm of her hand and real gold, it fit him to a T. She positioned it next to her arm and was impressed by how it dwarfed her wrist. Then she noticed the numbers on the face were Roman numerals.

"Just Roman who likes Roman numerals."

Something about the fact that he chose that watch impressed her.

She set it back on the dresser as her gaze dropped to the wastebasket on the floor near her feet. Next to the bag of cold food sat that white napkin he'd taken out of his pocket and looked at for a moment before throwing it away. Her curiosity got the better of her, and she reached down to pick it up.

A dab of ketchup had dropped onto it, along with a piece of yellow American cheese stuck to it, which made it disgusting, but she still lifted it out of the garbage. It looked like any other cocktail napkin in the world, but turning it over, she saw writing on it.

Cheri Room 515

She didn't know why, but that made a pain form in the pit of her stomach. Had he been with this Cheri person in her hotel room three floors up all day while she slept in this room alone?

Tossing the napkin back into the garbage, she mumbled, "Nice job protecting me, Roman. How nice that you could fit in Cheri in Room 515."

Why did she feel anything about that at all? What right did she have to be jealous? She'd only known him for a forty-eight hours, and nearly twenty-four of that had been filled with her sleeping, so she actually only knew him for a day.

A single day.

One day and she hated the idea that he had spent time with some woman up on the fifth floor.

Kate knew what spent time meant. That made her even more jealous. Had he been upstairs having sex with a woman while she slept?

So what if he had? She had no claims on him. None at all. But how long had he known this Cheri woman? Had he called her to come over once Kate fell asleep? Or had she been someone he met downstairs at the restaurant when he went down to get her that cheeseburger?

That meant he knew her even less than he knew Kate, yet he'd slept with her?

Kate's mind raced as jealousy began to eat her up. Jealousy she felt childish even admitting to. But jealousy nonetheless.

Consumed by it, she walked over to the bathroom door and threw it open. Then she stormed into the steam filled room and stared at the closed shower curtain as a million things to say ran through her mind.

"Roman, I hope I'm not inconveniencing you in any way."

She listened for him to answer but heard nothing but the sound of the shower running. Had he heard what she said?

"Roman, if you have something better to do, you don't have to stay here in this hotel room with me."

Still no answer.

Then the white shower curtain slowly opened and he stuck his head out. Water dripped off his black hair and down over his face and neck, and he stared out at her with a look of complete confusion all over his face.

"What's wrong, Kate? Did someone come to the door? Did something happen?"

"No. I just wanted to tell you that if you have other things you'd rather be doing, don't feel like you have to stay here with me."

Roman ran his hand over his face to wipe away the water and the shower curtain fell away to reveal his entire upper body. Kate tried not to stare, but she couldn't tear her gaze from his muscular chest and washboard abs that led to the defined V that angled in toward…

Damn, that's a nice body. That's even nicer than I imagined. That is one fine body.

He noticed her staring and smiled. "Why are you in the bathroom when I'm taking a shower if nothing happened?"

His question roused her from daydreaming about how hot he looked standing there, and she instantly felt defensive. "Asks the man who walked in on me while I was taking a bath."

"Then I guess we're even?" he said with a stupid grin that irritated her.

He'd probably smiled like that with Cheri from the fifth floor. Cheri who he'd spent the entire day with while she slept alone down here in the room.

Cheri who was probably a blonde. With a name like Cheri, she had to be a blonde. Women with names like that were always blonde with great bodies and men hanging off them. Good looking men like Roman.

Kate focused her attention on Roman still smiling at her like any of this was funny. "So don't feel like you have to hang around if you have something else you want to do," she repeated, trying to avoid looking at any part of his body but his face.

It was a nearly impossible task now that she'd seen him without clothes on. With water running over the peaks and valleys of his muscular body.

"I'm not sure what you're talking about, but I have nothing else I want to do. I told you. I'm not going to let anyone hurt you, Kate."

He waited for her to say something, but nothing came to her. Well, nothing she wanted to say out loud. Jealousy and arousal rushed through her like some kind of toxic mixture she knew wouldn't end up sounding right if she spoke, so she clamped her lips shut.

"Just give me a few minutes and I'll be done with my shower, okay?"

None of what she'd just done felt okay. None of the jealousy that coursed through her felt okay either. The only thing that was remotely okay in all of that was how incredible Roman looked standing there naked with water rolling over his gorgeous body.

She didn't say anything else and when he closed the shower curtain, she turned on her heels and left the bathroom, slamming the door behind her. Utterly sure she'd never been so stupid, she flopped down on the bed and covered her eyes with her arm.

"So dumb. Get it together, Kate. You're losing your mind."

Now anger folded itself into the mixture of jealousy and desire. Anger at herself, though. She hadn't completely lost the ability to think logically. Roman had every right to do whatever he wanted with whomever he wanted. Even if the person he wanted had the name Cheri.

And the truth of the matter was he hadn't done anything but try to help her. For that, he deserved her thanks, but even more, he deserved far better than the ridiculous scene she'd just put on in the bathroom.

Kate had no idea why she became so jealous. "I barely know the guy," she mumbled to herself as she lay there on the bed. "What's wrong with me?"

The bathroom door opened, and she looked up from underneath her arm to see Roman standing there fully dressed once again but looking so good with his dark hair still wet. God, did this guy ever not look incredible?

Embarrassed by her behavior, she didn't want to say anything now. Better to let him talk first so she could gauge just how idiotic he thought she'd acted in there.

Roman ran his hand through his wet hair, smoothing it off his face, before he walked over to the dresser to get his watch. Pausing a moment, he looked down at where he'd left it and then slid it over his hand and closed the band around his wrist.

"Now that you've had a chance to rest, I need you to tell me everything you know about why anyone would be after you."

She hadn't expected those words to come out of his mouth. Kate had been preparing to defend herself for the spectacle she'd just put on for him in the bathroom, so she breathed a sigh of relief that he wanted to discuss her problems with the law instead.

Sitting up, she made sure her robe covered everything it should and said, "Well, there's not much to tell other than my boss and one of his clients were murdered on Tuesday. Jonas, my boss, had warned me that if anything happened to him because of that case that I couldn't trust the police. I guess he was right since they've plastered my face all over the TV and think I'm a suspect."

"Why would he say you couldn't trust the cops?" Roman asked as he walked in front of her to sit down in the chair near the window.

Quickly, she tried to remember another time Jonas had an issue with the police. As a personal injury lawyer, he didn't often deal with the police as adversaries on cases. That role was saved mostly for insurance companies. The cops just filled out the reports he used when he went after other people for pain and suffering, the two things he always said had made his life what it was. She'd always thought those were two odd words to use to describe a life.

She turned to face Roman and shrugged. "I don't know. He didn't have a problem with the police, for the most part. Jonas wasn't a defense attorney, so the police were never the focus of his cases."

"What kind of lawyer was your boss?" Roman asked with a hint of distaste in his tone.

Kate knew what everyone thought of personal injury lawyers. She'd heard it a million times since she began working for Jonas. Ambulance chaser, blood sucker. And she'd heard the jokes about the only good lawyer being a dead lawyer and how Shakespeare had been right when he said they should kill all the lawyers.

But Jonas did good things for people. He wasn't someone who tried to make millions on other people's suffering. He just wanted to help those who needed it.

Feeling defensive, she said, "He was a personal injury lawyer, and before you say anything negative about that, please remember my boss is the victim here."

Roman simply nodded and pursed his lips. "Okay, point taken. But why would a personal injury lawyer tell his assistant not to trust the police if anything ever happened to him? That says something odd was going on. What was the case he and his client were working on? Clearly, that connection is the important one."

"I don't know. Jonas wouldn't let me know any of the details of that case."

A look of suspicion settled into Roman's face. "You were his assistant but he wouldn't let you know about a case he was working on? Was that normal?"

Shaking her head, she admitted the truth she never understood from the moment he began hiding things from her. "No. Jonas never did that before this case and never did it on any case that came in after that."

"How long was he working on this case?"

"Seven months," she answered, wishing at some point in all that time that she'd listened to her gut and looked into what Jonas was up to.

Maybe if she had, Jonas and Samuel Darnell would still be alive.

"So for more than half a year, your boss was working on a case he wouldn't share with you, his only assistant? What reason would he have not to let you know about this particular case, Kate?"

The suspicion she'd seen a minute earlier in Roman's face had turned into a look of judgment she couldn't understand. "What are you saying? That I did something?"

Roman slowly shook his head. "No. I'm just asking why a lawyer wouldn't tell his only assistant about a case when he'd never before or ever since acted like that on any other case."

Kate didn't like the way he sounded like judge and jury when he said that. Standing up, she looked down at him and told him the same thing she'd said before.

"I have no idea why my boss wouldn't let me know about this case. I don't know why he told me if anything happened to him that I shouldn't trust the police either. All I know is he's dead, his client's dead, and I'm wanted by the police for something I had nothing to do with. You say you want to help me, but it doesn't seem like it right now, Roman. It seems like you think I did something to deserve the police coming after me. Is that what you think? Do you think I'm a murderer?"

She waited for him to say something in response to her outburst, but instead, Roman just sat there staring up at her like he was mentally weighing every word she'd just said. She wanted to lash out and scream that he had no right to judge her like that. That just because he looked like every cop she'd ever seen and may very well have been a cop at some point didn't mean he should trust the cops more than her.

But she knew the reality. Roman was the only person who might be able to help her out of whatever mess she'd found herself smack dab in the middle of. Even more, Kate knew she couldn't get out of the mess on her own.

So, whatever she did, she had to convince Roman that she hadn't killed Jonas or Samuel. No matter what the police said.

Chapter Eight

"So there's no other reason why the police would be looking for you?" Roman asked and watched Kate carefully, looking for any sign or tell to let him know she may be lying about this case.

He had no idea if she'd done anything to deserve the police looking for her other than the fact that until two days before she'd been Jonas Flynn's only assistant who they justifiably could think knew the details about this case she claimed he never told her about.

Her mouth dropped open in shock, but she recovered quickly and shook her head. "No. I'm a boring, law abiding citizen. Let me tell you how boring I am. I don't have a car, so I've never gotten a speeding ticket. I don't have a dog, so I've never let a pet shit all over the neighborhood. I haven't gotten high since back in high school, so unless the New Orleans police suddenly have a lot of time on their hands and feel like busting people for the foolishness of their teenage years, the pot I smoked isn't why they want to find me. They're after me because they think Jonas, Samuel, and I were involved in some love triangle. At least that's what they're saying to the press."

As he studied the way she moved her hands when she got angry about something, he had the surest sense that boring would be the last thing anyone would call Kate Sheridan. She had a fire inside her that begged to be allowed to breathe fresh air. He wondered if she even knew how strong she was.

That aside, he suspected she was hiding something and a love triangle with her boss and one of his clients seemed doubtful. Whether what she was hiding would mean anything to this case or not he didn't know, but everyone had secrets.

And Kate definitely was concealing something. Now he just had to figure out what.

As for the cops, he had a hard time squaring what he knew about every cop he'd ever known and her suspicion that the local police had it out for her. While that kind of thing made for good movies and sold newspapers, he'd always found the truth to be far less exciting but no less impressive.

Police, whether local yokel cops or big city officers, tended to err on the side of good and honor in his experience. As much as she wanted to believe there was some conspiracy against her led by the New Orleans Police Department, he just didn't buy it.

"What proof do you have that the cops are somehow involved in this case?" he asked and then waited for her to tell him something, anything to convince him she was onto the truth with her theory.

Her eyebrows drew in toward her nose like angry slashes. Obviously, she didn't like his question, but that didn't change the fact that he needed an answer.

She began talking with her hands again, waving them around wildly as she became more frustrated with every moment he didn't jump up and agree with her.

"They came after me at that seedy motel. Why? What would make me a suspect?" she asked, punctuating her question by pointing at him.

"You were Jonas Flynn's only assistant, Kate. You naturally would be a suspect, along with every other person in his life."

"Ah ha!" she exclaimed, pointing at him again. "Right there I can prove that's wrong. Jonas had a girlfriend. Why isn't she the one whose face is being flashed all over the television? If there was going to be a threesome or a love triangle or whatever they're claiming, wouldn't she be the logical third person and not me?"

She did have a point. A romantic entanglement theory would lend itself to one of the victim's girlfriends more than it would Kate, someone who merely worked with Jonas.

"Okay, that makes sense. Do you have any other proof?"

Glaring at him, she twisted her face into a scowl. "Jonas told me not to trust the cops if anything happened to him involving this case. It's like he was predicting the future."

"That's not proof."

"Well, why would he tell me that then? Maybe he knew something about the cops that we don't know. Maybe that case had something to do with a cop. Maybe he knew they'd protect their own if what one of them did ever came out," she said, clearly grasping at straws for anything that sounded even remotely possible.

"Until there's some proof, I can't believe that."

His dismissal of all her theories infuriated her, and she began to pace back and forth through the room. "Why? Because you're one of them or used to be one of them so you think they're angels? Let me introduce you to the real world, Roman. It happens every day. Cops are just as liable to be crooked and dirty as anyone else. They aren't impervious to being bad. That badge doesn't mean they have some kind of protective shield around them that evil can't get through. Trust me."

"I've never been a cop. That's not why I'm having a hard time believing all of this. I just don't see any proof that the New Orleans Police Department is trying to frame you or do anything else other than solve these two murders."

He knew saying that would anger her even more, but he had no intention of lying to her. He also knew that he didn't seem to be doing what he'd been sent there to do. As part of Project Artemis, his job was to protect women in danger, and he believed in that one hundred percent.

He just wasn't so sure this woman was in danger. However, he didn't know all the facts yet, particularly regarding what this case her boss was working on with his client. Without that information, he couldn't determine exactly who may be looking to cause Kate harm.

"Proof? You want proof, huh," she said, marching into the bathroom and slamming the door.

She definitely had a fire inside her. Roman just wondered if he'd given it too much oxygen this time. He had no idea what kind of proof she'd find in the bathroom, but whatever she found in there, he worried what she'd try to do with it.

The anger in her eyes warned him that she'd

probably try to do something dangerous. This woman seemed to have a penchant for flying off the handle, so as he waited for her to come out, he considered how to react to whatever she sprung on him.

The bathroom door flew open, and Kate stormed out fully dressed. Pointing angrily at him, she said, "You want proof? Fine. I'll get you proof. If you're here when I get back, then you'll see. If not, then have a nice life."

Get back? Where the hell did she intend on going at four in the morning?

As she hurried toward the door to leave, he jumped up and headed across the room to stop her. Grabbing her by the arm, he said, "Where do you think you're going?"

She looked up at him with eyes full of rage before yanking her arm from his hold. "I just told you. I'm going to get proof that the police are involved in this."

He stood there stunned at how reckless she was. "No way. You're staying right here where I can protect you."

"And not believe me! I deserve the chance to vindicate myself. I can see it written all over your face. You think I'm lying to you."

She began to move toward the door again, intent on actually leaving and going out where the cops could find her, along with anyone else, like the person who had killed her boss and his client and may well be searching for her at that very moment.

"Kate, it's too dangerous. I can't let you go," he said as he blocked her path with his body.

Her mouth dropped open, and she stared up at him in shock. "Let me? I'm a grown woman. No one lets me do anything. Now move out of my way."

She tried to move him, grunting as she pushed against his body, but he simply shook his head. He had no intention of letting her leave to go anywhere.

Frustrated, she pushed on his chest but didn't budge him an inch. "What do you have under that shirt? A steel shield?"

Roman couldn't help but smile, partly at her compliment and partly at her frustration. "Just what everyone else has. Now let's sit down and you can tell me more about your boss and this client of his."

Her hands fell away from his chest, and her shoulders sagged in defeat. "No. Let me go."

"Kate, I'm not letting you leave this room. You won't be able to get by me, so you might as well just accept that fact and sit down and talk to me."

She twisted her face into a grimace and grumbled, "Fine."

After waiting for her to turn back toward the bed, he watched to make sure she sat down and then took a seat in the chair again. "Okay, let's talk this out. What—"

He didn't even get his whole thought out before she bolted toward the door, reaching it before he did. Flinging it open so it slammed against the wall, she ran out into the hallway. Roman tore across the room to reach her before she got to the elevators or worse, the stairwell.

Chasing after her, he broke into a sprint and caught her just as the elevator doors opened. She tried to get away, but he grabbed hold of her and squeezed her to him, hoping to keep her from squirming out of his grasp.

"Let me go!" she cried out so loud that he expected one of the hotel's guests to peek their head out the door to see what was going on.

"Stop it now, Kate. I can't let you go, so stop fighting me on this," he said as she continued to do just that.

If she kept trying to escape, he'd have no choice but to restrain her. He didn't want to, but she left him with no other options.

"Help! Help!" she yelled loud enough to wake the entire floor.

He hoped to God no one heard her or keeping her safe would become next to impossible.

Clamping his hand over her mouth, he whispered, "You gave me no choice here, Kate. The more you scream, the more chance that someone's going to call the cops. Do you want them to come here and find you?"

He felt her mouth open and then a second later her teeth sunk into his middle finger. Pain shot through the rest of his hand, but he didn't know if he could trust her not to scream again, so he stuffed his other hand into her hair and tugged hard.

Kate's eyes filled with tears because he knew how tightly his hold on her hair was, but still she kept her teeth on his finger. Locked in a stalemate, he tried to keep calm as the pain in his hand began to migrate up his forearm.

"I can let your hair go, but only if you stop biting me, Kate. I don't want to stand out here in the hallway with my hand over your mouth, but you can't scream again. Do you understand me? If you scream, someone's going to call the cops."

She nodded and slowly opened her mouth, releasing his finger from between her teeth. Then she said something, her words all garbled by his hand covering her mouth, but he saw he'd finally gotten through to her with the combination of pain and fear. Damnit, he hated having to resort to things like threatening the person he was supposed to be protecting. Why did she have to be so difficult?

Now he just had to worry about her running away. Looking deep into her eyes, he tried to find some evidence that she wouldn't bolt as soon as he let her go. "Do you promise not to run if I let you go? I can't release you if you're just going to try to get away again. I don't want to carry you back to the room, but I will if you don't give me a choice."

Nothing in the way she looked at him said she wouldn't run the second he removed his hands from her, and he couldn't take a chance that she'd do something stupid, so he scooped her up and threw her over his shoulder. At first, she seemed stunned, so he made it halfway back to the room before she finally reacted.

"Put me down!" she said, again far too loud for the middle of the night in a hotel hallway.

At least now if someone poked their head out to see what was going on, he could pretend they were having a lover's spat. Hopefully, a hotel guest would believe that.

"Stop making so much noise. We'll be back to the room in a few seconds," he said as he turned the corner and saw the door a few feet away.

Instead of yelling, she turned to punching his lower back, landing her fists on the very spot where he'd cut himself climbing out the bathroom window at the Bayou Motel. Over and over, she pounded that very spot so tender until he felt a terrible stab of pain race up his side.

He got the door to their room open and dumped her onto the bed before staggering back against the wall in agony. Although he knew what he'd find, Roman ran his hand over his side through his shirt and brought it up in front of him to see blood on his fingers.

Kate sat on the bed glaring at him until she saw him wince in pain and then saw the blood. Jumping up, she ran over to him.

"Oh, my God! You're bleeding! What happened? Why are you bleeding? Did I do that when I punched you?" she asked in rapid fire succession, not giving him a chance to answer any of her questions.

Taking a deep breath, he pushed past her and walked into the bathroom to get a better look at his injury. It couldn't be too bad since he hadn't been bleeding the whole time, and when he'd checked it in the shower less than an hour before, it hadn't looked like much at all.

Then again, he hadn't had someone landing punches over and over on that very spot before his shower.

Kate followed him into the bathroom and stood back as he lifted his shirt over his head. Tossing it to the side, he saw the large red stain on it and knew when he looked at his side it wouldn't be good.

Her gasp when he removed his shirt told him it may even be worse than he'd suspected.

"Oh, Roman, I didn't…I mean, I didn't think when I was hitting you," she said quietly.

Looking into the mirror, he saw tears well in her eyes. Christ, this woman was a handful. If she wasn't giving him grief about something he had no idea about as he took a shower or running away and then beating on his back when he was forced to carry her to the room, she was crying because she'd hurt him.

Roman didn't want to see her cry, so he waved away her concern. "I'm fine. It's just a little scratch."

Her mouth dropped open at his understatement. "A little scratch? Have you seen it?"

He knew it wasn't just a minor thing. That nail or screw or whatever it was in that bathroom window had torn into his side pretty well. He felt it when it happened and knew it would hurt more later. Now after having Kate use his body for a punching bag, it was much worse.

Turning toward the mirror, he examined his side, wincing as he poked his finger in the cut to see if it was deep enough that it would need stitches. The gash didn't feel too deep, so he could probably get away without seeing a doctor to fix him up.

"Stop touching it," she cried as she looked on in horror. "You're making it worse!"

Frustrated and in pain, he shot her a look in the mirror. "What made it worse was someone hitting me because she was having a temper tantrum all the way down the hallway."

Kate hung her head and quietly apologized. "I didn't mean to, Roman. I'm sorry. You did throw me over your shoulder like a sack of flour. What was I supposed to do?"

He threw her another look, this one even angrier. "Come back to the room and not act like a crazy person?"

She opened her mouth but didn't say anything. Finally, after a few seconds, she gave him a real apology. "I am sorry. I never wanted to physically harm you. Honestly, I didn't do this on purpose."

How was he supposed to stay mad at someone who said that with tears in her big blue eyes? He didn't want to be angry with her. All he wanted to do was help her.

Why did she have to make that the hardest thing he'd ever tried to do?

"It's fine. Just help me find something to stop the bleeding," he said as a trickle of blood began sliding down toward his waist.

His apparent forgiveness made her spring into action, and she began scurrying around the bathroom looking for a clean washcloth as Roman stood there watching her and wondering if maybe she truly was crazy. One minute she was fighting him, and then the next minute she couldn't help enough.

He had to admit, though, as much as he hated the way she fought him on everything, when she acted sweet and kind, he liked her a whole lot more.

Probably more than he should, in fact.

Chapter Nine

THE MORE KATE stared at that horrible gash in Roman's side, the worse she felt. Physically, it made her want to throw up, but emotionally, the sight of it just proved once again that he'd tried to help her from the very moment they met. He'd not only suffered through her behavior but truly suffered because he'd been doing what he claimed the entire time.

Protecting her.

She cringed at how she'd punched him all the way down the hallway. She'd done this to him. Kate looked everywhere in the bathroom but found not a single clean washcloth. Between the two of them, they'd dirtied them all.

Tearing open the shower curtain, she saw the white washcloth he'd used. "I can't find any clean ones. What about the one you used when you took a shower?"

"Yeah, fine. I just need something to press on the wound so my pants don't fill up with blood."

Still wet, the washcloth felt cool in her hands

as she turned to hand it to him. She struggled to keep her gaze on his face because some kind of morbid curiosity kept taking over and forcing her eyes to settle on that horrible cut on his side.

For his part, Roman stayed as calm as he had for virtually the whole time he'd been around her. Except for when he had to clamp her mouth shut because she wouldn't stop screaming and then when he had to carry her back to the room because she'd made it clear she planned to run as soon as she could, he'd been the rational one to her insanity.

All of which made her feel like shit.

Looking away toward the toilet, she again apologized. "I'm so sorry, Roman. I truly never meant for this to happen. I didn't think my fingernails touched you."

When he groaned in pain, she couldn't help herself and turned around to see the washcloth already half-stained in red. His face writhed in agony, making her want to fix what she'd done.

"Turn around," she said, as she placed her hands on his shoulders and began to maneuver him in a way that would allow her to help him while not letting him see his side.

He fought her, though, stopping halfway around. "What? No. I'm fine."

Even though his expression made it clear he didn't want her help, she had to give it. She'd done this to him, and she needed him to see she wasn't just a whole lot of meaningless I'm sorry's.

"Roman, please let me do this. I can help you. It's the least I can do," she said in her sweetest voice.

"I'm fine, Kate. Just let me do this myself."

"Just turn around and stop fighting me, for God's sake!"

With shock in his eyes, he relented and let her turn him so she could easily get to the wound. "Damn, you're either snapping at me or bossing me around."

She opened her mouth to tell him to keep quiet while she cleaned his side, but her first up close look at what she'd done made her gasp in horror. For as bad as it had looked from a few feet away, seeing it now made her truly sick to her stomach.

He heard her sharp intake of breath and looked back at her. "I'm fine. Just let it go."

His words were full of bravado, so she quickly worked to get her head together and took the washcloth from his hand. Dampening it with warm water, she gently pressed it to his skin.

The touch of the cloth to his wound made him flinch, so she quickly pulled it away. "I'm sorry. I didn't mean to hurt you."

"It's fine," he said through gritted teeth.

"So how did this happen? Is this an old

wound?" she asked as she rinsed off the cloth.

He shook his head. "I got caught on the windowsill leaving that shithole of a motel room you were staying at," he said as she pressed the damp cloth to his skin again.

Instantly, she felt even worse than before. He'd gotten hurt helping her get away from the cops, even though he didn't believe she had anything to fear from them, and then she pummeled him, reinjuring him.

As she gently cleaned the skin around the wound, she said, "I'm sorry, Roman. I didn't know. If I did, I wouldn't have…"

"Don't worry about it. It's not the first time I've been hurt, and it won't be the last," he said in a clipped tone.

Once she'd cleaned him up, she rinsed off the cloth once more and said, "It's clean, but it should have a bandage over it. And you should probably get a tetanus shot."

"It's fine. I'm okay."

"Let me call down to the front desk, at least. I'm sure they have bandages here."

Roman stood up straight and turned around to face her. "I'll be fine. I've got stuff in my bag."

He walked out, leaving her holding the bloody washcloth and feeling like shit for what happened.

Looking in the mirror, she shook her head at

her reflection. "Real nice, Kate. The guy saves you, and how do you repay him? You act like a spoiled brat and make him bleed. Nice."

She knew what she had to do. There was no other way. She'd already done enough damage to him.

Roman pressed tape around the edges of a gauze pad over his wound and pulled his shirt down before sitting in the chair at the far end of the room. Kate walked over to stand in front of him. He looked up at her like he expected her to say something more about how sorry she was for everything she'd done, but the time for that had ended.

Now she needed to say goodbye.

"I know you said you're here to protect me, but I don't need it. Thank you, but I'm fine on my own. I'm involved in this of my own doing, but you aren't and you've been badly hurt already because of me. I don't want that, so thank you, but I'm going to handle things from here on out. Good luck, just Roman. Take care."

She turned and began to walk toward the door, but she expected him to follow her again to stop her. He didn't. Instead, he continued to sit in the chair and let her go.

That shouldn't have surprised her. She had been the biggest pain in the ass he'd probably ever encountered in his job or anywhere else, for that matter.

And for that, she truly was sorry.

From behind her, she heard him say in that deep voice that never failed to make her feel safer, "You'll be lucky if you make it a block from the hotel."

She stopped and turned around to face him. "Thank you for your concern, but I'll be fine."

Roman gave her one of his smiles that she'd remember for the rest of her life. "That's my line."

Kate looked at him and thought to herself that he really could be cute sometimes. And sexy. And a good man. Too bad she hadn't met him when she wasn't on the run and wanted by the police for the murder of two people. Maybe they could have gotten together.

"So what's your plan then?" he asked with a look of skepticism in his eyes.

She hated to admit it, but she didn't have a plan. When she didn't answer, he put his hands behind his head with a brief wince and said, "So you have no plan?"

God, this man had the ability to shift from sexy and sweet to irritating as all hell in a matter of seconds. That she wouldn't miss.

Defensive, she put her hand on her hip. "I have money saved, so I'll be just fine. I'll just grab some files before anyone gets to the office and be out of town in hours."

Roman shook his head. "The cops are looking for you, for whatever reason, so you won't be able to just stroll through the front door."

She raised her hand to stop him before he went any further. "I know a back way in, so I'll just stroll in that way. Problem solved."

For the briefest of moments, she reveled in her triumph over his negativity about her going out on her own. He may have been big and strong and very helpful in a number of situations, she had no doubt, but she wasn't without skills herself. As a single woman in a big city, she'd learned to handle herself. More than once, she'd had to think on her feet. This situation would be no different.

Roman slowly leaned forward and positioned his elbows on his knees. "And as for your money, forget it. They've already put a freeze on all your accounts if they're really after you. It doesn't seem like you've thought this whole thing through, Kate."

He was taking all the wind out of her sails. Deflated, she sat down hard on the edge of the bed and sighed. "Fine. What am I supposed to do? I have to get that proof."

"Why? Who does it help for you to get proof that your boss didn't trust the cops?"

She didn't want to admit the truth, but she wanted the proof for him. Something about him thinking she may be guilty or played a part in the death of Jonas and Samuel bothered her. She couldn't explain it since normally she reserved that kind of respect for people she knew for years and had grown to trust.

This person she'd known for only two days. It made no sense that his opinion of her guilt or innocence made any difference to her.

But it did, and every time he looked at her like she might deserve the police coming after her made it all the more important that she show him she had nothing to do with these murders. That her distrust of the police stemmed from something real and not just the crazy ramblings of a woman on the run.

"It helps me, Roman. I want to have that proof is all," she said, not sure she wanted to admit the truth of why she planned to risk everything to go to the law offices and find the file for Samuel Darnell's case.

Roman eased himself back against the chair and shook his head. "That makes no sense. You know if you're guilty or not."

Focusing on her hands in her lap, she said, "Well, it doesn't have to make sense to you. You're not part of this anymore."

He didn't say anything to that, so she pushed down the fear of going out on her own that had begun to form into a tight ball in her stomach and told herself she could do this. She had to. She had no choice.

"Kate, I told you when I walked into your room at that fleabag motel that I was going to protect you. That's my job, and I don't plan for you to be the first assignment I fail at, so I can't let you go anywhere without me."

Frustration pushed fear out of her mind for the moment, and she stood to look at him. God, he looked so in control as he sat there, probably still bleeding from that gash in his side. Even injured, he seemed so calm and ready for anything.

If every word out of his mouth didn't irritate the hell out of her, she could admire him for that calmness. As it was, she wanted to lash out at him for thinking he could or should stop her from doing anything in this world.

"Why do you keep telling me you can't let me do things? What makes you think you have any say whatsoever in what I do or don't do about this or anything else? You come waltzing into my life saying you want to protect me, and you think that means you can dictate where I go and when? No way. Nope."

Kate felt her emotions begin to unravel, but she didn't care. She may have liked Roman more than she wanted to admit even to herself and she may have felt bad about what she'd done, but this issue of giving her permission to do things was her line in the sand, the hill she would die on, if need be.

Hopefully, that death would only be figurative.

But whatever happened, she fully intended on doing what she wanted to do and not because some man she'd just met let her.

She waited for Roman to say something, but he remained silent and just stared at her like she was some creature he'd never encountered before. Maybe he'd never met a woman who stood up for herself. She had no idea. All she knew was there would be no letting her do anything.

A grown woman didn't require permission to run her life as she saw fit.

Instead of saying something, like an apology for treating her like some kind of subservient child who needed his permission, he stood up and began walking across the room. Kate watched in a mixture of confusion and fear as he came toward her. For as much as she believed every single word she'd said, she didn't truly know this man or how he'd react to her impromptu declaration of her own independence.

Would he force her to obey him now? Or would he just walk out and go back to his boss to report that Kate Sheridan was definitely not a woman who needed their kind of help.

All of this raced through her brain as he slowly moved closer.

Roman stopped just inches away from where she stood and stared down at her with a look in his eyes she couldn't place. For a moment, she thought it could be admiration or appreciation, but she couldn't be sure. She waited for him to say something, frozen there as she tried to imagine what his response would be.

He opened his mouth to speak but then his face twisted into an expression of anguish and he reached out for her, grabbing her shoulders. Kate's thoughts immediately focused on his injury, but before she could ask him what was wrong, he fell back onto the bed behind him, taking her down with him.

They landed on the bed with her on top of his chest and their legs entwined. For a moment, she wasn't sure if he'd passed out from the pain or something else happened. Roman's eyes were closed, so she couldn't be sure.

"Roman? Are you okay?" she asked, touching his face to check if he was conscious.

His eyelids fluttered open and he winced. "I'm fine."

"You aren't fine. You just fell over in pain from that cut on your side. That's not fine," she said before she realized in horror that she might be pressing against his side. "Oh, my God! Am I hurting you?"

She tried to pull away, but he held her to him. "You're not hurting me."

He felt so strong against her that she didn't want to move. They lay there with his arm around her, Roman holding the two of them to one another. "Just give me a second and I'll be fine, Kate. Could you stop being angry with me for that long? I promise you that as soon as I'm up on my feet you can tell me how much you don't want my help all you want."

All the worry and guilt she'd felt earlier washed over her and exhausted her suddenly. Resting her head on his chest as she had when she felt asleep the night before, she closed her eyes.

"I'm sorry I've been so difficult. I am. I guess I'm just more independent than most women."

He didn't respond, and as she listened to the sound of his breathing and felt his chest rise and fall beneath her head, she decided she didn't need him to say anything.

But she did want him to know she had no regrets about who she was.

Opening her eyes, she lifted herself off him and leaned on her elbow as he looked at her with those dark eyes of his that never seemed to give away his feelings about anything.

"I'm not sorry for being that kind of person, Roman."

While that was true, she felt the need to add something else. "I am sorry for a lot of things you've had to go through because of me, though. When you look back on this job, I hope you'll remember that."

He smiled and looked up at the ceiling before returning his focus to her. "Kate, I'm not going anywhere, so I won't be looking back on this job as if it stopped here. Just as you don't plan to have anyone tell you what to do, either do I. Maybe we can come to some agreement that lets us both be who we are without making the other person be something they aren't?"

"Was that what you were going to say before you collapsed?"

"Something like that, yeah."

Kate took a deep breath in as she thought about his question, inhaling the scent of his shirt and his skin that smelled so uniquely him. Clean and masculine. She did like having him around, even if he tried to make her do things she didn't want to do.

And as much as she didn't want to admit it, she needed his help. The police still had her on their radar, and they would find her if she didn't get out of the city soon. Without Roman, she might be forced to contact her friends and family for some way to escape, and she didn't want to do that. He'd likely have an idea on how to get away safely.

She did owe him for all he'd gone through to help her. True, it was his job, but unless he was getting hazardous duty pay, he likely didn't expect to get cut up crawling out a cheap motel bathroom window.

"Okay, I think I can agree to that. No more you telling me what you're going to let me do, right?"

Roman smiled and nodded his agreement. "Right. And no more fighting me on every little thing. I meant what I said when I promised to protect you, Kate. I would never do anything that would make me go back on that pledge."

Maybe because she'd never had anyone who wanted to protect her the idea of someone like Roman wanting more than anything to take care of her just sounded unbelievable. She didn't know why she fought him on everything he'd tried to do, but she could try to change that part of her since he wouldn't be ordering her around anymore.

"It's a deal," she said and then sat up next to him. "I admit I'd like to stay here and just lie around for the rest of the day, but we need to get moving if we're going to get to my office building before everyone starts to come into work."

Roman nodded once more and slowly sat up. "Then I guess we better get moving to your office, but you need to promise me you'll follow my lead. It's not me telling you what to do. It's just that I'm more experienced with breaking into places in the middle of the night."

Intrigued, she chuckled at the idea of him on the wrong side of the law. "Really? Now this is a side of you I hadn't expected, Roman."

He stood up and rolled his eyes. "You have no idea."

Kate opened up her purse on the dresser and dangled keys in front of her. "But there won't be any need for any breaking and entering tonight."

"We're not going to go through the front door. We'll have to find another way so we won't be seen," he said, dismissing her suggestion.

Moving through the keys on her keychain, she held up the one to the back door of the building. "Well, I have that covered too. The back door work for you?"

He arched one dark eyebrow and smiled. "Okay. Maybe I underestimated you, Kate."

"Don't beat yourself up about it. There's a long line of people in my life who've done the same thing. I might not have all the answers, but sometimes I come up with one."

Roman opened the hotel room door and looked out into the hall before turning back to look at her. Extending his arm, he said, "Then I'll let you lead the way, but you need to make me one promise."

She stopped in the doorway and looked up at him. "And what's that?"

"If we get into any trouble, you follow my lead."

"Deal."

That she could agree to. In fact, as they began to walk down the hallway together toward the stairwell, she thought that she could agree to a lot of things with Roman when he acted like this. The memory of his muscular body naked in front of her in the bathroom and then him under her on the bed made her wonder if she wasn't thinking with the right part of her body when it came to him, though.

But for the moment, she liked having him next to her doing what no one else had ever done.

Protecting her.

Chapter Ten

A FTER MAKING THEIR way down the hotel stairwell and through the attached parking garage, they covered the ten blocks in just under twenty minutes and reached her office building on Loyola Avenue. Along the way, she filled him in on a few things she felt he needed to know, particularly that many a night she had worked late and never once did she run into any security, even when she didn't clock out until one or two in the morning.

Roman knew they didn't have much time before people began showing up for work. He followed Kate through the back service door of the fourteen story building and directed her toward the stairs when she began walking toward the elevators, earning him a look of utter disbelief.

"Are you kidding? My office is on the ninth floor," she said in exasperation that they'd have to walk the entire way.

"We can't risk the night security seeing someone using the elevators," he whispered in her ear as he gently pushed her up the first few white concrete steps in the stairwell painted to match.

"Why? I work here. It wouldn't be anything strange for me to show up at any time during the day or night," she complained in a tone that verged on whining.

"Just trust me on this. Walking is the way to go."

He waited for her to fight him on this point as she'd fought him on virtually everything else in the past couple days, but to his surprise, she just sighed loudly and trudged up the steps without saying another word.

Until they reached the third floor.

Huffing and puffing like she hadn't climbed three flights of stairs before in her life, she turned toward him and shook her head. "I need a second. I swear to God I don't think I'm going to make it the whole nine floors."

"Do I have to carry you?" Roman joked, hoping she didn't take him seriously since his side still ached.

Screwing her face into a grimace, she began walking up the stairs again. "No. You do not have to carry me, thank you. I just needed a second to catch my breath."

He wanted to tease her and say she didn't look as out of shape as she seemed at that moment, but he didn't want to ruin the good thing they had going on since they'd reached a détente of sorts back at the hotel. Walking behind her, he had to admit she had great legs and a nice ass, even if she couldn't climb stairs very well.

As they reached the landing on the fifth floor, a noise that sounded like someone jiggling the handle on the door started her, and she reached back to grab his hand. "Someone's coming!"

He stopped and waited to see if it would open. All the time, Kate's hand tightly squeezed his. After a few seconds, nothing happened, so he tapped her on the shoulder.

She turned to look at him, her eyes filled with a look of terror. "What do we do?" she whispered in a panicked voice.

For a long moment, he watched for the door to open. If it did, he'd get in front of Kate and protect her from whoever appeared. When no one did, he breathed a sigh of relief.

"It's okay. Probably just the security guard. Let's keep going but if you have to say anything, make sure you whisper, okay?"

Still clutching his hand, she didn't let go as they began to ascend the next flight of stairs to the sixth floor. When they reached each door, she stopped for a moment like she feared someone would come through at any second. Roman doubted that's where they'd run into trouble. Far more likely, if they had any problems, it would come when they got to her boss's office.

Finally, they got to the ninth floor and Kate perked up at the fact that at least they didn't have to climb any more stairs. Turning her head to look back at him, she smiled.

"I didn't think I'd make that last set of stairs," she whispered. "How is it you're not exhausted?"

"Good genes," he said with a smile.

"But what about your injury?" she asked, pointing at his side.

He had felt it twinge a little a few flights below but nothing he couldn't handle. Shrugging, he just shook his head.

"Maybe I should go through first. You know, just in case the security guard is there," he suggested as she began to twist the door handle.

"Why? What are you going to do? Knock him out?" she asked wide-eyed.

In truth, he didn't know what he'd do if they opened the door and found a security guard standing on the other side. He didn't like getting other people involved in cases, especially when he already was breaking the law.

However, he couldn't have a guard calling the police before they retrieved the information they'd come for, so if it meant he had to incapacitate the guy for a short time, he'd do it. His job was to protect Kate, and that's what he'd do.

No matter what it took.

"No. Well, if I have to, but…just be careful when you open the door. Don't go through it without looking around first," he said, praying to God she'd listen to him on this.

"Okay. Jonas's office is at the back. As soon as you go through the door, it's on the right."

She slowly opened the door and did exactly what Roman had told her to do, looking left and then right before walking through to the dimly lit floor of office suites. He followed closely behind, noting the location of the elevators on the opposite end of the floor and that there didn't seem to be any other way out than the stairwell.

They hurried to the office at the back of the building, and Kate used her key to her boss's office to let them in. Closing the door behind them, he watched as she made a beeline to the desk near the window thankfully covered with closed blinds.

She turned on the lamp on the left corner of his desk and looked back at Roman. "Jonas was a history buff, so when he saw these lamps online he bought them because he said they made his office look like an old timey southern lawyer's office."

Roman looked at them and didn't see how they were any different than other lamps he'd ever seen in offices. Gold tone with linen rectangular shades, they didn't seem old timey or southern to him.

"You should have seen how pleased he was when he turned them on for the first time," she reminisced as she sat in the chair behind his desk. "He was just as pleased as punch."

For the first time, he noticed Kate only occasionally had a southern accent. Curious, he asked, "Why don't you sound like everyone else in New Orleans?"

She looked up as she spun around in the chair toward the filing cabinet next to the desk and asked, "What do you mean by that?"

"You don't have a southern accent like everyone else in New Orleans. Like the desk clerk at the hotel. You don't sound anything like him. You only sound like you're from here when you say certain words, like when you said he was as pleased as punch. Why?"

Flashing him a smile, she said, "I was born in Illinois. My family didn't move down here until I was thirteen. I think the rule is if you move somewhere after you're twelve, you sound like the place you came from. I've picked up some of the accent, but I guess I still sound like I'm from up north."

She opened up the filing cabinet and lifted a laptop out of the top drawer. Surprised to see that come out, he said, "That's a strange place to keep that, isn't it?"

With a nod, she closed the drawer and set the laptop on the desk. Opening it, she explained as she began to tap on the keyboard, "He was an odd combination of old and new. I guess it seems strange, but even with his quirks, Jonas was an okay guy."

"What seems strange is that he didn't take his laptop with him when he left the office."

Kate stopped typing for a moment and shrugged. "I guess. That was another idiosyncrasy of his. He had the ability to remember any detail he came across. What do they call that? Photographic memory or something like that. So he didn't really need his laptop if a client called him when he was at home."

"Then what's going to be on the laptop that will prove anything?" Roman asked, suddenly worried her boss had kept all the important details in his head and they'd risked coming there for nothing.

She grinned up at him. "I said he remembered everything. I didn't say he wasn't completely OCD about making sure there was a copy of it. As I said, quirky. Anything Jonas ever heard, read, or saw ended up in a file on this laptop. But I'd bet a hundred bucks most people don't even know he had this since he kept it hidden in that file cabinet all the time. I'm likely the only person who knew he used it."

Quirky indeed.

"That must be why the cops didn't take it when they searched here. I can't imagine they'd leave a laptop full of potential evidence."

Kate pointed at the empty spot in front of her on the desk. "They took his desktop computer. I'm guessing they think they have everything they need. But they aren't going to find anything on it other than receipts for everything he bought for the office, payroll for me, and his tax information."

She continued tapping away on the keyboard and then opened the top desk drawer to grab a jump drive. She stuck it into the laptop as Roman watched out the door for anyone coming toward the office.

On edge, he wanted her to hurry and couldn't understand what she was doing with the laptop all this time. "We need to get out of here, Kate."

Looking up from whatever she was reading on the screen, she said, "I don't want to just take the laptop."

Roman shook his head, confused at her statement. "Why?"

"I don't know. I thought maybe the laptop could be traced."

He chuckled and shook his head again. "Only in the movies. Not in real life, unless he's got it set up like that, which I doubt, so just take the damn thing and let's go."

Now that she knew that kind of tracing a computer probably wasn't an issue, she slammed the laptop closed and as she rounded the corner of the desk, she turned off the light. For a moment, she looked around the office as Roman wondered what she could be doing just standing there.

Her voice filled with sadness, she said, "Jonas was a nice guy. He didn't deserve what happened to him. I'm going to miss working together with him. He gave me a job right out of school when I had no experience. He was a good person."

Not wanting to hurry her through the makeshift eulogy she seemed to need at that moment, nevertheless, he didn't feel good about them staying any longer in that office. If the security guard had been the one checking the door on the fourth floor, he'd make it up to the ninth floor soon. He didn't want to run into anyone who might sound the alarm.

He touched her on the shoulder and smiled when she looked back at him with tears in her eyes. "I'm sorry, but we need to get out of here right now."

Sadly, she nodded her understanding. "Okay. I just wanted to say my goodbyes."

Roman ushered her out into the hallway, and they hurried toward the back stairway they came up through. As they reached the door to the stairwell, he saw someone walking in the dark toward them.

"Someone's coming! Hurry," he said as he opened the stairwell door and pushed her through.

Behind them, a man yelled, "Stop! Who are you? What are you doing here?"

Kate's eyes opened wide and filled with fear. "That's the security guard! He must have seen us!"

Grabbing her hand, Roman began rushing down the stairs, pulling her along behind him as he took them two at a time. They reached the eighth floor landing and heard the door on the floor above them open before the man ran into the stairwell.

"Stop! You're not allowed in this building! Who are you?" he yelled as Roman's heart began to pound wildly.

They still had seven flights of stairs to run down, and if the security guard had a partner, they might be caught anywhere between there and the back door. He could handle one guard or even two, but if one of them called the police, they'd likely be met when they hit the street behind the building and taken in for breaking and entering in addition to theft, even with Kate's keys.

Her hand clutched his so tightly he didn't worry about them being separated, but as he bounded down the stairs, his legs much longer than hers, he worried she'd trip and fall. Looking back as they hit the fifth floor landing, he saw her holding the laptop to her chest, clinging to it like a life preserver.

Then he looked up as he heard the sound of shoes hitting the steps and saw the guard following them down the stairs. Much slower than them, he still might catch up if she fell, and Roman didn't want to risk it.

He stopped on the next landing and turned toward Kate. "Get on my back. I'll carry you until we get out of this building."

"No!" she said, shaking her head. "You can't. Your side, Roman."

"Don't worry about my side," he said as he spun around and crouched down so she could jump on his back. "Just get on and hold on tight because I'm going to take these stairs as fast as I can."

Only two floors above them, the security guard called out, "The police are on their way! Don't move!"

Kate didn't wait for Roman to tell her twice and climbed onto his back. Pushing the laptop against his chest, she wrapped her arm around his neck and her legs around his waist.

"Okay, I'm set! Go!"

He took off, jumping the stairs three at a time now as the sound of the security guard's shoes tapping against each concrete step echoed around them in the stairwell. Kate's leg rubbed against his side over and over, sending streams of pain through his torso, but Roman didn't stop until they reached the back door and got out into the street.

Lowering her to the ground, he handed her the laptop. "We need to keep running. Can you do that in those shoes?"

She looked down at the black boots with two inch heels and then up at him. "Not a problem. You obviously know very little about women. We can run in stilettos if we have to."

"Good. Then run."

They took off toward Canal Street on their way back to the hotel in the French Quarter, and even though Kate tried to keep up with him, she simply couldn't run as fast as he could. He kept looking back to see if the security guard planned to chase them outside the building and finally saw the man push the back door open and look up the street toward them.

Kate saw him look back and turned her head, causing her to trip over her own feet. She fell forward and landed hard on the ground and on the laptop.

Roman looked back and saw the man begin to run after them. He picked Kate up off the ground and grabbed the laptop.

"Run!"

She looked back and stopped as the guard continued to run toward them, so Roman pulled her along. Kate finally started running again after he barked at her to move, holding tightly onto his hand.

"Is he following us?" she asked frantically.

He looked back and saw the man about two blocks behind, but he didn't want to scare her by telling her that. "I don't know. Keep running. I'll tell you when you can stop."

They ran for another block before he turned around one more time and saw the man had given up. They were in the clear.

For now.

As THEY REACHED the hotel, they slowed down and began to walk again. Kate still held his hand and asked, "Can we please take the elevator up to the room? I can't handle any more stairs right now. My legs feel like cooked spaghetti."

Roman hoped when they walked into the lobby they wouldn't run into the police standing there waiting for them, but he didn't want to make her walk up the stairs again, even to the second floor. She had, after all, not fought him on anything since they left the room over an hour ago, so at least he could give her this one thing to make her happy.

He looked down at her and smiled. "Okay, we'll do the elevator, but if there's anyone suspicious in the lobby, we won't have a choice. We'll have to take the stairs."

The smile she gave him lit up her face. "Deal. See, I don't have to fight with you all the time."

No, she didn't. And he liked this Kate who agreed with him.

For the second time, they walked into the Allton Hotel lobby with its white marble floors, huge crystal chandelier, and luxurious furnishings in the waiting area. This time, they held hands, and Kate pressed her body to his as they passed the check-in desk and that same clerk he'd met the first night.

"Good morning, Mr. Madson," the desk clerk said in an entirely too chipper early morning voice.

Roman gave him a smile but said nothing, preferring to keep silent as he and Kate walked to the elevators. Although no one stood waiting for any of the three doors to open, just like the last time they stood there waiting to go up to their room, he wrapped his arm around her and she buried her face in his shoulder to hide from anyone who might walk up to them.

No one did, and when the doors to the center elevator opened a few moments later and they walked in, she didn't move away from him.

Instead, she pressed her face into the space in between his shoulder and chin. Her skin was warm against his neck, and as the elevator rode up to the second floor, he felt her lips touch his skin beneath his ear.

Closing his eyes, he let himself revel in how good it felt to have a woman this close again. Not just any woman, though.

This woman.

He wanted to feel every inch of her against him. Even though he knew he shouldn't want that, he couldn't help himself.

No. He didn't want to help himself.

Never before in Roman's life had he been so willing to throw caution to the wind for another human being. His world had been built on knowing when to risk it all and what to expect in return when he did. It's what made him the successful soldier he'd been and the man Persephone and Nicholas could always count on, no matter what the case.

Now his thoughts turned to the basic fact that although he barely knew Kate Sheridan, she made feelings he'd sworn he'd never feel again come alive inside him. Those emotions, so risky in his line of work, now threatened to overwhelm him as she stood clinging to him.

So close that he felt the beat of her heart against his side. He'd promised to protect her when they first met because it was his duty as a member of Project Artemis.

As they stood alone in that elevator after nearly being caught at that office building, he knew that had changed. Now he silently swore that he'd protect her not out of duty but because he cared for her.

It made no sense, but then again, he'd never thought emotions made much sense anyway.

"I'm sorry I nearly messed everything up back there," she said quietly, her soft lips moving against his neck and making him want to feel those lips on his right there in the elevator.

"You did great back there, Kate," he said, gently pressing her against him. "Even better, you didn't fight me."

The elevator dinged to let them know they'd reached the second floor, and the doors opened. They stood there for a moment, neither of them moving, until Kate pulled away from him and walked out into the hallway.

Roman was left wishing that moment never had to end, but now that it had, he needed to focus on the case. Kate was depending on him to protect her, and to do that, he needed to know what Jonas Flynn kept on that laptop.

Chapter Eleven

KATE JUMPED ONTO the bed and opened the laptop, eager to delve into what Jonas had been investigating. Roman closed the door behind him and took his spot in the chair near the window. Whatever that had been between them in the elevator made her not want to look up as Jonas's laptop warmed up, but she felt her partner's stare on her as she avoided his gaze.

Partner. For the first time, she actually felt like they were partners in this mess. Not that she thought they were equal partners. She knew better than to fool herself. Roman brought far more to the table than she did, but maybe if she found something useful to give them a clue to follow she could prove to him that she wasn't simply a woman caught up in a disastrous mess.

And even more, she could show him that she wasn't just some crazy woman who believed the cops were out to get her, or worse, a murderer he should turn in the next chance he got.

"Find anything yet?" Roman asked with a lilt

to his voice that told her he'd caught her daydreaming.

She turned her head and leveled her gaze on his face. "Patience, grasshopper. This laptop has been through hell tonight. For God's sake, I landed on it full force back there. Give it a chance."

A slow smile lit up his face. "Just checking. You looked a little lost for a minute. I'm not a computer genius, but I can help if you need me to."

Pretending to be offended, Kate screwed her face into a scowl. "I don't need help getting into a laptop, and certainly not my boss's laptop. I'm not a complete idiot, you know, Roman."

The smile didn't leave his face as he held his hands up in fake surrender. "I didn't mean to upset you. I was just trying to help."

As the welcome screen came up on the laptop, she smiled and blew on the tips of her fingers before rubbing her hands together. "No worries. I got this. Now to make some magic."

Roman chuckled. "Kate's going to make magic. Everyone step back."

She ignored his attempt at being cute, even though she couldn't deny that she liked when he acted like that. Seeing him smile and acting almost silly made her feel like he might be okay with her. After being so difficult and injuring him, she hoped this change meant things were improving between them.

That was other than what just happened in the elevator, which she didn't want to think too much about or her emotions would start running away with her.

Focus, Kate. Stop thinking like an oversexed teenage girl and get down to business.

Tapping on the keys, she began reading through the names Jonas had given his files. Ever the eccentric, he chose old TV show names, but Kate had no problem deciphering his secret code.

She hovered over the first yellow file and mumbled the name. "Barney Miller."

"What?" Roman asked, obviously listening carefully to what she was doing.

Kate looked up and shook her head. "Nothing. Just a file name."

He repeated his question. "What?"

"Nothing. Just Jonas's way of hiding things. Now give me a few minutes to see if I can find anything."

Roman's dark eyebrows came in toward his nose, and his eyes narrowed to squints. "Fine. If you need me, I'll be watching TV."

Before she could apologize for being so short with him, he turned away and pointed the remote at the TV, effectively shutting down their conversation. Not that she wanted to continue talking since she had to start figuring out her boss's notes, but she hadn't wanted him to think she was brushing him off.

He flipped through a few channels before settling on some old movie, so Kate returned her focus to Jonas's file named Barney Miller. Clicking on it and expecting something to do with the New Orleans Police Department, she saw it contained a single document with the name Fish.

"Fish?" she said out loud, unsure why anything in this folder would have that name.

Maybe Roman would know.

"Any idea why Jonas would call a file in the Barney Miller folder Fish?" she asked, interrupting his movie.

He turned his head to look at her for a moment before he turned back to look at the TV. "One of the characters was named Fish. The old guy who sounded like a human version of Eeyore."

Kate hadn't seen enough episodes of Barney Miller to understand Roman's explanation, so she didn't bother asking him anything else and just clicked on the document to see what it was about. In it, she found nothing but numbers. Some looked like dates, while others made no sense at all. They didn't appear to be dollar amounts, so what could they be?

She considered asking Roman for his help, but everything in his body language told her now was not the time, from the way he kept his arms crossed tightly across his chest to the way his shoulders turned away from her sharply. Making a mental note to ask him later once he looked more receptive, she moved on to the next folder named Hawaii Five-O.

Even before she clicked, she knew this would be about the New Orleans Police Department. Jonas hadn't been very clever with this one. Opening the file, she saw two documents. Apartment Defects and Flics.

Jonas must have been in a hurry when he typed the second file name because he missed the k in Flicks. Not that she had any idea what the word flick referred to.

Her curiosity piqued, she opened that document and found a list of five sets of letters that appeared to be initials. Were they initials indicating people's names or the names of other things, like towns or something else?

R.G.

H.H.

A.J.

K.S.

M.M.

Frustrated, Kate stretched her legs out in front of her under the laptop. What the hell did Jonas mean by naming this file flics and what did these letters mean? She'd been so sure she could figure out whatever he wrote in these notes, and now that she sat there staring at this second document, she had no idea what he meant.

The files hadn't given her anything useful yet, but she wasn't defeated by any means. Surely, the file named Apartment Defects would make more sense.

Kate clicked on it and sighed loudly as she read a partial address and a list of problems in someone's home. Had Jonas mistakenly put a document about his home repairs in with his work files? No, that made no sense. The address had nothing to do with where he lived, and he didn't own any other properties, as far as she knew.

Wherever this place was, it certainly wasn't anywhere she'd ever want to live. 1073 Richmond Street had improperly installed windows that allowed water to seep into the residence and into the walls. In addition, Jonas had noted it had missing drag strips and hold downs. Kate had no idea what either of those were. Continuing on, she read the apartment had even more problems. Faulty electrical work, including wiring that hadn't been completed to code, plagued the entire building. Even worse, a balcony on the third floor had been found to be structurally unsound due to a lack of proper supports.

Where was this horrible place? Kate scanned the document again and found no city or state mentioned.

"Find anything useful yet?" Roman asked, jarring her from her thoughts.

Kate sighed. "I don't know. This folder has two documents in it. One doesn't seem to make any sense at all, and the other just seems to be a list of things some poor homeowner has to deal with at their home."

"Is this the Barney Miller folder?" he asked, turning in the chair to face her.

"No. Hawaii Five-O. Not that I have any idea why he would name it that," she explained as a feeling of dejection began to come over her.

"Great show," Roman said, as if that helped at all.

"Well, I'm happy that you and my boss share a love of old TV shows. Unfortunately, I have no idea what any of this means."

Roman stood and walked over to stand next to the bed. "Here, let me see if I can make anything of it."

Kate couldn't help but feel disappointed that her big chance to prove she could offer something of use to their partnership had gone down in flames in such a short time. As much as she wanted to figure out just what was behind Jonas and Samuel's murders, part of her hoped Roman wouldn't be able to decipher what her boss meant in these notes because she didn't want to feel completely useless.

He sat down next to her on the bed, forcing her to move in toward the center, and took the laptop from her hold without another world. God, he could be so bossy!

Settling in, he began scrolling through the Fish document as Kate mumbled, "Sure. Go ahead. Do your thing."

Roman didn't pay any attention to her, so as he began to read through the documents in both files, Kate sulked. So much for showing him she could handle herself.

So much for proving her innocence.

After nearly ten minutes of him saying nothing, she couldn't stand the silence anymore and craned her neck to see what he was reading. Her eyes read down the page that contained the info about flics, whatever they were.

"I figured that file would be about the cops, but I couldn't make heads or tails of what Jonas put in there."

"Right church, wrong pew," Roman said before turning to face her. "Hawaii Five-O wasn't about cops."

Confused, she shook her head. "No, it was. I might not know anything my boss was trying to show in those documents, but I've seen that show once or twice. He would have used it to indicate something about New Orleans' finest."

She had no idea what he was talking about with his church and pew comment, but she knew her old television shows. Her mother had an odd obsession with programs from before Kate was born, so many a nights she missed the shows her friends were watching because her mother decided some seventies show was more interesting. That very reason was why she begged her parents for a TV for her fourteenth birthday.

So even though Roman seemed to have all the answers, this time she had him.

Smiling, he shook his head like she just had. "No, Hawaii Five-O was about an elite group of state police officers who answered exclusively to the governor."

He sounded so damn sure of himself that she didn't want to argue about this anymore. In truth, she couldn't say he was wrong.

Huffing her irritation at the whole subject, Kate folded her arms across her chest. "State police. Cops. All the same, if you ask me."

"As I said, right church, wrong pew."

"Well, that doesn't mean that I don't have to worry about the cops in this town being after me. New Orleans cops would gleefully go along with whatever the state police told them to, so it's the same church and maybe the other end of the same pew. Six and one half dozen of another."

Her frustration began to make her sound like an idiot. She knew that, but it didn't stop her.

"I'm not saying you don't have to worry about the police, Kate. I was just correcting a common mistake people make about Hawaii Five-O."

"Are you some kind of Hawaii Five-O expert, or did you study all the sixties and seventies cop shows, Professor Know It All?" she asked as she leaned back against the headboard.

"Well, my major was police shows, but I minored in TV shows set in the islands," he answered with a chuckle. "Just wait until we get to anything related to Magnum P.I."

Smart ass.

Kate had never met a man who could combine being sexy, cute, and arrogant all at once. It made it very hard to dislike him. Impossible really.

Swallowing her pride, she quietly asked, "Are you able to figure out anything from these things Jonas wrote?"

"No, but I'm not giving up."

He may not have felt like throwing in the towel, but she felt like an utter failure and wanted nothing more than to escape from this whole entire mess. She knew she couldn't, but that didn't change the fact that she wanted to.

"Well, have at it. I'm going to grab a bath. Maybe it will give me some epiphany."

Roman didn't say anything, so she slid off the side of the bed and headed toward the bathroom. Five minutes later, she stood naked and ready to step into the tub, hopefully to drown all her worries underneath a mountain of bubbles that grew by the moment in front of her.

But before she could begin to enjoy her own personal spa time, Roman called out, "Kate! Come here!"

Quickly, she grabbed a towel and wrapped it around her. Hurrying out into the room as she knotted it between her breasts, she rushed over to next to the bed to see what all the yelling was about.

"Is the place on fire? What's going on, Roman?" she asked as she looked around their hotel room for what had excited him.

He looked up from the laptop and pointed at the screen. "Look! Bingo!"

Leaning in to see what he was talking about, she read the document he'd been looking at and her mouth dropped open. She turned to look at him and found she couldn't even find the words.

"I know," Roman said with a smile. "It's like your boss is talking from the grave. I know it's not the entire case wrapped up in a bow, but at least we know why he worried about the cops if anything happened to him."

Kate turned back to read Jonas's words telling them that Samuel Darnell had come to see him after a series of run-ins with the New Orleans police and the Louisiana State Police. He believed he was being harassed because his cousin had been a whistleblower in a sexual harassment case against the department.

But Jonas found out that his cousin had nothing to do with why the police suddenly became interested in him. The cops weren't interested in a claim by some woman that one of New Orleans finest got handsy with her when she worked as some clerk for the department for a few months three years ago.

Roman touched the laptop screen at the very end of her boss's writing, and Kate read his words out loud. "This case isn't about the client's cousin. This is about something else, something much bigger. I think this goes all the way up to the top."

Letting out a sigh, she barely caught the towel as the knot between her breasts came undone and almost gave Roman a show. She scrambled to keep her body hidden as excitement about what she just read made her want to jump around the room celebrating.

"I was right! I knew he hadn't lied to me about not trusting the cops," she said, smiling so broadly that her cheeks began to ache. "Now do you believe me?"

Roman's gaze slid down from her face to where she held the towel closed in front of her. "I never said I didn't. But now we need to figure out what this case is about and what top your boss was talking about."

"The head of the police department," Kate declared, sure that she was right this time.

After thinking about her idea for a long moment, he looked up at her and let his gaze settle on her face. "Then why title one of the files Hawaii Five-O? That says state police to me."

"Same difference. Cops."

He shook his head. "No, although I did look up the word flic. It's French for policeman. If all of this is related to Hawaii Five-O, the top is the governor."

His statement made her breath catch in her chest. What would Governor Williams have to do with Samuel Darnell, a carpenter from Lafayette?

"Well, I'm going to get dressed again and get back into Jonas's laptop, so I'll be right back."

As she hurried back into the bathroom to put her clothes on, Roman yelled, "No bath, then?"

Kate closed the door behind her and began to dress quickly. She wanted to read every last word her boss had written and left on that computer to find out what the hell had happened to end up with him and Samuel murdered.

There was no time for a bath now.

Chapter Twelve

ROMAN AWOKE EARLY and instantly felt the effects on his back from sleeping in the chair the whole night. Tilting his head left and right, he cracked his neck and felt relief begin to trail down his spine. His side still ached, but he'd have to ignore that.

His eyes focused and he saw Kate on the bed still asleep, the laptop right next to her. She'd spent hours scouring her boss's files and had drifted off in the middle of reading.

Much of what she found he still needed to figure out, but that would have to wait until after he had some breakfast. Standing, Roman stretched his body and headed to the bathroom to make himself at least presentable to go downstairs to the restaurant.

Five minutes later, he stood in front of the mirror scrubbing the last vestiges of sleep from his face and staring at the man he saw before him. Three days ago, he knew what his life needed. At least he thought he knew. Now, everything seemed different.

Changed all around because of her.

Roman shook his head, still not believing what his head and heart kept telling him. He'd never believed in love at first sight. Who thought that shit really happened in real life? That was the nonsense of romance movies men had to watch to make their girlfriends or wives happy. It didn't happen anywhere but in the movies.

And yet, there he stood not twenty feet away from a woman who'd somehow, with her insistence on arguing everything and impetuous need to prove she didn't need his help, made him want her more than he'd wanted anyone in his entire life. It made no sense, but there it was.

He didn't exactly know what to do about it either. Not since Emily died had he even spent more than a night with a woman before leaving forever. He'd learned the painful lesson of his life with her.

Who he was and what he did had always been too perilous for him to let love in. He had a duty, first as a soldier and now as a member of Project Artemis, and that responsibility put him in harm's way too much to commit to anyone or anything else but the mission. He'd accepted that truth and lived by it.

Until Kate.

Now everything in his being seemed to have

abandoned that central idea of his life for the possibility of what he might have with her. But he knew better. Nothing had changed from the time he lost Emily until now. He couldn't promise a woman anything, no matter how much he wanted to.

That's why he'd stayed away from relationships all this time. And he'd been successful at arranging his world to accommodate the reality that he couldn't commit to a woman and the job at the same time.

It had to be one or the other, and for so long, he met no one who made him want to even entertain the thought of not being the person he'd been all these years.

Not until Kate.

Roman narrowed his eyes in anger at his reflection. "You know what happens when guys like us lose our focus. You know people get hurt. And still you stand here thinking about her like it can ever be anything more than what you've always had with women."

Splashing water on his face, he silently chastised himself for being foolish, disgusted with this newfound pie-in-the-sky attitude he had adopted in the past few days. This job was no different than any other, and if he didn't keep his focus, Kate or he would get hurt.

Or worse, both of them.

And not in some boo-hoo my heart is broken way either.

He now knew what the cops would want Kate for, and knowing how the police worked, if they got their hands on her, she had no chance. He still didn't believe they were guilty like she did, but once she became part of the case, she'd be caught up in the legal system and there'd be nothing he could do.

That's not how he intended this case to end. They needed to find out more about what her boss was looking into.

So tonight they'd leave the hotel they'd been in for the past four days and begin following the money. He didn't want to stay at the Allton much longer since it would only be a matter of time before the cops sniffed out their location. He'd let her sleep a little more while he got them some breakfast, and then they'd plan out their next moves.

Roman walked out of the bathroom and glanced over at where Kate lay still sound asleep. Curled up next to the laptop, she looked content there, like she'd fallen asleep many a night exhausted from work. He had to admire her for that. Her dedication to her boss definitely impressed him.

Shaking his head, he tried to rid himself of those feelings for her. He couldn't afford to fall for her. No. He needed to keep focused on this case and that was it.

By the time he reached the lobby, he'd almost convinced himself he could push away those feelings he'd begun to have for her. True, he'd never had to do it before, but he knew how to handle his emotions. He'd been through a war, for Christ's sake. If he could handle months on end in a dangerous foreign land under enemy attack, he certainly could control how he felt about one woman.

The server in the restaurant took his order for scrambled eggs, toast, bacon, and coffee for two and scurried back to the kitchen to get the cook started. No one else sat in the dining room, so Roman figured it wouldn't take long to get the food and sat down at a table near the door.

For the first time since their run to Jonas Flynn's office, he felt like he could relax. They knew a lot more about the case and once they got some food into their stomachs, they could make a plan. As long as they kept out of sight and avoided the cops, they'd be fine.

He had an idea exactly how to do that too. Time to ring up a buddy of his from years ago.

The server returned as he sat lost in thoughts about Butcher Richards, his friend from their days in Afghanistan, and said in a very thick southern accent, "Let me turn the TV on for you, hon.

That way you're not sitting there forced to stare at the four walls."

Roman looked up at her and smiled as she tried to reach above her head to turn it on while she explained that someone had stolen the remote control. She stood only about five feet tall and had to be almost that wide, so she wasn't able to reach far enough without standing on a box. Even worse, every time she tried to, her uniform rode up so high on her thighs that he nearly got a show.

She grunted and groaned as she stretched to no avail, so he walked over behind the servers' station where she stood and tapped her on the shoulder. "Let me. I've got a few inches on you."

Looking up at him, she smiled with a twinkle in her eye. "Oh, you definitely do, hon. I'd guess more than just a few inches too."

He chuckled at her not-so-subtle attempt at a double entendre and flipped the old TV on. "Any particular show you want, ma'am?" he asked.

"Oh, whatever you like, hon," she said as her gaze wandered up and down his body, stopping for a moment longer on his crotch than anywhere else.

Choosing not to change the channel, he smiled and scooted by her as she stood watching him walk back to the table. He didn't care what showed up on the TV. He just wanted to get his food and go back to the room.

Not even a minute later, he looked up and saw Kate's picture as big as life on the screen. Underneath it were the words SUSPECT IN DOUBLE MURDER in big bold letters. Jumping up from the table, he saw the server come out of the kitchen with a tray of food in her hands for him. He quickly handed her a twenty and took the tray from her.

"Thanks, hon. You okay? You look like you just saw a ghost," she said as she stuffed the money into the cash register.

He left without answering her question and rushed back through the lobby toward the elevator. He saw the desk clerk he knew again, but this time, the man stared at him strangely before directing his gaze to the TV in the lobby waiting area. Looking back, Roman saw he was watching the same news program that had been on the TV in the restaurant.

Forcing a smile, he hurried toward the elevator, but he knew the clerk had put two and two together and recognized Kate's face. Roman balanced the tray in one hand as he repeatedly pressed the up button, his heart pounding as he knew every second he stood there and Kate slept upstairs, the chance that the cops would find them multiplied.

A minute later, he reached the second floor

and tore down the hallway to the room to wake her up. The clerk had likely already called the police, so they had only minutes to get the hell out of there.

Dropping the tray on the table just inside the door, he leaned over the bed and shook Kate's shoulders. "Hey, wake up! We have trouble. We need to get out of here right now!"

Confused, she sat up and looked toward the window at the darkness outside. "Why? What time is it?"

"Forget the time," he said as he grabbed her bag and tossed it on the bed. "You're a person of interest in those two murders now, so your face is all over the TV downstairs. I think the front desk clerk knows it's you. We need to get out of here."

She jumped out of bed, slammed the laptop shut, and quickly slipped her shoes on. "Did he say something to you?" she asked as she ran into the bathroom.

"No, but I got the feeling by the way he looked at me that he made the connection that the person he saw me with the other day was the one he was looking at on the TV, so we need to get going now."

"Where are we going?" she asked as she hurried out of the bathroom and gulped down a mouthful of coffee.

He grabbed his backpack and took out his

phone from his pocket to make a call. "I'm working on that right now."

Rushing down the hall, he guided her away from the elevator when she began to walk toward it and instead they headed for the stairwell as he waited for his friend to answer.

"Who are you calling?" Kate asked while she ran down the stairs to the parking garage.

"A friend we can trust," Roman said as someone answered the call.

"Hello?" the familiar voice said into his ear.

"Hey, Butcher, it's Roman. I'm hoping you're still hanging out in the Big Easy. I need a big favor."

His old Army buddy laughed loudly and said in his thick, Louisiana accent, "Holy shit! How long's it been, Roman? Yeah, I'm still on my old stompin' grounds. What's up?"

Kate and Roman ran down the stairs as he explained, "I need somewhere quiet to crash for a few days. You still have that place on the lake you always said I could use if I was ever in the city?"

Butcher laughed again. "Yeah. You're in luck. If it was next month, you'd be stuck bunking with my sister's fuckwit husband, but until then, the place is all yours. I'm doing a job in Dallas for the next two weeks."

"Great. Do me a favor and text me the address to this number," Roman said as they burst through the stairwell door into the parking garage. "I owe you for this, Butcher. I won't forget it."

"No way, Roman. I'm here today because of you. The least I can do is let you crash at Chez Butcher. Do you want me to arrange a visit from someone soft and curvy while you're kicking back out on the lake?" his friend asked with a hint of curiosity in his voice.

Roman looked at Kate and smiled. "No, but thanks. I think I'm covered on that front. Sorry we won't be able to have a beer together, but next time?"

"Enjoy it, buddy. It's nothing but peace and quiet out there. Whatever you need to escape from in this world, that's the place to do it. You remember where I told you I keep the key?"

Scanning the parking lot for a car to steal, Roman smiled at the thought of peace and quiet again. "Thanks, man. I appreciate it. Under the hedges in front of the house, right?"

"Right. Just lift up the loose sod and the box with the key will be right there. Let me know if you need anything."

"You're a lifesaver, Butcher. I owe you."

"Bullshit. Just have a good time and enjoy yourself for once, man. And let me know if you change your mind on some company. I know someone who would be perfect for a few days."

"I'm good. Thanks again, man."

Roman ended the call and made a beeline toward an old brown sedan. Finding it locked, he lifted his right elbow and smashed through the driver's side window. Glass fell all around him, but he didn't have time to care. Opening the door, he pointed at the opposite side of the car as Kate stared in shock at the shattered driver's side window.

"Get in!"

Brushing the glass off the seat, he hopped in and unlocked her door before bending down to hotwire the engine. He hadn't done this in years, but in seconds, he heard it start.

Happy he hadn't lost his touch, he sat up as Kate complained, "Why did we have to steal a car older than me?"

Roman ignored her and shifted the car into reverse. As he backed out of the parking spot, she said, "Why couldn't you find something nicer?"

"As much as I'd like to get into how it's practically impossible to hotwire newer cars, we don't have time. Hang on," he said as he floored the gas and drove out of the parking garage.

Handing her his phone, he said, "When Butcher texts the directions, read them to me. I'm heading toward his place on Lake Pontchartrain. In the meantime, you're going to have to get me going in the right direction."

"Okay. Let me think for a moment."

He looked over at her as he raced down St. Louis Street. "We don't have time for thinking. Just tell me how to get there, Kate!"

Pushing her down in the seat, he turned the wheel so the car took the corner sharply onto Basin Street. She stammered out a few words before Roman barked, "Get down so no one can see you!"

"You don't have to yell! I'm down. I'm down. What street are we on now?" she asked frantically.

Leaning forward, he looked up through the windshield to find the street name but saw no signs. "Damnit! Where are the street signs in this town?"

"I don't know," Kate yelled at him. "I never look at them, so I don't know. Just keep going and there must be one coming soon."

He weaved in and out of a line of cars that suddenly appeared and finally at the next corner saw a street sign. "Orleans. Or is it Basin? Damnit! The signs are all fucked up."

Kate pointed out the window. "Orleans? Good! Take Orleans and head toward I-10."

I-10? Roman searched for a sign to tell him where to go. Again, no goddamned signs that he could see. "There is no sign for the on ramp."

Peeking her head up, Kate pounded on the window. "Right! Take the right and then the ramp onto the highway."

He followed her directions and cut across the lanes to head onto I-10. Looking in the rearview mirror, he checked for any sign of the cops following them and saw nothing but a few cars behind them and no police cars.

Kate still sat crouched on the floor, and Roman didn't want to risk it letting her up just yet. "Stay down for a while longer. I just want to make sure we aren't being followed."

"That's okay," she said with a wry smile. "It's not too bad down here, other than the shards of glass and the empty cigarette packs. Whoever's car this is, they treated it like a garbage can."

"Just a few minutes more. What exit am I looking for off this road?" he asked, trying not to smile at how frustrated she sounded.

"You'll need to look for Lake Pontchartrain Causeway. Your friend just texted the address, so since I'm assuming this heap of junk doesn't have GPS, I can just use your phone to find the house. Give me a few seconds and I'll have it for you."

He couldn't stop himself from smiling at her irritation at his choice of cars to steal. "Next time, I'll try to find a newer make and model. Does that make you happy?"

Rolling her eyes, she grimaced. "What will make me happy will be a shower and a change of clothes. Any chance your friend has a female friend or a wife who's my size?"

Roman watched the road and thought about her question. He had no idea about Butcher's private life. That's not the kind of friends they were.

"I'm not sure. Maybe. I don't know."

"Real close, huh?"

The kind of friendship he and Butcher Richards had stemmed from their time in war. They were brothers in arms, far more than mere friends. Others might think they weren't close because neither one of them knew about their personal lives.

But they knew something far deeper about one another. No matter what, they were there for each other when the need arose. That's the kind of close they were.

CHAPTER THIRTEEN

KATE DIDN'T KNOW how long she sat on the floor of the passenger side of that brown 1980s piece of crap car Roman had hotwired, but when her legs began to cramp up and send shooting pain up to her hips, she had to move.

"Hey, is the coast clear yet? I'm tired of doing my stowaway act down here. Can I get up?"

Roman nodded as the car turned left. "Yeah. We're almost to his house."

Happier than she thought she could be at hearing those so simple words come out of his mouth, she pulled herself up onto the passenger seat and stretched her legs as she looked out the window. In all her time living in New Orleans, she'd never come over to this side of Lake Pontchartrain. The sight of the enormous million dollar homes and their perfectly manicured properties told her why. She had a feeling she couldn't even pay the cover price to get into this area of the city.

"So you know a bajillionaire?" she asked while

they drove past each gorgeous home.

He laughed, like she'd said something outrageous. Maybe he didn't know how much the houses around there cost, but she didn't have to be a realtor to understand it took some serious cash to afford a place on the lake in Mandeville.

"I'm not kidding. These homes are certifiable mansions. Your friend must be loaded," she said, staring at the double staircase up to the porch on the house they drove past.

"What's the address again?"

She checked the text. "1819. It should be just up ahead. So you didn't answer me. Is he a bajillionaire? They must pay you guys a bunch to swoop in and do your knight in shining armor thing."

Turning to look at her, he raised his eyebrows at her mention of his job. "He and I don't work together. We knew one another in the Army. He was my captain."

Who knew the US Army paid their people so well? If she'd known there was so much money in enlisting, she might have considered it. Since she'd never made enough at her job as a legal assistant to even drive out near homes like these, she had to believe she'd made a mistake in her employment choices.

"So was he higher in rank or lower than you?" she asked, suddenly curious about this man she knew so little about who had come into her life just days before.

Roman pointed out the window at a house and pulled into the driveway. "I wouldn't call him my captain if I was higher rank than him."

The disgust in his voice came through loud and clear, irritating Kate. Feeling defensive, she tossed his phone into his lap as he shifted the car into park.

"Sorry. Those of us who are mere civilians don't know the Army nomenclature. Whatever he was in the service, he clearly has money. This house might not be a mansion like the ones further down the street, but it's still nicer than anything I've ever lived in."

She hadn't exaggerated. As she stared at the raised Acadian style home in front of her and looked at the mere two block distance to the lake, she knew this friend of his had spent a pretty penny on this property. As anyone in real estate could attest to, the most important thing was location, location, location.

And this house had it in spades.

Roman didn't seem fazed in the least by the impressiveness of the home in front of them. Instead of gawking at the stairs that led up to a gorgeous wrap around porch, he instead acted workmanlike, walking around the house like he was searching for something. Kate looked around to see if anyone else was watching him act so strangely.

Thankfully, no one else seemed to be around to see him. Walking up behind him, she asked, "Uh, are you checking for the water meter, or is this just the way you act when you arrive at someone's house?"

He glanced back and gave her a scowl. "I'm looking for the key. Maybe you don't announce it to the whole world?"

Jeez. What changed to make him so cranky all of a sudden?

"Can I help?" Kate asked, trying to be helpful.

"No," he answered tersely. "Just stay out of sight and wait for me."

The shortness of his answer stung. She thought they'd developed into a team who did things together, but since they left the city, he'd changed somehow. Kate couldn't put her finger on exactly what was different, but it was unmistakable.

She did as he said and stood behind the air conditioning unit. As she hid from neighbors' eyes, she wondered if her life would ever go back to the way it had been before all this madness. She'd never been anyone important—certainly no one people would notice—and even though more than once she'd wished for a more exciting life, this hadn't been what she meant at all.

A new boyfriend and some more interesting ways to spend her nights were all she'd hoped for. Being on the run for her life hadn't been any part of her fantasies.

Roman poked his head into her hiding space and waved her out. "Found it. Let's head in."

Kate hurried past him and practically ran up to the front door, not hating those stairs as much as the thousand or so others she'd been forced to deal with in the past couple days. He took his own sweet time making his way to where she stood, and she saw by the smirk on his face that he'd noticed how she didn't complain this time.

He turned the key and opened the front door. As she walked past him, she said, "Not one word about my running up those stairs. Got it?"

Chuckling, he didn't respond and simply walked into the house behind her. Kate stopped just a few feet in and stared at the all-white décor. She'd expected something different. Something far more masculine. Maybe something with more exposed wood. This friend of Roman's must have had a woman in his life who had a say in the design of his house because all Kate saw around her was beautiful.

"I think I'm in love," she murmured before walking straight ahead through the open floor plan toward the all-white kitchen.

She'd never seen a more gorgeous kitchen in

her life. At least not in real life. This place was the kind of home you saw in magazines.

Swiveling her head left and right to take in all the incredible details in the chef's kitchen, she eyed up the six by six foot white marble topped island with a six burner gas stovetop and enormous hood above, stainless steel double ovens and refrigerator, and beige and brown stone backsplash. She could live in this room for the rest of her life and be more content than she'd ever been before.

Roman walked away, seemingly unimpressed by his friend's home so far, and she wandered around falling more in love with every step. When she walked into the master bath, she stopped and held her breath at what she saw.

As with the other rooms, the bathroom had been decorated in white, and similar to the kitchen, brown accents warmed up the space. A deep marble tub sat against a beige and brown marble tiled wall that hid the glass shower enclosure.

Oh, how she yearned for the moment when she'd slide into that tub and wash off the remnants of the past few days.

She didn't feel right calling dibs on the master bedroom, so she found another of the four bedrooms and fell onto the bed as exhaustion overcame her. Between running down two flights of stairs not ten minutes after being awakened from a sound sleep and then having to crouch down on the floor of the car they stole to get out of the city, it had been one hell of a day already.

Hopefully, life would settle down for a few days so she could catch her breath.

KATE OPENED HER eyes and for a moment didn't know where she was. It took a minute or so to remember she and Roman had come out to his friend's house on the lake and she'd fallen asleep in one of the bedrooms.

Now all she had to figure out was what time it was. Rolling over, she looked out the window and saw darkness. Had she slept all day again?

She listened for a moment for any sign of her partner in crime, but she heard nothing but silence. Maybe Roman had fallen asleep also. Not that she could blame him. He'd gone through almost as much as she had, by her side from almost the very beginning of this nightmare.

Or adventure. She didn't know which better described what they were stuck in.

Beside her lay Jonas's laptop, so once she fully woke up, she set to figuring out how to follow the leads he'd left for her in his files. What made Samuel Darnell so interesting that the cops bothered him over and over? Were the state police really involved like Roman believed, and if so, how? Time and time again, she searched for information and found a dead end. No wonder Jonas hadn't gotten any further.

Frustrated, Kate didn't know where to find the answers. She angrily pushed away the laptop as she wished she had the ability to figure out what her boss couldn't before he died. He deserved her to at least do that for him, but so far, she'd failed miserably.

Maybe she just needed to get some fresh air. Maybe that would give her some perspective that would help her solve this mystery.

She rolled off the bed and padded across the hardwood floor out to the kitchen. Everything looked the same as it had when she walked through earlier. Clearly, Roman hadn't decided to make something to eat.

After walking around the entire house, she still didn't find him, so she looked out the window to see if the old brown car still sat in the driveway. Still there. Well, at least she could be reasonably sure he hadn't abandoned her.

Not unless he planned to walk back across the Causeway. Then again, for all she knew about him, he might. She wouldn't have thought that yesterday, but something about him had changed today.

The sun had set and a chill in the air had set in, sending goosebumps along her skin as she stepped outside onto the front porch and began walking down the steps to search for him. A full moon shone across the water of Lake Pontchartrain, and lights from the million dollar mansions along the lakefront cast a golden glow on the shore. The scene looked so calm, she stopped to take it all in for a moment. Peace and calm felt so wonderful after what she'd been through.

Her mind wandered to the possibility that someday it would be the norm for her again. She wouldn't argue with having that peace at a house like this one either.

She walked down toward the lakeshore and saw Roman sitting alone near the water just past a giant oak tree nearly covered with Spanish moss hanging from every branch. He must have sensed her as she crossed the road to join him because he looked back at her and watched as she approached him. Kate felt his eyes on her, making her nervous since he seemed like a different man now.

Unsure what to say, she fell back on a joke to break the ice. "So this is how you protect a woman in danger? You leave her alone in a strange house? I woke up and had no idea where I was."

She punctuated her comment with a chuckle, but it didn't work. He didn't crack even the tiniest smile and simply just stared at her as she spoke. When she finished, his face remained stony.

Not that he'd ever been a really emotional guy, but this person seemed entirely foreign to her now. What had changed?

She wanted to ask but didn't know how to. He wasn't exactly the chattiest kind of man at any time. Since no matter what she said seemed to irritate him, she figured she might as well just go the direct route.

"What's wrong, Roman? You seem different ever since you woke me up this morning."

He drew his eyebrows in and then looked away toward the water. "No difference. Just trying to figure out what our next move should be."

No difference and yet he couldn't even bother to face her when he said that. Nope. She wasn't buying it.

Had he finally reached his limit with her arguing?

"I tried to do some more research, but I keep running into dead ends, so I figured I'd see what you were up to. You weren't in the house, so I figured I'd look outside and saw you here."

His response to her explanation? Utter silence.

Something had changed between them. The problem was she didn't know why.

She walked around him so he didn't have a choice but to look at her. Staring into his emotionless face, she quietly said, "I'm sorry I've been such a pain. I don't mean to be. I guess I'm just used to being on my own."

Roman said nothing for the longest time but didn't look away, so she had to fight the urge to fill the empty space in the conversation. Hell, who was she kidding? A conversation took two people talking. One person doing all the talking and being stared at by the other person resembled more a scene out of some psycho killer movie than a conversation.

Finally, he smiled, the corners of his mouth lifting just a tiny bit. "You're not a pain, Kate. There's nothing wrong with questioning things."

"Well, if you're not angry about that, what's wrong? It seems like ever since this morning, you've been upset about something."

He shook his head and shrugged, as if nothing was bothering him. "I'm not upset. I would have liked a little more time to make a plan, but the desk clerk put an end to that idea. It's not bad, though. Butcher's house is a whole lot better than even the Allton."

Since she had him talking, she wanted to take advantage of the opportunity to keep him communicating, so Kate sat down next to him. "How do you know this Butcher guy? He must be pretty trusting to let you stay at his house like this."

Roman tilted his head left and then right, as if

he was debating the truth of what she said. "I don't know if I'd call Butcher trusting. That might be the first time I've ever heard him described like that."

"His house cost a fortune. That he's given us free reign of it for as long as we stay sounds pretty trusting to me. Is that because he was your captain and he knows you?" she asked, becoming more and more curious about this friend of his.

"I guess," Roman answered in a faraway voice. "When you spend time with someone as people are shooting at you, I guess you grow to trust the people you serve with."

Kate knew nothing of that. She'd never even seen a gun up close until she caught a glimpse of Roman's sticking out of the back of his pants and then later saw it sitting on the hotel bathroom vanity. She didn't even know anyone who owned a gun before him. Before the other day, the nearest she'd come to a gun had been those in the movies and on TV.

She couldn't even imagine what it must be like to have people shooting at you. The mere thought of it sent chills down her back.

"What's that like? Is it as terrifying as it sounds?" she asked, genuinely wanting to know what he'd experienced.

Turning his head to look at her, he remained silent, studying her for a moment before he answered. "The first time it's the scariest thing you'll ever go through. You pray to God you'll make it out alive. You're afraid like you've never been afraid before in your life."

"And after that?"

Roman narrowed his eyes and squinted as he looked away toward the water. "After that, you get used to it. You have a job to do, so you do it. People are depending on you, so there's no time to be afraid."

She shook her head in disbelief. "No way I could do that. I'd be paralyzed with fear the first time and every time after that. I'd never be able to get used to it. I'm a coward."

His expression turned serious, and he frowned. "No, you're not, Kate. You're definitely not a coward. You're braver than even you realize."

The intensity in his tone surprised her, but his words sounded like he was proud of her. She had no idea what she'd done to deserve that, though. If she wasn't arguing with him, she was questioning his choices. Neither showed any bravery, in her opinion.

"I don't know about that. I just know I couldn't handle people shooting at me all the time, even if the US government paid me enough to afford a house out here. No thanks."

Chuckling, he looked back at Butcher's house.

"He didn't make that kind of money as a captain in the Army. Trust me. I know."

"So who is this Butcher guy? Does he work at Project Artemis like you?"

Roman leaned back on his palms and smiled. "No. He's in security now since he left the military."

"So why does he trust you so much to just let you crash at his house with me? I'm assuming you didn't mention that I'm on the run from the cops. Is it because you guys served together? Because I'm not sure many of my friends would let me take over their house if they were away. Then again, maybe I just have bad friends."

"There aren't many people in this world who would do this for me. Butcher and I more than served together. We watched out for one another over there. We were brothers in arms and that's carried over to our civilian lives."

Kate had a feeling Roman wasn't telling her the whole story, but as usual, he didn't seem to want to give her more details than he'd already offered. So she took a wild guess.

"Did something happen between you two? Does he owe you some debt or something?"

He looked into her eyes and nodded. "You could say that, I guess. I didn't do anything that any other of his men wouldn't have done. He was that kind of leader."

Now she understood. Butcher and Roman were more than friends. They were blood brothers.

"You saved his life, didn't you? That's why he trusts you with this house. Is that it?"

She searched his eyes for the truth and found it. That's why. Roman wasn't just another of his men.

"I didn't do anything special. We all would have given our lives for one another. That's what being a Ranger means."

"What did you do?" Kate asked, hanging on every word he spoke now.

Roman's eyes grew distant, and he looked out toward the lake in front of them. "We were conducting an assault on a compound and everything was going exactly as it was supposed to, but then in a flash, suddenly gunfire started coming from every side. We knew we had to get the hell out of there and regroup, but we were under attack. Butcher took one in the leg and went down. Three other guys got hit, so four of us knew what we had to do. I picked Butcher up and carried him out of that hellhole and they got the other three."

She gently touched him on the arm, and he turned to look at her like she'd interrupted a memory. "You say that like it was something ordinary. You saved someone's life, Roman. I bet it wasn't the last time you did that either. You've got hero written all over you."

Waving away the compliment, he shook his head. "I did what I was supposed to do. Now with this favor he's doing for us, Butcher and I are even."

"I don't even think you and I are even. You saved the man's life. Trust me. As someone who's been on the receiving end of your help, I'm willing to bet he doesn't think you're anywhere close to being even."

He didn't respond, and Kate knew full well he wasn't just pretending some fake humility. This was who Roman Gregory was. But she wanted to know more.

"Why are you doing this for me? You stuck around when I know you thought the cops had every reason to suspect me of being part of Jonas and Samuel's murders. Then when we found out what my boss was onto, you risked yourself and stole a car. You aren't a law breaking kind of guy, so why are you doing this?"

"It's my job, Kate. I told you. I'm not going to let anyone hurt you. That's my mission, and I've never not successfully completed a mission."

"How did you get involved in this Project Artemis?"

He smiled, and this time it went all the way up to his eyes. "It's a far less interesting story than you're probably imagining."

"Try me. Something tells me it's way more interesting than anything in my life."

"Says the woman who's currently on the run and in the middle of some government conspiracy."

"No fair using my current circumstances against me. Stick to telling your story. How did you get started with Project Artemis?"

In his usual humble way, he shrugged as if what he was about to say wouldn't be far more impressive than anything she'd ever heard before. Just the fact that he willingly put himself in harm's way to help a woman he'd never met outweighed everything she'd ever seen anyone do.

"They recruited me. After I left the Army, I spent some time in security like Butcher, but guarding wealthy financiers and their mistresses didn't do it for me. I wanted something else, and when Nick Hanson, one of the people in charge of Artemis, came to me to join him and a few others he'd recruited, I liked what I heard."

None of this surprised her. Roman had an honorable streak a mile wide in him.

"Why did you leave the military? I get the feeling you're the perfect type for the Army."

He took a deep breath and let it out slowly. "I left because it began to feel like nothing we did mattered anymore. I signed up and did my two tours in Afghanistan, but I needed something more. Something that let me know I was making a difference in the world."

Kate watched as Roman's expression grew dark. She could only imagine the horrors he'd experienced over there and didn't want to make him miserable by asking more questions about his time in the Army. Better to turn the conversation to something lighter.

"So this Nick guy told you he wanted to protect women in danger and you, being the kind of guy you are, jumped at the chance to help people?"

His eyes grew wide at her description of him. "The kind of guy I am?"

God, he really had no idea what kind of man he was. "You know, the hero type. That's why you didn't like being some wealthy guy and his girlfriend's security detail. There's nothing noble about it, and if you're anything, Roman, you're noble to your core."

He thought about what she said for a long moment. "You say that like there's something wrong with being noble."

"No. It's one of the best things I've seen in a person in a very long time, but it's not common by any means. Not anymore. You're a throwback to a time long gone, I think."

Her answer didn't seem to make him any

happier about how she'd described him. Instead of continuing the conversation, he grew quiet, and Kate didn't know what she'd said to make him clam up like that. She hadn't wanted to offend him by saying he was noble. She meant what she said when she told him how nice it was to see that in someone.

Just when she thought he'd start talking again, he stood up. "I have work to do. You should come in. We can't risk anyone seeing you out here."

Kate wanted to ask what she'd done wrong, but he didn't give her a chance as he turned and began walking back to the house. She hurried to catch up to him, wishing they could return to their conversation, but to no avail.

The moment was lost.

CHAPTER FOURTEEN

ROMAN KNEW HE couldn't leave Kate alone, but suddenly as he walked back to the house, he wanted to be anywhere else in the world. He didn't want to discuss what he'd done for Butcher or why he jumped at the chance to work for Nick and Persephone at Project Artemis. The way she said he was a throwback to a time long gone only pointed out the obvious differences between them.

She saw herself as an independent woman who didn't need anyone to save her, and in her eyes, he was some kind of relic from a time when men like him tried to suppress the freedom of women like her.

Not that he was a man who would do anything to protect a woman and a man who believed in honor and duty.

The way she described him made it sound like there was something wrong with who he was.

He didn't want to think about that anymore. Time he got back to work on this case. The sooner he helped Kate clear her name, the sooner he could get back to the estate and the next assignment.

"Hey, can we talk?" she said behind him as they walked through the front door.

Without looking back at her, he said, "I have work to do. If you ever want to get back to your life the way it used to be, I need to talk to my friend who might be able to help us."

"The guy who owns this house? How can he help?" she asked, following him through the living room and into the hallway.

Roman didn't bother to explain that he didn't mean Butcher when he referred to his friend. He knew more than one person, for God's sake. Just because he used the word friend didn't mean he meant Butcher.

"Roman? Did you hear me or are you just ignoring me?" Kate asked just before he closed the bedroom door behind him.

He sat down on the bed and called the estate hoping to talk to Xavier. If anyone could help them, he could. Roman knew next to nothing about computers, but his fellow Project Artemis member spent his days and nights consumed with them. The one member of the team who rarely got sent out on assignments, he helped whenever anyone needed to know more than what they could find out through a basic search.

Nick answered, as Roman had expected, happy to hear from him. "Hey, Roman. I'm glad you called. We were beginning to wonder about you. How are things going down there?"

"Things got a little more involved in the past day or so, but other than that, everything's fine. I was calling to talk to Xavier. I've got something I could use his help with."

Chuckling, Nick said, "Ah, something our in-house hacker can help you with? I saw him earlier today, but I don't know if he's on the estate. Give me a minute and I'll have Tess see what she can find out."

While his boss searched out Xavier, Roman reclined back on the bed and closed his eyes to enjoy the peace and quiet. Not that he disliked sharing a room with Kate, but he had to admit being alone came with its own benefits he'd missed since he left the estate.

"Roman? I had a feeling you were going to be calling me today," Xavier said in his usual way that made him sound so relaxed and casual.

"Oh yeah? Are you clairvoyant now?" Roman joked.

"Nah. I leave that otherworldly shit to Julian. He's the one who always seems to know what people are thinking even before they tell him. It's downright spooky, if you ask me. No, I just had a feeling I'd be hearing from you sometime soon.

Call it a gut feeling."

"Well, your gut was right. The case I'm working could use some of your magic. Do you have a few minutes?"

"I do if you don't call what I do magic. You know it's anything but. Hacking takes real skill. It's not that hocus pocus shit at all."

Roman could tell by the sharp tone in Xavier's voice that he'd offended him. Rarely did he sound anything but downright chipper, so the angry undertone in his words stuck out like a sore thumb.

"Pardon my French, man. I've been in New Orleans for too long. You know how everything down here is voodoo. I didn't mean to say your skills are magical."

For how prickly he could be, Xavier couldn't stay angry for long. It just didn't seem to be in the guy's DNA. He liked having a good time too much to be miserable.

"Aw, I can't be upset with you, Roman. Out of all of us, you're the most serious, so I know there's no way you were busting my balls. I get that. So what can I do for you?" Xavier said, his charm returning once again.

"Thanks. We've gotten as far as we can, and every time we try to get further, we hit a wall."

Xavier laughed. "That wall you keep hitting is what someone trying to hide something wants you to hit. That's where I come in. So tell me about what you're working on."

"I'll send you all of what we have. Follow the money seems to be the idea," Roman said, swinging his feet off the bed.

"Politicians and money. Story as old as time, especially when you're talking about Southern politicians. They're as crooked as they come," Xavier said.

"Let me know as soon as you find something. In the meantime, I'm laying low with the client at a lake house just outside of New Orleans."

"I'll let Persephone and Nick know. Stuck alone with a beautiful woman on a lake? Sounds like a vacation to me."

Roman brushed him off. "Yeah. Right."

"Don't get me wrong. You deserve it, man. Of all of us, you're the one who works the hardest since you never give yourself even a moment's break. Enjoy a few days of peace and quiet and whatever else you and she decide to do."

"Bye, Xavier. Let me know as soon as you find out anything, okay?"

He stuffed his phone back in his pocket and took a deep breath. With Xavier working on this case, Roman expected to make some headway soon. Now if he and Kate could just lay low at Butcher's house for a while, hopefully this assignment could end without anyone getting hurt.

A banging noise outside the bedroom door made Roman jump up off the bed and head out, his gun drawn. He rushed down the hall and searched the living room but found nothing out of order.

He heard the noise again behind him and spun around toward the kitchen to point his gun directly at Kate's head. Her eyes opened wide in terror, and she dropped a frying pan on the counter. So that was the noise he heard.

"What the hell are you doing pointing that gun at me?" she screamed as she shot her hands up in the air to surrender.

A quick scan of the room told him nothing was wrong, so he slowly lowered his weapon. "I heard a noise."

Kate picked up the frying pan and waved it in the air as she barked at him. "So you thought you should pull out your gun? Because someone making dinner for you is certainly dangerous. You can find my picture up in post offices across the country. Wanted for sautéing. Armed with a spatula. Considered dangerous. Proceed with caution."

"I'm sorry."

Roman stuck his gun into the back of his pants and ran his hand through his hair. He hadn't meant to frighten her. He just heard a noise and reacted the way he'd been trained to.

"Why are you getting a frying pan out?"

As she rummaged through Butcher's drawers looking for something, she explained, "When I'm antsy, I like to cook. Since I'm downright terrified, you may get the best meal of your life. Your friend's fridge is pretty well stocked, actually."

"You don't have to be scared, Kate. I won't let anyone hurt you."

He meant that. Even though he'd only known her for a couple days, he silently swore if anyone tried to hurt her, he'd kill them. And he didn't make that pledge lightly.

"Says the man who just pulled a gun on me for wanting to cook dinner," she said with a slight smile.

"Not exactly," he said, sitting down at the island in the center of the kitchen. "So you're making dinner for us? What's on the menu?"

She turned and headed toward the other side of the room. "I'm thinking my world famous shrimp scampi."

"World famous?" he teased as she stuck her head in the refrigerator. "Are you a celebrated chef too?"

Leaning back, she threw him a nasty glance. "Keep it up and you'll get bread and water for dinner while I eat all the shrimp scampi."

"What? Am I in jail now?" he said with a chuckle, enjoying how she reacted to his giving her a hard time.

Her arms full of ingredients, she kicked the refrigerator door closed and made her way back to start preparing their meal. Kate dumped an onion, a garlic bulb, a stick of butter, a bag of raw shrimp, and a single lemon onto the top of the island.

With a smile, she asked, "Are you a scampi over rice kind of guy or scampi over pasta kind?"

Roman didn't answer quickly enough as he tried to remember the last time he had shrimp scampi and what it had been served over, so she narrowed her eyes to a squint and leaned forward toward him.

"I'd say you're a pasta guy. Am I right?" she asked with a quizzical look.

He didn't really care what she served the meal with, so he nodded and let her think she was right in her guess. "Pasta sounds good."

Without saying a word, she spun on her heels and marched over to the counter to reach up into a cabinet. Roman stared up at it, surprised at how stocked Butcher kept his kitchen. Did he routinely cook for himself, or did he just keep the place ready for friends who asked to crash for a few days? He had a hard time imagining him being much of a cook, to be honest.

No matter how much she stretched, she couldn't reach the top shelf and the boxes of pasta remained just an inch away from the tips of her fingers. After a few moments of frustration, she looked back at him and asked, "Can you get this for me? I'm about a millimeter too short for your friend's cabinets."

Happy to be of assistance, Roman walked over and easily grabbed a box of linguini. He'd never liked that particular pasta, though, and grimaced at the thought of eating it that night.

Kate stood looking up as he held the pasta box in the air. Her body pressed against his as he stood there in front of the cabinet loving the feel of her next to him.

"Not a fan of linguini? I think right next to where that was there's a box of angel hair."

He replaced the box on the shelf and pulled out the second box of pasta. "Yeah, let's go with the angel hair."

Handing it to her, he remained frozen to where he stood, looking down at her smiling at him as she said, "Okay, angel hair it is. But I'm going to have to move out of this corner if we actually want the dinner cooked."

"Oh, yeah," he said, closing the cabinet door and then stepping back out of her way.

"Not really a kitchen kind of person, huh?" she said, chuckling at him.

He couldn't disagree. At least not at the moment since he appeared to misunderstand the basics of spatial relations and conversation. He didn't usually act so damn awkward, but then again, it wasn't every day that a beautiful woman made dinner for him.

It had been long enough that he couldn't remember the last time a woman made the effort to do anything for him. More accurately, when he allowed a woman to do anything for him. Keeping people at arm's length made gestures like the one Kate was about to make rare.

And that was no one's fault but his own.

Kate began preparing the ingredients for the meal, starting with the garlic. After mincing four cloves, which filled the room with its fragrant odor, she turned on the gas burner. Then she drizzled virgin olive oil and tossed two spoonfuls of butter into a large frying pan.

Stirring the mixture in the pan, she asked, "Can you look up in the cabinet in the corner for white wine? It's there, but I forgot to take it out."

He walked around the island and searched for what she needed. He found the white wine and turned to hand it to her just as she said, "Oh, I need red pepper flakes too. I've got the salt and pepper, but I need the red kind too."

"Got it. Red pepper flakes," he mumbled as he pushed aside seasoning bottles on the bottom shelf of the cabinet.

Once he found them among the dozens of possibilities in herbs and spices, some he'd never even heard of, he closed the cabinet door and asked, "Anything else?"

"Nope. Just the red pepper flakes. I just need a little bit, but it's an important part of the recipe. I really adds that special touch to it."

Kate stood in front of the burner stirring the oil, butter, and garlic together in the pan, so he leaned over her and placed the bottle of red pepper next to the stove. She smiled at him and returned her attention to cooking, but he remained behind her just watching and enjoying the delicious scent of the meal as it filled the air.

After a minute, she looked back at him and smiled again. "Is something wrong? Why are you standing back there? Come around and sit on the other side of the island so we can talk like normal people do in the kitchen."

Is that what normal people did? He honestly didn't know anymore. He'd been on his own for so long that the kitchen was now merely the room that contained food of some sort and appliances to heat it up. Even at the estate he strove to be alone as much as possible, including meals.

Not that he'd found a lot of success in that recently.

Taking his seat again across from where she

stood cooking, he watched her as she added the shrimp to the garlic mixture and stirred them around the pan for a few seconds before disappearing from sight to search the cabinet below. She popped back up a moment later with a large pan and filled it with water before putting it onto the burner to boil.

"Do me a favor and open the box of angel hair, okay?"

He did as she asked and handed it to her. "Here you go."

Twisting her face, she studied him for a second before saying, "You look like a big pasta eater. A man your size needs a lot of food, I'm guessing. I think I'll do the whole box."

"What are you going to eat?" he joked.

Her face lit up with a smile. "I'll keep a few strands for myself. So since we're to the point where we can kid with one another, why don't you tell me something about yourself, just Roman?" she asked, resurrecting the nickname she'd given him back at the fleabag motel when he wouldn't tell her his full name.

Avoiding her gaze, he quietly said what he believed to be the truth. "There's nothing to tell. I was a Ranger—am a Ranger—and now I work for Project Artemis watching women make shrimp scampi."

Kate rolled her eyes. "I knew there was a sense

of humor underneath all that seriousness, but there's got to be more to you than your job for the past decade or so. What were you like as a kid? I bet you were all into sports and stuff like that, weren't you?"

He shook his head. "I don't know. Not so much. Just football and baseball."

His answer made her stop stirring. "Not much? That's two of the biggest sports. Did you play both in high school?"

"Yeah."

The water in the pot began boiling, so she poured the angel hair into the bubbling water. "Yeah. So you played two huge sports in high school, which probably took up most of the school year. But you didn't play much sports. I don't get you, Roman. You don't have to be so humble all the time. You were probably a BMOC and didn't even know it."

"BMOC?" he asked, repeating the letters she'd just said. "What's that?"

As she turned off the heat on the skillet, she explained, "It means big man on campus. BMOC. I guess most people would say you were a BFD—a big fucking deal. Either way, I'm guessing it was a case of the girls wanting to be with you and the guys wanting to be like you."

She had no idea how wrong her assessment of his high school days was. True, he had shined in sports and those years weren't filled with teenage angst and misery like so many people's were. But that was mainly because he'd kept to himself most of the time.

Kate waved the spatula in the air, as if she'd read his mind and didn't believe he hadn't been a BFD or a BMOC back then. "Let me guess. You don't think you were, but if I met people you went to high school with, they'd treat you like some kind of minor royalty if they saw you again."

"You done?"

The smile faded from her face. "I wasn't trying to make fun of you or anything, Roman. I just wondered if you were a superstar back then."

She turned her attention to the food and turned off the burner under the pasta pan. Taking a spoonful of pasta water, she dumped it into the skillet with the shrimp and then drained the angel hair. A minute later, he had a plate of shrimp scampi with angel hair pasta and a glass of white wine in front of him.

"Dinner is served," she said, forcing a smile.

Roman didn't want to cut off the conversation like he did. He never meant to stop things like that. He just always did. All that time alone had made him pretty bad at interacting with others.

He took a bite of the meal she'd made and

couldn't believe how incredible it tasted. With only a few items, she'd whipped up a shrimp scampi better than any he could ever remember having.

"This is delicious, Kate. You outdid yourself with this."

She beamed at his compliment. "It's nothing. Well, it's my world famous shrimp scampi, but I'm trying to follow your example and being humble."

Raising his glass, Roman made a toast to this woman. In the short time they'd been around each other, she'd injured him, nearly driven him crazy, and made him want more for the first time with a client.

"To Kate and her meal—both incredible."

They clinked their wine glasses together and each took a drink. Both of them fell quiet and focused on eating for the rest of the meal, but Roman wanted to know more about her now.

"Since you know all about me, tell me about you, Kate Sheridan," he said as he pushed the empty plate away from him.

She finished the last of her meal and picked up both their plates. "Me? I'm just Kate."

He didn't believe for a second she was just anything. Since he hadn't felt this way about anyone in years, he knew she had something great about her.

As she rinsed the dishes at the sink, he said, "Turnabout is fair play. Tell me about you."

Kate took her time and turned around slowly after almost a minute. "I moved to New Orleans when I was thirteen, and I graduated high school wanting to be a lawyer. But as so many of us can say, I got sidetracked by a boyfriend during college. I can't even remember his name now. How sad is that?"

While he'd never let himself get sidetracked by his feelings before, Roman found it charming to think that Kate had thought she was so in love that she gave up going to law school. It made her seem softer in some way.

"I wouldn't say it's sad. You were in love."

She quickly protested that idea. Shaking her head, she said, "I wasn't in love. If anything, I let my hormones get the best of me. Not my finest hour."

"So this man of your dreams didn't pan out. What happened after that?"

"I dropped out of college because I had gotten so far behind in my classes. After a year or so, I knew I couldn't just mope around, so I went back to school to be a paralegal. I got my associate's degree a year later, and Jonas Flynn hired me right out of school. That was the only job I'd ever had as a legal assistant. And now, I'm on the run from the cops and making shrimp scampi for the man whose job it is to protect me."

"So even though you got distracted, you ended up doing what you wanted after all. I can't think of anything more Kate than that."

Blushing from his compliment, she lowered her head and pushed the spatula around on the counter before turning to toss it in the sink. Roman hadn't seen this shy side of her before. He couldn't stop himself from thinking there was a lot to Kate he hadn't experienced yet.

And he wanted to see those other sides more than he knew he should.

Chapter Fifteen

D INNER HAD GONE over well, as she knew it would since she'd made her favorite recipe, so Kate assumed they'd continue their conversation after she got the kitchen cleaned up. She knew she'd thought wrong, though, as she turned around after washing the last dish and saw an empty chair where Roman had been sitting at the island just minutes before.

Discouraged, she wondered if she had said something wrong again. It seemed like she was always doing or saying something that made him back away. Just when she thought they were past the point where whatever about her that made him uncomfortable bothered him, he turned into a ghost once again.

Maybe he didn't feel like she did. The thought had crossed her mind. It wouldn't be out of the ordinary for someone like him who helped women in need as a job to have a hard and fast rule about getting involved with a client. It probably made sense for him to keep every woman he worked with at arm's length. How effective could he be at protecting someone if he had feelings for her?

Kate slumped against the kitchen island and wondered if she should just be honest with him. She quickly dismissed that idea. The mere thought of trying to have that conversation— trying to tell him that even though she knew they were complete opposites that she had developed feelings for him—just the thought of it made her cringe.

Never in her life had she heard or seen that kind of honest admission of how someone felt turn out successfully. Only in the movies and in books did that happen. In real life, you told someone you had feelings for them and they more often than not sat with a forced smile as they mentally scrambled to find a gentle way to let you down easy. While she'd never herself admitted she had feelings to a man before he did, she'd witnessed enough emotional car crashes with girlfriends to know a session of true confession wasn't what she wanted to do with Roman.

Even if the image of him staring at her with his mouth agape as she told him how she felt made her think it might all be worthwhile just to see him like that.

But no, that's not the kind of woman she was. Independent, yes. Courageous in the face of people after her, maybe. Emotionally brave, though? No way.

She knew her limits, and bearing her soul to a man who routinely turned away whenever she got close was at least three steps past her hard line. Kate had no illusions about the kind of men she found attractive.

Tough, quiet, even sullen, they tended to be the brooding kind of guys other women ran away from like they were on fire, and for good reason. Those men required a strong woman who didn't need to be fawned over day and night. They never failed to be there when you needed them, but they weren't exactly sweetness and light, and they rarely remembered birthdays and anniversaries.

Roman was exactly the type of man she'd always wanted. Looking around the living room and not seeing him anywhere in sight, she couldn't help but think that every time anyone had ever said to her to be careful what she wished for in a man, they'd been more right than they could ever know.

Pushing the idea of actually telling him how she felt about him out of her mind, she resigned herself to continuing dropping subtle hints and hoping he reciprocated at some point. It wasn't brave or brash, but it was her style and she couldn't change it for him or anyone else.

No matter how much she wished she could.

Kate looked around at Butcher's home and shrugged. "Another night at home alone. Oh well. At least I know the terrain of that landscape."

She wasn't tired, but still she headed for the bedroom she'd claimed earlier in the day. At least if she spent her time in there it didn't feel like she was constantly chasing after Roman trying to get him to speak to her. That's not how she wanted to spend her night.

Instead, she settled into bed and prepared to watch back-to-back episodes of Dateline. She'd never really been a huge fan of television shows devoted to solving mysteries of lost people or murderous boyfriends or girlfriends, but recent events in her life now made them more interesting. She just hoped she didn't end up as the subject of one of them someday.

The first episode involved an ungrateful niece who had slowly poisoned her uncle in order to receive his estate worth nearly half a million dollars and a life insurance policy of over two hundred thousand dollars. After almost an hour of wishing the awful woman dead for her horrid behavior, Kate sat back on the pillows and watched as they sent her to prison for the rest of her life.

Not exactly cheery nighttime TV but at least she could be sure others in the world were going through worse than her.

The next episode focused on that famous child who had gone missing in Portugal a few years back. Still to that day, no one had ever found her body or any trace of her anywhere on Earth. After fifteen minutes of that, Kate changed the channel. An hour of that story would make her want to throw herself into Lake Pontchartrain.

Glancing over at the clock on the nightstand, she saw in big red numbers it was way too early to go to bed. Nine o'clock was a fine time for farmers to go to sleep but not her, especially since she didn't feel tired.

But what else could she do? She had no idea where Roman had hidden himself, and leaving the house didn't seem like a good idea since she had no idea if the people who may be after her had figured out where she was yet.

Resigned to an early night, she slid under the covers and pulled them up over her head as she mumbled, "Guess it's time for sleep, Farmer Kate."

"LET GO OF me! Let go!" she screamed, desperately trying to pry her arm free from the man's hold.

She sat bolt upright in bed and searched the dimly lit room for anyone near her. She saw no one. The sound of her heartbeat pounded in her ears, making it impossible to hear anything else.

Her mouth was parched, so dry that she couldn't imagine how she screamed at all. Licking her lips, she tried to moisten them, but nearly panting in terror didn't help much to fix the problem.

Had she screamed? Or was that all just a nightmare?

A very vivid nightmare of a man grabbing her while she slept in that very bed she sat in now.

As she struggled to separate reality from her dreams, Roman flung open the door and ran in, stopping dead right in front of the bed. His head swiveled left and then right as if he was searching for something, and Kate noticed he wore a different pair of pants and a shirt she hadn't seen on him before that moment.

Had he gone out shopping when he disappeared from the kitchen?

Finally, he said, "I heard you scream. What happened?"

"I don't know," she said shaking her head in disbelief. It had all felt so real. "I guess I had a nightmare."

At hearing there wasn't some murderous killer there in her bedroom, Roman's shoulders sagged. If she didn't know better, she would have said he looked disappointed.

"I thought something happened to you," he said, taking a step back toward the door.

"No. Sorry. I guess it was just a nightmare."

He stood there staring at her for a few moments before turning toward the door. "Okay, good night," he mumbled gruffly.

But she didn't want to be by herself in that room for the rest of the night. She wanted someone next to her so if she had another nightmare she wouldn't wake up terrified and alone.

Just as he opened the door, she said, "Don't go. Stay with me?"

It came out as a question because she truly didn't know if he'd say yes. For as much as he said it was his job to protect her, he seemed to only want to do it from a distance. Staying with her all night would shrink that distance he kept between them to almost nothing.

Although Kate had a feeling if Roman could find a way of putting space between them as they spent the night together in that room, he would.

Slowly, he turned around and without saying a word, nodded as he closed the door behind him. That he agreed to stay surprised her. She'd expected him to find some way to do his duty while putting himself anywhere but in that room with her.

Roman looked around for someplace to sit, but other than the bed, the only other place to sit was on the floor. She had a sense that he considered that choice as he looked down once and then a second time toward his feet before taking a step toward the bed.

"You can sit here with me, Roman. The bed is actually pretty comfortable," Kate said with a smile.

A few seconds passed by as he thought about her offer, and then he sat down next to her on the other side of the bed. He still didn't say anything, which only encouraged her to fill the empty space with more words.

Looking down at his long legs stretched out in front of him, she said, "Those clothes look new. Where did you get them?"

"I ran out after dinner and found a store. I got you some things too. I took a guess at the size, but if anything, they'll be too big, not too small."

She had a feeling she should be insulted, but the way he said that with sincerity made her not want to argue with him now. Turning to face him, she said, "Thanks. I'm sure they'll be fine. I guess you figured after a few days we either needed to wash our clothes or find new ones."

Roman grimaced and shook his head. "No. I got us clothes so if anyone has seen us and described us to the police by describing our clothes, then we won't look the way they think we should."

That made sense. In fact, changing their clothes made perfect sense now that he explained it that way.

"Oh. Well, thank you just the same."

A few moments went by in utter silence, and all Kate could think was there had never been two people alone in a bed who had less chance of sleeping together than the two of them. Roman seemed more standoffish than ever, if that was possible, and she couldn't imagine anything she could say that would make him warm up to her.

Just as she'd suspected, he'd found a way to make it feel like even though they sat so close on that bed their legs touched, it felt like they were separated by a million miles and a world of silence.

Dejected, she let out a sigh and slid under the covers before turning her back to him. "Good night, Roman."

"Good night."

That's all he said.

She lay there feeling his left leg press against her back and her butt, chastising herself for not knowing what to say. If Eve were there, she'd already have him stripped naked and she'd be riding him like he was some wild stallion.

Kate didn't have to wonder why she was still single. What was happening, or not happening, right before her eyes told her all she needed to know.

A million thoughts ran through her mind.

Did he care one bit about her? It felt like he had back at the hotel. He seemed to when they were lying in each other's arms on her bed then. Had she done something to turn him off?

That question itself spawned at least a few dozen more. She'd injured him, barked at him, tried to run away from him, and those were just the highlights. Other than those examples, she'd been difficult since the moment she met him, although she still didn't know how she was supposed to act when a strange man walked into her motel room. It wasn't every day that kind of thing happened. To expect her to just be some trusting soul without asking questions seemed a tad ridiculous and foolish.

Unable to simply lay there, she rolled over and looked up to see him sitting there just staring down at her. How strange. She'd expected him to have his eyes closed or at least to have been staring off into space and not at her as she slept.

"Why are you looking at me, Roman?"

Without missing a beat, he replied, "Why do you ask so many questions, Kate?"

His answering by asking another question, especially that one, surprised her. "Because I'm an inquisitive soul. I thought there was nothing wrong with me asking so many questions."

"There isn't. I just figured you might like a taste of your own medicine," he said with smile that also surprised her.

Could it be possible he wasn't unhappy about staying with her?

"A taste of my own medicine? I'm trying to figure out what exactly my questions cure, but I can't find anything, to be honest."

"Certainly not your curiosity, which seems endless."

Kate's mouth dropped open in shock at his teasing her. He was actually being cute and playful. "That's the first time in nearly five days since we met that you made a joke. Well, it wasn't actually a joke, but it was you trying to be cute. You should try to do that more often. I like it."

"I'm not a cute kind of guy," he said after a few moments. "Serious people tend not to do cute too well."

Liking this side of him, she pushed on his leg with her hand. "Well, you should try it more often. You're pretty good at it."

Roman smiled and ran his tongue slowly over his bottom lip. "Just pretty good? I guess I'll have to try harder next time."

She watched as the moisture from his tongue made his lip glisten in the dim light. That right there seemed like a definite sign he liked her. Didn't it?

Quickly, she scrambled to think of something clever to say to keep their conversation going. Of course, nothing came to her. Not a word. Not a clever phrase. Nada.

Exhibit two in the case why Kate Sheridan was still single.

"Nothing to say, Kate? No question for me to answer?" Roman asked in a tone she'd never heard him use before.

It sounded downright…flirty.

Was she completely misreading the signs, or was he flirting with her there in the bed they shared?

"None that I can think of," she said in return, giving him her best smile in case he had any thoughts at all of making a move.

Which she wished more than anything at that moment that he would.

And then he said nothing. No flirty retort. No lip-lickingly cute anything. He just fell silent.

That was it. Disappointed or discouraged or whatever she was feeling, she sat up next to him and didn't stop herself when the truth of how she felt and how he made her feel came spilling out in all its messy glory.

"What is with you, Roman? At dinner tonight, we were having a great time, and then poof! You disappeared. No see you later, Kate. No I'm going to head down to the lake and enjoy the sound of the water. Nothing. I had no idea where you went. I just knew you didn't seem to want to be near me. Again. Now you come in here all ready to do your protective hero shtick, and when you find out I just had a nightmare, you look disappointed. Then flirty cute Roman comes out for a little bit—by the way, I really like him, so if this is a case of multiple personalities, I'd love it if you could tell him to come back. And just when I think we're making some headway, you go radio silent on me again. What the hell is going on with you?"

Kate had to take a breath after letting all that out, and she waited for him to say something. Anything. But all she got was silence and his usual staring at her with those dark brown eyes that gave no hint as to how he felt about anything.

"Whatever. Fine. Feel free to go back to your room or wherever you were before you came in here. I'll be—"

Before she could lie and say she'd be fine, he leaned over and stopped her words with a kiss that curled her toes. His lips softly pressed against hers, gently taking what he wanted from her as she eagerly offered him as much as he cared to have. Stuffing his hand into her hair, he pulled her to him so their bodies melded together.

He felt warm and powerful against her, and as he settled her onto his lap, she found out how much she affected him. His tongue slid lightly over her lips into her mouth to tease hers, sending a jolt of need straight to her core.

She wanted him before she knew how incredible he made her feel. Now she needed to have him inside her.

CHAPTER SIXTEEN

ROLLING HER HIPS over him, she moaned into his mouth. "God, this feels so good."

He leaned back away from her and smiled. "I haven't done anything much yet. Just wait until we get to the good parts."

Kate looked down at his lap. She'd already felt how hard the good parts were. Waiting for them wasn't top on her list of things to do at the moment. Feeling him as he pressed his body to hers and she rode him like that stallion she'd been thinking of before sounded much better than waiting.

"No more waiting, Roman," she said softly as she pulled his mouth to hers and kissed him hard with all the need she had built up inside.

His hands slid down her side to her hips, grasping her firmly to hold her still. God, she wanted him to move so much faster. Why did he insist on taking his time? Did the man have no understanding of how much she wanted him?

Taking matters into her own hands quite

literally, she leaned back away from him even as he held her in place and undid his pants. He watched as her fingers slowly unzipped them and then spread the fabric apart to reveal his black cotton boxers underneath.

She looked into his dark eyes and searched for a sign as to how he felt, but as always, she saw nothing. If she was to believe his eyes, he felt nothing about what she was doing to him.

His body told a completely different story, though. As she lightly ran her fingertip down the front of his boxers, she felt how hard he already was. He wanted her as much as she wanted him, so she reached under the fabric and felt him twitch against her hand as she wrapped her fingers around that hardness.

Now she saw a different look come into his eyes. Need filled them like she'd never seen before that moment, and he took hold of her and flipped her onto her back in one fluid motion.

Part of her wanted to protest that she hadn't finished teasing him, but he didn't look like a man who wanted to hear another word questioning him at that moment. Intensity filled his face as he made quick work of her pants and shirt, leaving her lying there beneath him in just her bra and panties.

He ran his hands up her legs, spreading his fingers as he inched up her thighs toward where they met her body. She wanted him to touch her so badly it hurt. But he stopped just before he reached that spot she knew would give her what she needed and smiled down at her.

"The look on your face says you have a question for me, even at this moment, Kate," he said in a low voice edged with desire.

Sliding her hands over his, she tried to tug them higher on her thighs to no avail. Now she did have a question for him.

Her lips forming a pout, she asked, "Why are you trying to torture me?"

He leaned down and kissed her on the lips, whispering against them, "I wasn't, but it was all worth it to see that adorable little pout you just did. I think that might have made me even harder, and that's saying something."

Enough teasing. She had a hundred ideas of things they could be doing that felt better, and she desperately wanted to try each and every one of them with him.

Scratching her fingernails down his back, she felt his thick muscles through his new shirt and wanted to rip the thing off his body. To hell with new clothes. He could walk around without a shirt. That would work. He'd look different than he had so others might not recognize him, and she'd get to see him half naked.

She didn't have to resort to tearing it off him,

though. He stripped out of it and his pants as she watched in awe as inch by inch his body came into view.

The hardness of his chest that made her wonder days before if he had a shield on under his shirt stood on full display for her now. Clearly, this man had either been blessed by God or spent a good amount of time in the gym.

Whichever it was, the effect was breathtaking.

Kate felt the overwhelming need to run her hands over his broad shoulders, the muscular pecs, and his chiseled abs. She'd never seen a body like this. At least not in person and just inches away from her.

As if he could read her mind, he settled his body between her legs and eased down on top of her, whispering, "You look surprised. I thought you saw most of me when you interrupted my shower."

The need to touch him took over, and she let her hands roam over his soft skin as she marveled at how beautiful his body truly was. "I guess I wasn't paying close enough attention," she said staring at where her hands drifted over his gorgeous abs.

"You like what you see?" he asked in a teasing tone that got her attention.

Looking up into his eyes, she nodded. "Oh yeah. I think you might be perfect, Roman. It's a little intimidating, if I'm being honest."

He drew his tongue across his lip and smiled. "Even though I don't talk enough and you want to argue with me about practically everything?"

Her gaze slid from his face and roamed over his hard body. "I think this more than compensates for those things."

As she let herself ogle the most beautiful body she'd ever seen, her gaze settled on that gash in his side. She touched the area around it, hoping it wouldn't be hot and tell her it had become infected, but she found the skin cool against her fingertips.

He flinched when she tried to see it up close. Worried she'd hurt him again, she looked up at him and asked, "Are you okay? Are you in pain? Because if you are, we can stop."

Roman shook his head and leaned down to press his lips to hers in a kiss that took her breath away. Pulling away, he said, "Don't worry about that. We have other, more important things to focus on."

His lips trailed down over her neck and to her breasts as all the while Kate kept wondering if this was a dream. If it was, it certainly was better than that nightmare she'd had before.

Wanting him, she hooked her thumbs in the waistband of his boxers and tugged them down over his hips. His cock sprung free and pressed against her thigh, sending a jolt of desire through her. She wanted to feel him inside her so damn badly.

Roman smiled wickedly. "Enough with the foreplay? I like a woman who knows what she wants."

His deep voice rolled over her like silk, and then he quickly slid her panties off, tossing them off to the side. She felt his legs moving, but she was focused on unhooking her bra. Finally naked, she returned her attention to him and in the next second his mouth was on hers in a kiss that made her want him more than she thought possible.

She didn't have to wait long to get exactly what she desired. One slow thrust of his hips and Roman filled her so fully she had to catch her breath. He smoothed the hair away from her face and stared down into her eyes like nothing else in the world mattered more than being there with her and making love to her.

Slow and steady, he slid into her to the hilt, touching a spot she'd never known existed inside her. Each time he filled her up, it felt like they were made just for each other, perfect pieces fitting together to create a whole.

The sound of his breathing filled her ears, and its warmth heated the skin of her neck as he pumped into her. Her fingers tugged at his hair, eliciting a guttural noise from him that sounded so utterly sexy she pulled harder just to hear him make it again.

Kate scratched her fingernails down his back and sunk them into his hips to urge him to go faster. For a moment, he hesitated, but she moaned, "Don't stop. God, don't stop."

He didn't, and with every thrust of his cock into her body, she inched closer to coming. Wrapping her legs around his waist, she pressed her heels into his spine and arched her back.

"God, I'm so close. Right there…"

He lifted his upper body off her and balanced himself on his hands next to her head as he stared down into her face, the intensity in his dark eyes so sexy she wouldn't have been able to look away if she wanted to. For one of the few times since she'd known him, she knew exactly what he felt because of the look in his eyes.

Need. The need to possess her utterly and completely for himself.

She'd never had anyone look at her like that. Other women had told her about having a man look at them like that and how incredible it made them feel, but never had it happened to her. It was what she'd always wished for in a man but never got.

Until now.

Dipping his head, he kissed her hard as his movements became more jagged, fucking her with short jabs instead of long strokes. She sensed he was close like she was and tilted her hips to help get them over that sweet precipice. Just a few more hard thrusts and Kate felt her orgasm rush through her entire body.

Roman groaned as her body tightened around him and came seconds later, his back arching as he filled her one final time. He looked like the epitome of maleness.

Strong. Powerful. Commanding.

And in complete possession of her, even if she didn't want to admit it.

The aftershocks from her orgasm still racked her body when he eased out of her and rolled off to the other side of the bed. Flush with ecstasy, she closed her eyes and let out a deep breath, utterly satisfied.

"Kate?" he whispered in a deep voice that hit her exactly on that spot he'd touched inside her.

She turned to look over at him and opened her eyes. He looked so different now she had a hard time remembering that man who so often wore that stony expression she'd gotten used to.

"Yes?"

Turning to face her, he smiled and she wondered how she'd ever missed how sexy he could be. "Are you okay?"

"I'm more than okay. You?"

His smile broadened, and he nodded. "I'm

more than okay too."

He wrapped his arm around her and pulled her close. Resting her head on his chest, she listened to the sound of his breathing, loving the way he felt so strong beneath her cheek. He kissed the top of her head, letting his lips linger for a moment before he tightened his hold around her.

And just like that, Roman returned to saying nothing, but now, Kate didn't worry about his silence. It comforted her in some strange way and made the moment mean more to her.

KATE OPENED HER eyes slowly as Roman's arm holding her gradually registered in her brain. She and Roman had slept together and now they…well, were sleeping together in her bed. He lay next to her with his eyes closed, and she struggled to believe what they'd done.

Not that she regretted it. No way. Sex with Roman had been the best she'd had in her lifetime. A woman didn't regret that kind of sex.

She looked over at him and knew he still slept soundly, so she eased out from under his arm and grabbed her clothes to go outside. For some reason, she felt antsy, like she wanted to move and do something. That she couldn't frustrated her, but she didn't dare to endanger the two of them.

At least she could get a breath of fresh air on

the porch.

Quickly dressing in the hallway, she headed outside into the night. Chilly for New Orleans, she wished she had a sweater to throw over her shoulders. Maybe Roman had gotten her one when he went out to buy them new clothes.

What a man he was. That she could even think he might have been that thoughtful felt completely out of the ordinary. She'd never been with a man who could rock her world in bed and still be someone she could depend on. Most men succeeded at one or the other, but to be good at both? She wondered if she was still under a haze from the great sex they'd had.

She wanted to tell someone about him. Wasn't it just her luck that for once she'd found a man who had everything she could possibly want and she had no one to share the news with.

Eve. That's who she could tell. She had a bone to pick with her about telling the police about what had happened to her anyway.

Fishing her phone out of her purse, she turned it on and pressed 2 to speed dial her. After only two rings, she answered in her usual perky way.

"Talk to me."

Kate looked around to make sure she was alone on the porch and whispered into the phone, "Eve, it's me. Do you have a minute to talk?"

"Jesus! Kate, where the hell have you been?

I've been over to your apartment like ten times in the past few days. I've been worried sick. Are you okay? What happened to you?" she asked, her voice frantic.

"I'm fine. Thanks for ratting me out to the police, though."

She began to pace at just the mention of the cops as Eve tried to explain why she'd done exactly what she'd been told not to do. "I'm sorry, hon. I got scared. That man following us in the Quarter freaked me out, and then when you ran, I didn't know what to do. Are you in jail?"

"No. I guess I should actually thank you because someone in the New Orleans Police Department called this group that helps women and one of their men came to the Bayou to help me."

"One of their men? What kind of man are we talking about?" Eve asked with far too much interest in that one part of her story.

Kate didn't exactly know how to explain Roman. Was he like a security guard for her? What exactly was he other than the man she'd fallen for and just slept with?

"His name is Roman and he's trying to help me figure out what to do about Jonas's murder. He found us a place to hide out for a little while so we can do some investigating."

Eve hummed in to the phone. "Hmmm,

Roman. Sounds like someone I'd like to meet. Good masculine name. Does this Roman look as hot as his name?"

"Very much so," Kate said with a smile that made her cheeks hurt.

"Oh my God! Tell me you haven't slept with him. Did you sleep with the man protecting you, Kate?"

Giddiness overtook her, and she walked around the side of the house away from the front door. "Shhh, don't say that so loud. He might hear you," she said, pressing her mouth to the phone.

"Is he right next to you? I want all the details! What's he look like? Is he hung like a horse? Give me all the info right now!" Eve squealed into the phone.

"He's gorgeous. Everything I could ask for in a man," she said, trying to be cool as she answered Eve's questions. "He's hung like…well, I don't know what he's hung like, but let's just say he left me boneless after we made love."

"Oh my God! Kate! I can't believe this. So are you two madly in love or what? Was it love at first sight? Tell me everything!"

She didn't know what the two of them would be after sleeping together. She hoped they'd be more than just two bodies who bumped into one another that one time. And she certainly didn't know if he loved her.

Honestly, she didn't know if she loved him either. It seemed too soon. They'd known each other less than a week. It took longer than that to fall in love with someone, didn't it?

"I don't know, Eve. I just know we need to find out what was behind the murders before we can think of anything after that."

"Okay, okay. I can see that. But the second you two figure out what else you are, I want to know. Got it?"

"I got it."

"So have you been able to figure out who killed Jonas and his client yet?"

"No, not yet. I tried to follow all the clues he left on his laptop, but I kept running into dead ends. I still don't think I can trust the police, though, so no matter what, do not tell them you heard from me, okay? I'm serious, Eve. Don't tell a soul I called you."

"I won't. I promise. How did you get your boss's laptop?"

Chuckling, Kate explained the caper she and Roman had done to get it. "We broke into his office and stole it. A security officer saw us and chased us down the stairs and out into the street. I swear it was the scariest and most exhilarating thing I ever did in my life."

"Good God, honey! This isn't like you. You're

all wild and crazy. Now I can't wait to head out with you the first night you get back. We'll have a blast!"

The thought of all of this being past her and returning to her life again seemed like a near impossibility as she stood on Butcher's porch looking out toward Lake Pontchartrain. She had no idea when that would happen or how it would come about, but she liked hearing her friend talk about it in such a positive way.

It made her feel like she and Roman were going to make it out of all of this alive and well.

Looking around, Kate suddenly worried she'd been out in the open for too long. She couldn't afford to risk anyone finding them there.

"I better go, Eve. Remember, don't tell a soul you heard from me. Promise?"

"I promise, honey. You take care of yourself, you hear? And let that Roman do his job. I know you. You've probably been fighting him every step of the way, right?"

Leave it to Eve to hit the nail right on the head.

"Not all the time," Kate said, only half-heartedly trying to defend herself. Eve knew her too well to believe she'd gone willingly into anything a man wanted her to do.

"Well, I want to meet him, so you two stay safe and come to see me the minute you get back.

I love you, honey."

"Love you too, Eve. Remember, tell no one I called."

"This time my lips are sealed. I swear. Take care, Kate."

She ended the call with a feeling of melancholy settling into her heart. She missed her apartment and her life. Hopefully, someday soon she'd get to introduce Eve and Roman when life returned to normal.

The night air chilling her, she hurried back inside and to the warmth of the bed Roman still slept in. Stripping out of her clothes, she crawled in next to him and loved when he reached around her to take her in his arms and pull her to his body.

As much as they'd felt perfect together during sex, this felt even more like they were meant for one another. Closing her eyes, she let herself enjoy how safe and protected she felt in his arms.

She didn't know how long she lay there pressed against him, but she could have spent the rest of her life in that very spot. Just as she began to drift off to sleep, she heard him moan softly behind her.

"Where did you go?" he asked in a sleepy voice as he gently squeezed his arm around her.

"I just took a walk outside for a breath of fresh air. I didn't mean to wake you up. I'm sorry."

Roman nuzzled her neck. "It's okay. I was just worried when I didn't feel you next to me."

Smiling, she sighed at how cute he could be. He said so little, but when he did say something, it said so much.

"Well, I'm back, so no need to worry. Go back to sleep. You deserve to get a good night's sleep."

His lips grazed her earlobe, and he whispered, "Always so bossy, Kate."

"It's one of my best traits. I knew you'd get used to it," she teased him as he pressed his hips forward and angled his cock against her ass.

"Mmmm. I could get used to something else I like much better."

She knew exactly what he meant and couldn't disagree. Sex with him was definitely much better than her lame attempts to boss him around.

And she could absolutely get used to it.

"Oh yeah? Got any suggestions?" she asked, turning her head to look at him.

Wide awake, he smiled and licked his lips. "Round two sounds good, don't you think?"

As he slid her under him, she couldn't think of anything that sounded better.

Chapter Seventeen

THE SIGHT OF Kate lying naked beneath him made Roman want to take her again, but this time without foreplay. She felt so good against him that kissing and whispering sweet nothings in her ear wouldn't do it for him. He wanted to be inside her again, making love to her like she deserved, filling her until nothing separated their bodies.

"You look like you have something on your mind," she said with a cute smile that made him feel guilty for what he'd been fantasizing doing to her.

"Just thinking of how good it's going to feel being inside you."

She winced and a tiny moan escaped her throat. "You don't say much, but when you do talk, you sure know what to say to get a girl going."

He trailed his fingertip down between her breasts and let it come to rest just above her belly button. "Good. I know other ways to get you going too."

Kate arched her back and opened her legs wider so his body sat in between them. "I do love a man who has skills," she cooed.

Her sweetness made him want to devour her all the more. Sliding down her body, he kissed the exact path his finger had traveled, staring up at her to see her face as he drew closer to the delicious goal between her legs.

The moment his mouth grazed her tender skin, her eyes rolled back in her head and she moaned his name. Hearing that made him hard as a rock, but he needed to take his time. Kate wasn't just some casual hook up, meaningless and easily forgotten. They may not have known each other for long, but she'd ignited a long dormant spark inside him that made him want more than just a throwaway roll in the hay.

Her fingers threaded through his short hair, tugging his head toward her to keep his mouth where it gave her the most pleasure. Her skin felt like silk against his lips, and she tasted like heaven. As much as he wanted to watch as he gave her another orgasm, he couldn't stop his eyes from closing as he reveled in her.

"Oh, that feels so good, Roman," she said in a dreamy voice.

But he wanted her to feel even better. Sliding his middle finger inside her, he hooked it and rubbed in tiny circles, remembering how Xavier had said this was the one thing that could drive a woman crazy. He opened his eyes and watched to see if his teammate had been correct.

Kate pressed her knees open even wider and arched her back, staring down at him as he caressed her tender skin. Tearing her hands away from his head, she sunk her hands into the sheets next to her and squeezed them tightly in her hands.

"Oh my…what are you…oh my God, don't stop…right there…" she moaned, her words heavy with need.

Moments later, her body tightened around his finger, and she came, a tiny squeal escaping from her mouth before she buried her head in the pillow and closed her thighs to the sides of his head. He pressed his mouth against her and rode her orgasm until the very last aftershock tapered off and Kate fell still beneath him.

Clearly, Xavier had been right. And all along he'd thought the nerd of the group had just been the world's biggest bullshitter. Well, he still thought that, but at least on this one thing, he'd been right.

"I don't think I can move my legs. Or my arms, for that matter. I'm the definition of boneless," Kate said with a smile. "Were you a porn star before this job?"

Roman couldn't help but laugh at her compliment. At least, that's how he was taking that comment.

Sitting back on his heels, he shook his head. "Nope. Definitely not a porn star."

She bit her lip in that cute way she sometimes did and asked, "Maybe it was a part time job then? Because I don't know what you did there, but that was incredible. Damn."

"Just something I heard about one day and thought I wanted to try out with someone who deserved it."

Her smile lit up her face. "Someone who deserved it, huh? I like that."

Roman slid up her body and kissed her softly on the lips. "Oh yeah. You're definitely someone who deserves that and more."

Wrapping her arms around his neck, she kissed him back with all the passion he could wish for. "I like that. You know what I'd like more of?"

She slid her hand down over his chest and abdomen to palm his cock before he could ask what her heart desired. Looking down between their bodies, he watched her stroke him and smiled.

"I like how you think."

Still wet, her body took him inside her easily. Kate kissed him and whispered against his lips, "You feel so good. I'm not going to be able to walk after this night."

Rolling her over so she straddled his hips, he looked up at her. "Good. Then I'll know I've done my part right."

Kate positioned her hands on his chest and leaned forward to kiss him again. "You don't have to worry. You're doing all the right things."

He held her hips firm and began to move her up and down on his cock, slow and steady. If it made her half as crazy as it made him, he wondered how she was holding back because all he wanted to do was jackhammer into her to feel that sublime moment when he finally came.

The seductive look in her eyes said she loved how he made love to her, and with every moan, he became more sure she felt as good as he did.

Dragging her fingernails over his ribs, she groaned, "If you'd let go of my hips, I'd ride you like you've never had before. I promise."

When she said things like that, he didn't want to hold back. All he wanted to do was ram his cock into her to make her come harder than she ever had with any man in her life.

"I'm trying to take my time, Kate. I thought women liked that."

Leaning forward, she whispered breathlessly in his ear, "I don't know what other women like. I just know when a man knows how to make me feel good, I don't want to wait, so feel free to fuck me with abandon, Roman."

Between the sound of those words and the feel of her warm breath teasing his ear, he wanted to do exactly that. He slid his hands down her body from her hips and grabbed a hold of her perfect ass, squeezing hard as he lifted his body from the bed to plunge into her balls deep.

She took a sharp breath in as he filled her to the hilt and then moaned into his ear, "Oh, God…fuck me."

Roman let go of all the restraints holding him back, and stuffing his hand into her hair, he tugged hard, pulling her up off his chest. She stared down at him with need in her eyes and rolled her hips.

"I want to watch you ride me, Kate. Time to put your money where your mouth is, love."

He watched as she began to fuck him in earnest, her body milking his cock as she rode him just as she'd promised. Never before had a woman made him feel so incredible, and even though he preferred to control the pace of sex, he loved seeing the look of desire on her face as she took him inside her over and over.

It didn't take long before he began to read the signs that told him Kate was close, so he grabbed hold of her hips again and took over, pumping into her to get her to that sweet spot he knew her body craved. She tumbled over it moments later and came hard, bucking her hips as her orgasm tore through her.

She collapsed on top of him and dropped her head next to him on the pillow. "God, that was unbelievable. I'm serious. I'm not going to be able to walk after tonight."

Roman continued to thrust into her body, enjoying the pulsating feel of the aftershocks from her coming on his cock. Nearly exhausted, she still rolled her hips with each push into her and murmured in his ear, "You feel so good. I want you to feel that too."

"Don't worry," he groaned as he inched toward his release. "I'll be there in a bit."

Cooing contentedly next to him, she sounded like the epitome of complete satisfaction, which sent his body into overdrive after just a few more strokes into her. Holding her still, he filled her with everything he had until his body was as exhausted as hers.

They lay there silently in each other's arms trying to catch their breath, and Roman wondered if he could do this with her. Not the sex, which he had no doubt he could do for the rest of time.

No. Everything else. The moments other than sex when he had to give more than his body.

Those were the times he'd never been good at. A woman deserved more than a man who kept his heart walled up. Kate deserved more. She deserved someone who could make her laugh when she felt blue. Someone who could tell her she could do it when the rest of the world told her she couldn't.

Someone who could open up and be the man she needed other than in the bedroom.

He just didn't know if he could be that for her.

And he knew all too well as he lay there with her curled up on his chest loving the feel of her body next to his that he should have goddamned thought about that before taking her to bed.

While he turned that thought over in his mind, he heard a buzzing sound somewhere in the room. Kate lifted her head off his chest and leaned over the bed toward where it came from.

"That's my phone," she said sweetly as she slid off him to grab her pants.

Still lost in thought, he only heard her speak but didn't process what she said. "What?"

Holding her phone up in front of her, she swiped her finger across the screen and explained, "It's just Eve. She must have forgotten to tell me something when we talked."

Now fully understanding her words, Roman sat up in bed and looked down at her. "Forgot to mention? When?"

Kate reached up to run her hands over his chest and kissed him. "When I called her while you were sleeping."

He pushed her hands away in horror and jumped out of bed to get dressed. "Jesus Christ, Kate! You called the person who told the police where you were? We have to leave! Now!"

How could she have been so careless? Furious, he didn't know what to say, even though he wanted to yell at her for how stupid she'd been.

Storming through the house as he slid his shirt over his head, he made a beeline to the kitchen to find his watch he'd taken off when he returned to the house earlier. Fuck! She had no idea what she'd done to everything they had there.

He returned to the bedroom to find Kate nearly dressed and began pacing back and forth in front of the window watching to see if anyone had arrived yet. Grabbing her cell from on the bed, he turned it off and stuffed it into his pocket.

"I'll keep this. You'll get it back if we make it out of this alive."

She followed him as he stormed around the bedroom to grab the laptop. "It's okay, Roman. Eve knows better than to tell the cops again. We can trust her."

He spun around, so angry he could barely speak. "What were you thinking calling her? If someone's after you, they've been waiting for that so they can trace the call. They're probably on their way right now. We need to get the hell out of here!"

She started to say something, but he pushed past her to grab his stuff from his room and walk out toward the front door. "Let's go."

"I swear, it's okay. She's good. I promise," she pleaded behind him.

"Stop talking, Kate. We need to leave."

She grabbed his sleeve and tried to stop him as they rushed down the stairs toward the old car. "Please, stop. We're okay. We don't have to freak out about this. Talk to me."

He turned around at the bottom of the steps and glared at her. "This isn't freaking out, Kate. This is us having to go because you just called someone on your phone and likely let anyone who wants to find you know exactly where you are."

Climbing into the car, he leaned down and hotwired it once again to get it started. Kate sat down in the passenger seat and started to say something, but he didn't want to hear it.

"Roman, it's the middle of the night."

His frustration with the mess she'd created threatened to explode out of him, so before he said anything, he reminded himself she hadn't intended to completely screw up everything.

Hanging his head, he pressed his face against the steering wheel. The coolness of the metal felt good on his skin and calmed him just enough to be able to speak to her without barking what he wanted to say.

"You don't seem to understand. The people who are likely looking for you at this very moment also likely have the ability to know when you make a call on your cell phone and where that call was made. When you called your friend, you helped them to find you. I'm trying to keep you safe, so now we have to leave this house and go somewhere else."

Finally, his words seemed to sink in, and she asked in a worried voice, "Somewhere else? Like where?"

Roman looked over at her and hated the answer to that question. "Like the place I found you at probably."

Her disappointment at hearing that showed on her face. Frowning, she began to speak, but he stopped her. "I just need to get this car to somewhere out of the way for now, okay? Don't say anything more. That's all I ask."

For one of the first times, she did as he asked without asking any questions or arguing with him. At least there was that saving grace. As he drove, he tried to find some upside to their having to leave Butcher's gorgeous home with every amenity they could want.

But he couldn't think of a single thing. Now they'd have to hide out in some shithole motel on the outskirts of town because there was no way they could risk trying to find a room in any of the nicer ones in New Orleans.

"Put your head down and pretend like you're looking in your purse for something."

"Why?" Kate asked, once again with the damn questions when all he wanted her to do was follow his directions.

"Because I have to pay this toll to get across the bridge and the less people see of you, the better. Now put your damn head down and do as I say."

He prayed to God she didn't ask another question or argue with him over this as he rolled up to pay the toll. The guy in the booth smiled at him, probably wondering where they were going in the middle of the night or more likely wondering what kind of person lived in one of those beautiful homes on that side of the lake and still drove a piece of shit car.

"Gorgeous night, huh?" the worker asked in a very thick southern accent.

Roman handed him the money and tried to keep his disgust tamped down. "Yeah, gorgeous. Have a good one."

"You too! Night, y'all!"

They drove off across the bridge with Kate's head still down, and as they reached Metairie on the other side, the car began to buck, jolting forward once and then again before it rolled to stop on a side street. A few seconds later, it made a wheezing sound Roman knew couldn't be good.

"What happened?" Kate asked, popping her head up.

"I don't know," he answered, feeling his anger begin to bubble up inside him.

He tried to start the engine, but it was no use. It was dead.

"Let's go. We need to get out of sight. Somewhere there aren't so many streetlights," he said as he threw the driver's side door open.

Stepping out into the street, he slammed the door shut and hurried around to Kate's side. "Come on. The longer we're out in the open like this, the better chance someone will see us."

She looked up at him in disbelief. "What are we going to do? Walk? To where? Where are we going?"

Roman had already had enough of this interruption of their night and her questions. Pulling her out of the car onto the sidewalk, he slammed her door shut and pointed down the street. "Walk. Quickly."

"Where?"

Just then out of the corner of his eye, he saw a police car turn onto the street where they stood. His heart began to pound as he scanned the area to find a way out. He saw nothing closer than a block away.

Sliding his arm around Kate, he began

walking with her toward the next intersection. "I need you to walk faster. There's a cop just down the street. Don't do anything to draw attention to yourself, okay?"

"Okay. I won't," she said nervously, clinging to his arm as they walked.

The blue and red lights on the cop car began to flash in the windows of a shop as they passed, and Roman knew they had to get out of there fast. "Kate, run! Don't let go of my hand, but run!"

She tried to look back to see why they needed to leave so quickly, but he pulled her along down the street toward the intersection and hopefully someplace they could hide until he figured out where the hell to take her. They made it to the street and he saw houses with yards.

As the police car came up behind them, they ran into the side yard on the second home in and raced toward the back of the house. The cop turned on the siren, which began to blare through the neighborhood, and Roman pulled on Kate's arm to make her run faster.

"Catch up! We need to find a way out of here!" he barked back at her.

She didn't answer, but he felt her hand slip from his hold and seconds later, he saw her on the ground writhing in pain as she held her foot. "I twisted my ankle."

Roman stopped and looked around for the

cop. "You need to get up, Kate. Now."

"I can't. I twisted it or something."

Lifting her onto her feet, he took her hand again. "We have to get out of here before that cop finds us. Try running."

She put pressure on her right foot and nearly collapsed to the ground. With tears in her eyes, she cried, "I can't! What are we going to do?"

They had no choice. They needed to get out of that yard before they were trapped. Scooping her up into his arms, he held her close to his body. "Put your arms around my neck and hold on tight. I'm going to get us out of here. Don't worry."

"I'm sorry, Roman. I'm sorry I messed everything up."

He looked into her tear-filled eyes and tried not to be furious with her for fucking up their perfect hiding place. "It's fine. Just hold on tight."

For five blocks, he ran at top speed between yards and parking lots until he saw a red neon motel sign. It wasn't a five star hotel or Butcher's place, but as long as it gave them somewhere to hide for the next day or so, it would have to do.

Roman gently set Kate down on her feet in the shadows at the end of the building and pointed toward the bushes nearby. "Stay in there and don't come out until I get back."

She nodded and frowned up at him. "I will. I

promise."

He hurried down to the motel office and found a nice young girl no older than eighteen working the check-in desk. She looked up from a magazine and smiled at him as he walked in, tucking her blond hair behind her ears.

"Well, hello there! How are you tonight?" she asked as she stood up to her full height.

"I'm good. I need a room for the next two nights," he said as sweetly as he could, still trying to hide his disgust at how bad this night had turned.

"Two nights. Sure. That'll be one hundred and twenty-two. Cash or credit?"

He handed her a credit card with another of his aliases and signed the bill when she slid it across the counter. "There you go. Thanks."

She handed him the red plastic keychain with the room key and smiled at him. "You're in Room 17. To get there, just go out, turn right, and head down the sidewalk. Have a good night, Mr. Stanton."

Forcing a smile, he mumbled, "I can only hope."

He returned to the bushes to find Kate leaning against the building and favoring her sprained ankle. "Come on. Just don't step really hard on it and you'll be fine."

Kate pouted. "You aren't going to carry me?"

"I'm trying not to attract a lot of attention. A man carrying a woman might make people notice us, so just take your time. We're in Room 17 just down here a few doors."

He opened the red motel room door and flicked the switch on the wall to turn on the light. The Louisiana Motel was only slightly better than the one he'd originally found Kate in. The room was basically a white ten by ten foot box with exposed pipes painted white in an effort to hide them that hadn't succeeded. An old, yellowed air conditioning unit sat in the wall up near the ceiling, its frayed cord hanging down beneath the unit. A particleboard dresser stood nearby with a mirror propped up against the wall on top of it. Next to that sat a full size bed with a hideous red and green floral bedspread covering it. Another piece of particleboard furniture that was supposed to be a dresser sat in front of the bed holding a TV that had first been watched in the eighties.

Kate followed him into the room and looked around. "It isn't so bad. It's definitely better than the Bayou. You have to admit that."

She sat down on the bed while Roman called Xavier again. If he found out anything they could use, maybe they wouldn't have to spend much time at all in this place.

"Sorry. I haven't gotten very far yet, Roman."

"I need something here, Xavier," he said,

pacing back and forth across the room in front of Kate as his anger began to boil over.

"Whoever's behind all this is good and well-funded. I'm going to need more time to make the connections. What's the hurry anyway? You're supposed to be enjoying a few days and nights at that lake house. Relax and kick back while I work on things."

Barely able to contain his disgust, Roman said, "We had to leave, so there's no more lake house and no more relaxing. I'm stuck in a shithole motel, so get going so I can get the fuck out of this place."

"Oh. Okay, man. I'll put a rush on things as much as I can."

Roman ended the call without even saying goodbye and tossed his phone on the bed as he continued to pace back and forth, choosing to remain silent.

This night had gone from bad to worse.

CHAPTER EIGHTEEN

FROM THE BED to the door and back again, over and over Roman paced without saying a word as Kate watched him grow angrier by the second. The smile he'd worn just a short time ago when they lay together in each other's arms after making love was gone, replaced by a scowl worse than any she'd seen on his face before.

That said something since she'd certainly tried his patience repeatedly since the night they met.

She wanted to say the words that would make things better, but every time she tried, he shut her down. Was calling Eve really that huge a mistake?

Opening her mouth to ask him that very question, Kate saw him draw his eyebrows in tightly and changed her mind about saying anything. Better to not make things worse. He looked like he might explode if he got any angrier.

Instead, she pulled the laptop across the bed toward her and opened it up to keep herself busy. Maybe if she made some headway in her research on Jonas's leads Roman would forgive her.

Before she could read a word on the page in front of her, he yanked the laptop away and slammed it shut in her face. Then he walked off with it, like she couldn't even be trusted to go online.

"What the hell? Why'd you take that?" she asked, furious at how he was treating her like some kind of prisoner, or worse, some kind of moron.

Roman glared at her and said nothing. But now she didn't want to stay quiet any longer.

"What's the problem? You said his laptop couldn't be tracked, so why can't I do some work while you pace back and forth fuming?"

He put the laptop on the flimsy dresser next to the TV and turned to glare at her again. "That's to make sure you don't do something stupid like try to message your friend that way."

God, he knew how to stay angry at a person, didn't he?

Looking up at him, she tried to find the kindness in his eyes she'd seen just a short time before. It wasn't easy since he insisted on pacing back and forth.

"Can you stop moving for a minute and talk to me?"

Her request finally got him to stop moving, at least for a second, but only long enough for him to snap, "No."

As he turned on his heels and started across the room again, she said, "I'm sorry I screwed up. I should've been smarter. I really am sorry."

But even that didn't make Roman stop pacing, and he said nothing in response to her apology, even though she meant it sincerely.

Maybe if she tried again. She had to reach him.

"I really am sorry, Roman."

That finally got him to stop right in front of her, but what she saw on his face didn't look like understanding or forgiveness. His frown deepened and he stared down at her angrily. "I'm sorry doesn't help, Kate. I'm trying to keep you safe, but I can't do that if you keep making mistakes like that."

His words stung, but the way he said them made it all ten times worse. She didn't hear a hint of caring in his voice at all. How could he be so cold and unfeeling after what they'd done together?

"So you're not going to accept my apology?" she asked, staring up into his eyes filled with anger.

He didn't respond to her question but just stood there glaring down at her.

"What do you want from me, Roman? I'm sorry."

Shaking his head, he finally answered. "I want

you to understand mistakes in my business get people killed. I have this thing with living. I like it."

"I made one mistake. I get it, but I think I deserve forgiveness."

He leaned down close to her face. "Which one do you think I should forgive, Kate? The one where I had to run after you before someone saw you and got you punching me for my reward, or the one where you screwed up and forced us out of a comfortable bed in a nice place to come here to Motel Roach and Flea?"

His expression was so angry she had to look away. "I'm sorry for both of those things, Roman. I am. I didn't mean to mess up. I feel like shit," Kate said quietly.

"Oh, so you feel like shit. Well, that makes it all better then. We'll be fine now that you feel bad."

"You don't have to be so sarcastic. I just meant that I'm really sorry, Roman. I'm sorry I've been such a hassle the whole time. I thought you understood."

Embarrassment washed over her as she felt him standing there still angrily looking down at her like she was some kind of criminal. She'd thought he liked her inquisitive way. That he'd found her spunkiness charming.

That despite everything that had happened

that he had felt for her what she felt for him.

She waited for him to say something, hoping he'd at least give her a reprieve from his anger if he couldn't forgive her yet, but he said nothing and simply returned to pacing back and forth across the room. Out of the corner of her eye, she could see that miserable scowl remained on his face even now after all she'd said.

It was no use. She'd screwed up so badly he'd never forgive her. Kate knew what she had to do. As soon as he stopped pacing and fell asleep, she'd leave and head out on her own. It's what she should have done all along. She may not have had a group to help her, but she had things she could use to try to figure out who had killed Jonas and Samuel.

She just wished she didn't care so much about Roman now that she had to leave him.

TWO HOURS LATER, he had finally stopped pacing and crawled into bed next to her. She got no sense that any of the feelings he'd shown her in the last bed they shared existed anymore as he silently turned his back to her.

Her heart ached to hear him say anything kind to her again. He lay there so close to her, and yet it felt like a chasm that couldn't be bridged stood between them. Just like before, he'd pushed her away, but this time, she wouldn't wait around for him to find his way back to her.

She listened for a sign that he'd fallen asleep and heard his breathing grow heavy. After a few minutes, she knew it was time and gingerly slid out of the bed, careful not to make any noise that could alert him to her intentions.

Tiptoeing around the room, she grabbed the laptop and then searched for Roman's pants to get her phone. She spied them on the end of the bed near his feet and knew she couldn't just reach into the pocket and grab them without risking waking him.

Frozen there at the foot of the bed, she stared at the covers for any hint that he may have awakened. When they didn't move, she carefully slid her hand into the front pocket of his pants and grabbed a hold of her phone to pull it out.

Now that she had all she needed, she looked across the room to see her purse. Once she had that, she'd be free to leave. For a moment, she turned back toward where Roman slept and let herself remember how much she loved being with him. It wasn't just the sex, either.

That had been incredible, for sure, but as much as she'd miss that with him, she'd also miss that honorable streak that ran a mile wide in Roman. She'd never had a hero in her life, and now that she had to leave him behind, she knew she'd miss that part of him the most because it was what made him truly a good man.

And men like Roman were hard to find.

Kate couldn't think about that now, though. She'd already let her feelings dictate too much of what she'd done since running away from Eve that night. The time had come to take care of herself and not rely on anyone, including the man who lay in the bed in front of her.

Even if she'd fallen in love with him.

Never before in her life had she regretted something even before she did it, but as she watched him lying there in front of her, she already knew she'd regret leaving him. It didn't matter, though. They were both better off apart.

Now all she had to do was convince herself of that.

With one final glance at him, she turned and tiptoed toward the door. She didn't know exactly where she would go, but it was better this way for both of them.

"Why do you have a death wish, Kate?"

At the sound of his deep voice, she stopped and looked back at him. "It's better that I do things alone."

Chapter Nineteen

R OMAN WONDERED IF he should just let her leave since she clearly didn't want him around, but he couldn't do that. Protecting Kate was his mission, but even more than that, he cared about her. He hadn't cared for anyone like this in a long time.

Even more, he liked the feeling and didn't want to be without it in his life any longer.

He got out of bed and walked over to where she stood clutching the laptop and phone he'd taken off her earlier. Looking down into her beautiful face, he shook his head and put his hands on her shoulders.

"I can't let you do this on your own, Kate."

She turned away so she didn't have to face him. "Whatever you guys are, you aren't expected to be my savior. You got me this far. You can tell your boss you did good."

He slid his arms around her, and when she refused to look up at him, he said, "Kate, I want to say something. Look at me."

She slowly lifted her head, and he said, "I can't let you do this on your own because I care about you. I can't stand the thought of you getting hurt."

Her eyes grew wide, and then she narrowed them as a look of confusion came over her. "Are you supposed to feel that way about the people you help?"

Shaking his head, he quietly said, "No."

"Then why?"

He kissed her to stop her from asking any more questions. At that moment, he didn't want to think about anything but how good her lips felt against his. For the first time in too long, he felt something for a woman, and he didn't want to lose that.

To lose her.

Pressing his forehead to hers, he admitted the truth. "Because even in this shitty motel room, I've never been happier anywhere else in the world and that's because I'm with you."

"Really?"

"Really. So I don't have a choice. If you go, I go. So if you're planning to leave now, you need to know I'm right beside you."

She smiled and sat down on the bed. "I guess there's no point in leaving then. Might as well stay in this luxurious suite we have here."

Roman took a seat next to her, taking the

laptop and her phone from her hold. "Might as well."

Kate turned toward him and took his hands in hers. When she looked up at him, he saw real regret in her eyes.

"I am so sorry, Roman. I didn't think when I called Eve. It was so stupid, but I never meant to ruin everything."

He stopped her with a kiss and then whispered against her lips, "No more talk about that. We're here together. That's all we need."

"Even though it's nothing as nice as your friend's house?" she asked sheepishly.

That was an understatement. One glance around the tiny, rundown room showed that. He couldn't hold her mistake against her forever, though.

Kissing her, he pulled her close into his arms. "It's okay, Kate. As long as the people after us didn't find out where we went, we should be fine."

Kate looked up at him and shook her head. "You said that wrong, Roman. They're not after you. They're only after me. I know you think this is your job to protect me, but you've already done so much. I would understand if you didn't want to do anything more. I mean, I was just about to leave. No one would blame you."

The truth of it was it didn't matter if he

didn't want to do anything more to help her. He had to, and not just because he worked for Project Artemis. He couldn't just let her go out there where someone could hurt her.

"I'm not going anywhere, so stop trying to push me away because it won't work."

With a chuckle, she said, "Says the man who has pushing people away down to a science."

"Exactly, so I should know. Now let's get to work and see if we can figure something out where to turn next."

"Where should we start?" she asked as she sat down on the bed on her side.

"I think we need to figure out how the governor is involved. Your boss felt sure it went all the way up to the top, so that's where we have to look," Roman said, sitting down next to her.

"We could head up to Baton Rouge," she suggested.

It sounded like a long shot to him. "We can't just walk into the Governor's Mansion and ask him."

Kate's face lit up. "No, but we can go to one of his campaign offices."

"Why would we find anything there?"

"I don't know, but if I can get a look on one of the office computers, maybe I'll find something."

"How? I can't imagine they're not password

protected," Roman said, still skeptical.

She kissed him and smiled. "New Orleans is a very small place when it comes down to it. I just a need a way to call someone, so I'll be needing my phone back."

Roman shook his head. "No way. Remember it getting traced? Burner phones only from here on out, and I want to know every last detail about who you're thinking of calling because I can't imagine this is something I'm going to agree to."

"Then get me a burner phone so I can make my call."

"Who are you going to call?"

"You'll see," she teased. "You get me that phone and I'll get us to someone who might be able to help."

He shook his head. "We're in this together, Kate. I need to know everything if I'm going to be able to protect you."

She smiled sweetly and nodded. "Okay. I want to call someone named Jasper Carrollton. He's someone I've known for years. If anyone can help us, it's Jasper. He travels in circles up and down the social ladder of this city. I've known him forever. I would trust him with my life."

Roman didn't know how he felt about this Jasper person. Bringing anyone else into what they were already involved in didn't sound like the best plan. Then again, they needed something to make some headway on this case.

"Okay," he said as he moved to leave. "Give me a few minutes to go buy a burner phone."

Kate reached out and tugged his hand to bring him back to the bed. "But first, maybe you should stay here for a little while."

He had an idea what she meant and liked the way she thought.

"It might be better if I stay out of sight for a few hours anyway. The cop might still be out looking for us," he said with a smile.

Lying back onto the pillow, she looked up at him with need in her eyes. "Then you definitely should stay here for a while."

The way she looked so sexy and beautiful and wanting him made him forget how awful that tiny motel room was. He crawled into bed and kissed her with all the need he felt for her. When he saw her standing there planning to leave, all he could think of was how much he couldn't let her go. She might get hurt, but even if she was able to take care of herself, he didn't want to lose her from his life.

He hadn't let himself feel this way about a woman since before he left for basic all those years ago. Then he'd been so young and naïve about life and the world. He believed in the concept of love and when he asked Emily to marry him, he thought his life had been planned and they'd live happily ever after.

That's how it was supposed to be. Then events beyond his control took over and ruined his perfect life. The woman he thought he'd spend the rest of his days with was gone, and suddenly he had no one but himself to rely on.

At first, he saw being alone as his punishment for not being there for Emily when she needed him most. Then after a while, it became a way of life for him and he couldn't imagine ever wanting another person to mean that much to him ever again.

The risk was too much. He might lose another woman he loved again, and he simply refused to let that happen.

So he remained alone.

Life in the service made it almost easy to never put down roots or let someone in. He could always justify not settling down by reminding himself of the danger he lived with every day. Better to be alone than leave a woman who loved him a widow to grieve him.

By the time he left the Army, being single had become a part of him. It was just who he was. Or more correctly, who he'd become over the years.

But the need to protect those who needed his help had remained and become a central piece of his personality, so when Nick offered him the chance to join Project Artemis, he didn't think twice. Whatever he doubted about Persephone Gilmore's desire to spend her millions on the idea, he never questioned how important that goal was and how much he believed in it.

He threw himself into each assignment he received, and as he had in the Army, he excelled. Not having ties served him well as it always had, but every so often he wondered how it would feel to have someone to love again. Protecting someone was one thing, but loving them was completely different.

That never happened in any assignment before he met Kate. Maybe it was because he never let himself fall for anyone, or maybe because he kept clients at arm's length and they couldn't imagine him as someone who could care for them like a man in love.

He could, though. No matter how far down he pushed the desire to love another woman, it always existed inside him. He acknowledged it sometimes when he lay in bed alone staring into the darkness of wherever he stayed. That recognition that he still secretly hoped that someday he would meet a woman who could love what he'd become after all that time didn't change the fact that he simply didn't believe he should let another one in.

Then Kate came into his life and all those reasons he had told himself over the years began to sound like excuses to not let himself be happy. He fought against letting those reasons go because they'd been part of him for so long that they were who he was.

How she broke through a wall he thought had become impenetrable he had no idea, but she had. Slowly at first, knocking a hole in it here and taking a few blocks down there. And then, without warning, that wall came tumbling down, leaving his heart exposed for the first time since Emily's death.

Now he couldn't imagine life without Kate. He didn't want to either. Just as everyone had warned him, it took the right woman and he fell head over heels before he knew what happened. He'd never believed them, never believed it could happen to him because he'd always made sure it couldn't.

Or at least he thought he had. He wasn't sure of much of anything anymore since he met Kate, other than he didn't want to live without what she made him feel ever again. And he'd do whatever it took to keep that in his life.

He watched her as she curled up next to him, her naked body pressed to his, fitting like she was made just for him. Wrapping his arms around her, he held her close and closed his eyes. That burner phone could wait a little while longer.

For now, all he needed in this world he had right there.

CHAPTER TWENTY

J UST AS SHE finished dressing from her shower, Kate heard the door to the motel room open. Peeking her head out, she saw Roman walk in and toss a bag on the bed.

"I'll be right out," she called from the bathroom as she tried to make her hair look at least presentable.

This whole living on the run lifestyle did nothing for her look. Clearly, she wasn't a ride or die type of chick.

Staring into the mirror, she mumbled, "You're more of a can we stay somewhere nice chick."

Her hair had decided that flat with a dash of frizzy would be the way she'd look that day, and it didn't matter how much she tried to give it some volume. Nope, it would just stay like it was, so no point in fussing with it any more.

She found Roman sitting on the bed with the phone in his hand as he activated the burner cell. She'd never seen this before, just like she'd never been on the run from the law before, so she watched intently.

Looking over his shoulder, she asked, "So who were you when you bought this? Roman or that other name?"

"Michael Trenton," he said flatly, as if she should know that name.

"Who's that? Another one of your aliases?"

He handed her the phone and nodded. "Yeah. That's one of my names. Here you go."

"At the rate we're going, you're going to go through all your names by the time this is over," she joked as he stood up to open a can of soda he'd brought back from the store.

Turning to face her, he smiled and shrugged. "No worry. I have a lot more. We'd have to be on the run for years to go through all of them."

That statement right there made her more curious about him than anything else he'd told her about his job or his life, but she didn't bother to ask him about it. Maybe later or when they were finally safe. For right now, she had to call Jasper.

One of her oldest friends, she felt certain they could rely on him to help them and keep it all quiet. She just hoped he was back in the city.

"I'm going to need my old phone to find the number."

She watched for any sign that Roman still didn't trust her, but he handed her the phone without a second thought or a single word. Scrolling through her list of contacts, she found the one she wanted and typed the number into the burner phone.

Jasper Carrollton. She'd known him since middle school, and they'd been friends from the first day he sat down at her table in the cafeteria and asked her if she wanted to be friends. After a few seconds of staring at him, she'd said yes. The rest, as they say, was history. If anyone could get her into the governor's campaign office, it was Jasper. He knew everyone, mostly because he'd slept with so many people, male and female.

In matters of love and lust, Jasper didn't discriminate.

On the second ring, he answered in his heavy southern drawl and she said, "Hey, Jasper! It's Kate. I need your help with something."

"Katybird! Baby girl, that's no way to begin a proper conversation. Don't I at least warrant a how do you do, Jasper?"

"I'm sorry. I'm a little distracted today, so I forgot my manners. How've you been, Jasper?"

"I'm fine, as always. Thanks for asking. I've been out of town for a couple weeks and just got back home this morning. What did I miss that got you into trouble?"

"How do you know I'm in trouble?" she asked.

With a chuckle, he answered, "Let's just say I know you, Katybird. So what do you need?"

"I need you to promise you won't breathe a word of this to another living soul."

He inhaled sharply, like what she said surprised him. "I can't believe you would even say that. You know me. I'm a vault. I think I'm insulted."

"Okay. I need to get into someone's office. The governor's campaign office downtown. Tonight."

Kate waited a moment before continuing. "And I need to get into one of the computers."

Jasper didn't say anything at first, and she wondered if he'd had some religious conversion or something while he was gone from town. Normally, he'd be perfectly fine with helping her on something like this.

"Interesting. Okay, give me a few hours and come by my house tonight at ten. I'll have what you need by then."

Relieved, she let out a big sigh. "Thanks, Jasper. I'm going to owe you huge."

"I'll add you to the list of people I can blackmail. It's a pretty prestigious group, so you should be honored."

"I love you. Thanks! I'll see you at ten. And Jasper?"

"Yeah, honey?"

"Thanks for being there for me."

"Always. Friends to the bitter end, right?" he said, saying the exact words they used to say to one another back in those middle school days.

"Right. See you tonight."

For the first time since she messed up by calling Eve, Kate felt like she was doing something that could help Roman instead of hindering everything he was trying to do for her. She tossed the phone onto the bed and smiled at him standing across the room near the door.

"Tonight, we get to head to the Garden District and one of the nicest houses there. Jasper will take care of us."

"Are you sure about this, Kate? Do you believe this Jasper should be trusted?" Roman asked, his expression full of worry.

She waved off his concern. True, Eve had gone against her explicit wishes when she told the cops about her being in trouble. And it was also true that she'd messed up when she called Kate last night, but Jasper was different.

"It's okay. He's good people. Not to worry. Jasper will handle things."

"Handle things?" Roman asked in a curiously sharp voice.

Worried he thought she had insulted him by insinuating her friend could help her better than he had, she hurried to clear up what she'd meant.

"Jasper knows a lot of people in town, and he knows his way around New Orleans society in ways I never could, and I live here. Don't worry. He can be trusted to keep his mouth shut. Nobody is better with secrets than Jasper."

For a moment, Roman said nothing, but the worry he'd worn on his face morphed into a grimace. Finally, a few seconds later, he asked, "So, you and this Jasper guy are close?"

"Yeah. We've known each other for years. Since middle school, to be exact."

"How close?" he asked in a quiet voice. "I mean, you did say you loved him."

Kate chuckled at his misinterpretation. "Oh, not that way. Jasper is like the brother I never had. He's a huge manwhore. I'm not his type, but we've been close friends forever."

"Why aren't you his type?" Roman asked, taking a step toward where she sat on the bed.

The question was a valid one since Jasper seemed to have very few things he found unappealing in anyone. She'd seen him with every variety, shape, size, and color of woman, not to mention men, so that they had never gotten together would seem rather noteworthy to someone who didn't know him.

But Kate knew the reason they'd never taken their friendship to a more physical level was the simple fact that for Jasper, true friends were few in his life, so he cherished the ones he had. Better to not mess up a good thing just for a roll in the sack, he'd say.

"I think we've been friends for too long, and for Jasper, I might always be that lonely girl sitting alone at the lunch table he met that first day. I was brand new to school and had no friends, and he walked right up and sat down in front of me to ask if I wanted to be friends."

Roman sat down on the bed next to her and nodded. "I'm sure you've changed since then, though."

Suddenly, she saw that look that said he was searching for something, and she understood why he was asking all these questions about her and Jasper. He wasn't nervous about him possibly giving away something that could help people find them.

He was jealous.

Kate wove her fingers through his and squeezed his hand. "I'm sure I have changed. Thirteen was not my best year on this planet, for sure. But trust me, Jasper Carrollton has no interest in me in any way other than friendship."

"It's fine," he said, staring down at where their hands sat on the bed between them. "I just like to know what I'm walking into with people. I hope we can trust him. That's the more serious concern."

"More serious than you being jealous that Jasper and I are more than friends?" she asked, struggling to keep the smile from her face.

He popped his head up and twisted his face into a scowl. "That's ridiculous. I'm not jealous. Just curious."

"Well, just curious, there's nothing between me and Jasper. You'd care if there was?"

Kate waited for Roman to answer her question, wanting to hear him say something that would tell her she'd been right to think he was far more jealous than curious. She saw it written all over his face, but she wanted to hear him say it.

But he just shrugged and looked away as he answered, "It would just be something I should know to be able to work this assignment correctly."

He could say all that mumbo jumbo about the assignment all he wanted. She knew better. He was jealous.

Never a huge fan of jealousy in men because it always made them seem weak and out of control when they exhibited that emotion, she found the idea of Roman being jealous sort of charming. The man never appeared weak and always seemed to have everything under control, as far as she'd seen, so in him jealousy came across as sweet.

And stubborn since he refused to admit he felt it at all. Typical Roman.

AT FIVE MINUTES before ten, they stood outside the stately home that had been in Jasper Carrollton's family since the nineteenth century. Hidden by a large bush, they waited as a group of twentysomething males passed by before walking around to the back door. Kate knocked gently as Roman stared out into the backyard at the in-ground swimming pool and hot tub just a few yards away.

"Your friend has some money. This house is huge and comes with some nice amenities," he said in a tone of appreciation.

Kate scanned the yard and a memory of her drinking too much and falling into the pool at one of Jasper's parties flashed through her mind. God, she hoped he didn't bring that up in front of Roman.

Or the other million and a half things she'd done that would probably make him want to run for the hills as soon as his work with her ended.

Turning back, she pushed that night back into the recesses of her mind and knocked on the door again. "Yeah, he comes from wealthy stock."

Roman chuckled and repeated the words wealthy stock. "As opposed to good stock?" he asked.

Smiling, she thought about if Jasper and his family could be considered good. They'd fought on the side of the Confederates, but that wasn't anything shocking in New Orleans. He'd once told her his great-great uncle or someone like that had been good friends with Huey Long back when he was governor and Jasper's relative was an illegal alcohol bootlegger during Prohibition. Even that didn't fall into the bad category in Louisiana. But some of the other, more unsavory stories she'd heard of the Carrollton family would probably land them somewhere in the grey territory of good versus bad.

For someone honorable like Roman, though, she suspected those things would make them bad, so she simply smiled and said, "It's all ancient history now. Jasper's just…well, Jasper."

She didn't explain that the sliding scale of morality might put even her friend into the bad column.

Raising her hand to knock once more, she saw him appear at the back door, smiling like always. She'd never met anyone who always seemed happy like Jasper.

He threw the door open and spread his arms wide at the sight of them standing there. "Katybird! Honey, get in here and hug my neck!"

For a moment, she felt Roman's body tense up against hers, but she ignored that and stepped forward to give her friend a giant hug. He'd be fine once he got to know Jasper.

"It's been too long, you. From now on, you

have to spend at least a whole month at home once in a while so your friends don't end up missing you so much."

Jasper held her at arm's length and let his gaze travel up and down her body. Frowning, he said, "You look like you've been slogging through hell lately. What's going on with you?"

"I'll tell you all that in a minute, but first, I want you to meet Roman."

She looked back at him and saw the most skeptical look she'd ever seen anyone wear on his face. Clearly, he wasn't impressed.

Thrusting his hand out, Jasper took a step toward Roman and smiled. "How do you do? Any friend of Katybird's is a friend of mine, so welcome. Come in, please."

It was the most restrained hello she'd ever heard from her friend, but then again, he knew how to read people, and Roman's face told the story that he didn't like what he'd seen so far.

For his part, Roman shook Jasper's hand and in his serious way said, "Thank you for letting us come here tonight. We appreciate your help."

So far, so good. A little somber, but Kate didn't mind Roman's style. She rather liked it.

"My pleasure. Let's go inside and sit down. Katybird, you need to tell me all about this business you need my help with," Jasper said as he escorted them into the house.

They walked through the chef's kitchen with every appliance a cook could ever want or need and through the formal dining room with the long cherry wood table and chairs for eight guests that looked like it belonged at some state dinner. As they made their way, Jasper pointed out things about the house to Roman. Kate had the sense it was equal parts bragging and pride.

"Above the dining room table on the ceiling is the crystal chandelier that was one of the first electric run lights in all of New Orleans. The Carrollton family always liked to be on the cutting edge, and anything to show up the neighbors," he joked.

Roman's face remained stony as it had been from the moment Jasper opened the door, but she saw the hint of a smile at that last remark. As they walked into the TV room, she touched his hand and gave it a squeeze. He looked down at her and that hint of a smile blossomed into a full-fledged grin.

"Okay, after we talk, I'll give you the full tour, but I'm pretty sure you don't want to see rooms like the salon, which still looks like it did when my great-grandmother designed it. Take a seat and tell me what you want to drink. You name it, I've got it, so the sky's the limit," Jasper said as they headed toward a large white couch flanked by brown leather chairs around a large rectangular teakwood coffee table.

"I'll have a white wine," Kate said, suddenly thirsty for alcohol.

"Nothing for me," Roman said with a smile that looked a little like it was forced. "Not driving, but one of us needs to keep our wits about us."

Jasper didn't seem offended, thankfully. "White wine for Katybird. I'll be right back. Make yourselves at home."

He disappeared a moment later, leaving them alone to talk. Curious what Roman thought, she turned to him and said, "This place is something else, isn't it? You know, he hasn't worked in forever. Thank God he comes from money or who knows what would happen to him."

Roman didn't respond but merely nodded, so Kate nervously continued talking.

"This house really is incredible. That stuff he told us about the chandelier is really true. This was one of the first houses in New Orleans to get electricity." Looking above at the ceiling where a far more rustic antique brass chandelier hung over the seating area, she asked, "What do you think?"

"Of?"

Kate leveled her gaze on him. "The house. My friend. Any of the half dozen things I've told you about the place. Pick one."

He took a deep breath in and let it out slowly.

"The house is incredible. I'd say your friend beats my friend in the house department hands down. As for Jasper, I don't know yet. I haven't been able to get a read on him. All I know is he has money, doesn't work, sleeps with lots of people but never with you, and even though I'm a man, I can say I don't think I've ever met any more attractive man in person in my life. Oh, and the chandeliers are nice. Not my style, but nice."

When Roman finally spoke, he certainly did have something to say.

Kate focused on the part about her friend's appearance, amused at how Roman had described him. Jasper certainly had been blessed in the looks department. From his thick, light brown, wavy hair to his crystal blue eyes and tanned, chiseled face, he was a knockout from the top down. And below the neck was pretty damn nice too. Never someone who had to worry about his weight, he kept in top physical shape and it showed. The fact that he could afford to dress well in the finest designers only accentuated what he'd been born with.

That Roman had chosen to mention his looks told Kate he still harbored some jealousy about her and Jasper, so she quickly moved to quash that once more. Taking his hand in hers, she brought it to her lips and kissed his knuckles. "He definitely is good looking. No wonder everyone in town can't wait to sleep with him. That and the money, of course. But not me, and he has no feelings for me that way either."

Roman smiled and gave her hand a squeeze. "You sure, Katybird?"

"Yes, and I think that sounds very strange coming from you. You're more of a Kate kind of guy, don't you think?"

He thought about the question for a moment and nodded. "I think you're right, Kate."

She wanted to lean over and give him a kiss to show him he had nothing to worry about, but at that moment Jasper returned with her white wine, his cognac, and a glass of water for Roman. He set each one down on the table in front of each of them.

"You should have something for when I make the toast."

They lifted their glasses in the air, and Jasper said, "To my dearest and oldest friend, who I suspect has gotten herself in deep this time. All the best!"

As the three of them clinked glasses and the two men around her took a drink, Kate wondered if his toast referred to the trouble she'd gotten into or her feelings for Roman. Jasper always had seemed to have a sixth sense about that kind of thing.

He sat down in the brown leather club chair

to their right and smiled. "So, guess whose picture I saw on the news this morning. How about you tell me what's going on?"

"It's better you don't know, to be honest."

Jasper shook his head and frowned. "Oh, Katybird, I hope you're being careful."

She patted Roman's arm. "Not to worry. Roman here is protecting me, so I'm in the best hands possible."

"I can definitely see you're in good hands. My question is, what did you get yourself into and why do you want to get into the governor's campaign headquarters?"

Kate turned to look at Roman as if to ask if she could tell her friend everything, and he nodded, giving his silent okay. Turning back to face Jasper, she gave him the condensed version of the whole ugly thing that had happened to her since she found out about Jonas's death.

"Well, I don't know what they're saying on TV, but Jonas and one of his clients is dead. At first, I thought the cops in town here had something to do with it because he'd warned me if anything happened to him to not trust the police. But now we think it's much bigger than just the New Orleans PD. We think whatever this case was that Jonas was working on with his client, it goes all the way up to the governor's office. That's why I need to get into his campaign office in town so I can look for some proof that we're right."

"I did see that they said Jonas had been murdered. They're looking for you as a suspect, Katybird. I didn't catch any more than that, but this is big. Are you ready for what could happen if you do find proof? Because that will be stumbling into one of the biggest hornet's nests you ever saw. Politics is an ugly business to start with, but in this state? It's downright cutthroat, honey. Trust me. I know. And not just from a hundred years ago either. These people play for keeps."

Kate swallowed hard and tried to keep a calm look on her face while her insides began to shake. Until that moment, everything had seemed almost too surreal, too bizarre to really grasp. Now that her oldest friend in the city and a man who knew many dangerous people in high places was lecturing her on how terrifying her situation was, she didn't know if she could go through with all this.

As all these thoughts tore through her brain, Roman reached down and took her hand in his, calming her instantly. He didn't say a word, but he didn't have to. Just knowing he would be by her side made her feel brave.

"So can you get us into the campaign office?" Roman asked in a low voice that showed no hint of fear or concern.

Jasper nodded. "Yeah. I can do that, but I hope you two know what you're doing. This is the deep end of the pool. I just need one thing from you before I do."

"Name it," Roman said without missing a beat.

Kate wondered what Jasper could want. He had more than enough money and influence. He literally wanted for nothing. So what could he possible ask for from Roman?

His face grew more serious than she'd ever seen him look. With a slight frown that frightened her, he said, "Take care of her. She won't admit it, but she needs it. I'll only help you two if you promise you won't let her get hurt."

Roman squeezed her hand and answered, "I swear on my life I'll protect her."

Never before had Kate believed something without a shadow of a doubt, but she believed him. He'd shown her every day since they met that he'd do just as he promised to protect her.

CHAPTER TWENTY-ONE

AT JUST AFTER eleven-thirty, Roman followed behind Kate and her friend Jasper as they made their way through the streets of New Orleans toward the governor's re-election campaign headquarters. He led them through back alleys and side streets for what felt like nearly an hour until they reached the plain looking storefront on a street Roman had never heard of.

He leaned forward and tapped Kate on the shoulder. "The governor has his re-election headquarters in New Orleans here?"

She shrugged. "Maybe all the prime real estate was taken? I don't know. I've never been in this section of town before."

Roman looked up at the street sign on a nearby pole. Clio Street. That didn't help much.

The storefront looked like nothing special. Just a few empty windows with a single red, white, and blue poster propped up in the corner of one of them that said RE-ELECT WILLIAMS FOR GOVERNOR. This was really where the governor of this state had his campaign headquarters in one of the biggest cities in Louisiana?

Unsure if trusting Jasper had been a good idea, he reached for Kate's hand and pulled her back toward him. In her ear, he whispered, "Something's not right here, Kate. This doesn't look like where a campaign office for the governor would be. I'm getting a bad vibe."

Smiling up at him, she sweetly patted him on the chest. "Trust me. If Jasper says this is the place, then this is the place. We're in good hands."

Just then, Jasper turned to face the two of them and pulled a silver key out of his shirt pocket. "Anyone interested in a little breaking and entering?"

Kate eagerly joined him as he opened the door, but Roman hung back a moment. He had a bad feeling about this guy. He was too clever, too funny for his taste.

Or maybe it was the jealousy. Kate hadn't been wrong about that. Never one for feeling jealous, he'd been nothing short of consumed by the emotion since he heard her tell Jasper on the phone that she loved him.

The guy had gotten them into this place, though, and now that Roman looked inside after they'd turned on a light, he had to admit it had all the makings of a campaign office. As far as he could tell, it looked like where a candidate's campaign could be run. It had chairs and metal desks, and the partitions made it look like any office he'd ever seen.

What he didn't see was a computer, though.

"Roman, close the door and come in," Kate said in a loud whisper from the back of the room.

He followed her voice in the dim light and found her and Jasper huddled over a laptop computer that looked like it had seen better days. Jasper's fingers typed away on the old keyboard, making him look like he knew what he was doing.

Not caring if he heard, Roman asked Kate, "What? Is he a hacker too?"

Jasper stopped typing for a moment and looked up, flashing him a cocky smile. "No. I just know what to ask for when I fuck someone. I could only get my girl to give me the passwords to get into the computer. After that, I can't help you. She did say, though, that the governor's people keep everything on here. Let's hope it's something you need."

Kate looked at him with a side glance he knew meant he'd said the wrong thing by questioning her friend, but Roman didn't care. His gut still said something was off about this whole thing with Jasper. The sooner they got what they came for and got the hell out of there, the better.

With one final tap on the keys, Jasper stood

up and announced, "Okay, girls and boys. I got you in, and now I'm out of here."

While Kate thanked him profusely and gave him a hug, Roman wondered just how far he'd gotten them. Walking around the desk, he saw on the monitor screen a sign he might have been wrong about Jasper. Right there in front of him were listed all the files contained on that desktop.

"Hey, is this the only computer here?" Roman asked as Jasper began to head toward the door to leave.

Looking around the room, he answered, "As far as I can see. I didn't ask my bedmate how many there would be. I just asked her how to get into the computers at the headquarters here. I've done that, so now I'm gone. Remember what you promised me. I'd suggest you two get out of here the minute you find what you're looking for."

Roman got to work as Jasper closed the front door behind him. With Kate standing by his side, he began to copy the files to the jump drive she'd taken from Jonas Flynn's desk in their last midnight caper to someone's office. As the files copied, he called Xavier.

"I'm sending you everything I can find that might help you figure out who's behind this. It might be a longshot, but it's worth a try."

"Great! What are you sending me?" Xavier asked.

"Files from the governor's campaign office," Roman said flatly, struggling to keep his voice even as his heart beat wildly in his chest at the excitement of what Xavier might find in the files.

"Holy fuck! Seriously? I'm not even going to ask how you got those files, Roman. You can save that for the drink I'm buying you when you get your ass back here."

The last of the files finished transferring to the jump drive, so Roman began sending them to Xavier. "If I get back. I have to go, but I hope to God you can figure out who is behind this from those files."

"They're starting to come in. Okay, stay safe down there. I'll let Nick and Persephone know what's up."

Roman pressed END and silently said a prayer that he would find something to help them in those damn files. Quickly, he turned off the laptop and slammed it shut, more than ready to get out of that office.

"Did he get them all?" Kate asked as Roman pushed her toward the door.

"Yeah. We have to go. Now."

Just as they got to the front door, she turned in his hold and rushed toward the light switch on the back wall. "Wait! The lights! We don't want anyone to see us coming out of here."

Roman watched her flick the switch and then

turn back to come toward him, but in the dark, he suddenly saw a shadow come up next to her and then a second one. She cried out as one of them grabbed her, and Roman rushed toward them. Before he could reach her, a fist slammed into his jaw, sending him reeling backward. A second later, he got his bearings and charged the man, sending him over a desk onto the floor. He got a few punches in before something hit him in the back of the head.

Before he blacked out, he heard Kate scream his name, but he couldn't reach her. As he faded into unconsciousness, he heard one of the men say, "We need to take them to the hangar."

And then he heard nothing.

ROMAN'S EYES SLOWLY fluttered open, and instantly, his head began to throb. He moved to lift his hand to touch where he'd been hit on the back of the head, but he couldn't move his arms. Struggling to see because everything in front of him appeared grey and blurry, he strained to focus on why he was immobile.

He sat on a hard, concrete floor with a rope holding his wrists tightly behind his back. A second later, he tried to move his ankles and found them bound also. As his eyesight cleared, he strained to make out where he was. He vaguely remembered hearing someone say they needed to go to the hangar, and now as he scanned the open space around him, he saw that's exactly where he'd been taken.

An airplane hangar.

Roman turned his head left and right to look for Kate, but he couldn't see her anywhere. Panicked they'd taken her somewhere else, he called out her name.

"Kate! Where are you? Can you hear me?"

Behind him, he heard a noise that sounded like her. He tried to see where she was, but he couldn't turn far enough.

"Kate! Talk to me! I can't see you," he called out.

"Roman? I can't see you either," she said in a tiny voice.

A mixture of dread and rage surged within him. Had they hurt her? Is that why she sounded so small and frail?

"I'm right here, Kate. Don't worry. I'm right here. You're not alone."

"I can hear you and you sound so close, but I can't see you," she said louder now, and he figured out they were both bound on the floor near one another.

"I'm behind you, I think. Are your hands and feet tied?"

She made a small grunting noise and then

answered, "Yes. My hands are tied behind my back. Oh God, my shoulders hurt so much."

Roman extended his fingers as far as they could reach, but he couldn't touch hers. She was just too far away. He couldn't give up, though. He had to find some way to get to her and then get them out of there.

"Where are we?" she asked, her voice laced with fear that struck directly at his heart.

"We're in an airplane hangar at an airport somewhere."

He listened for sounds outside and heard nothing. It had to be a small, local airport or airstrip. "I'm not thinking a major airport, though. There's no noise, no people around working on planes."

Without saying it, he knew what that meant. They weren't in New Orleans anymore.

The heavy sound of a large metal door opening alerted him to someone coming, so he quickly told Kate, "Don't say a thing. Don't answer whatever questions you're asked. Understand?"

She answered, her voice trembling, "Okay, I won't say a thing. Are we going to be okay, Roman?"

His heart tightened in his chest at the sound of her fear. He needed to make her feel like everything would be okay.

Even if he didn't know if it would be.

"I promised you I would protect you. I know things look bad, but trust me, okay? Just don't tell them anything. And no matter what you hear me say or what they do to me, don't tell them a thing. Promise me, Kate."

"I promise. I won't."

"It'll be okay. We'll be out of here soon and then we can go anywhere you want. Okay? We can go back to Butcher's and I'll make you dinner this time."

"I'm scared, Roman."

Her confession tore at him, and he silently swore to God he'd get her out of there safe and sound. Heavy footsteps grew closer and closer until finally Roman saw a man appear next to him. A hulking giant of a person, he stood so tall that Roman had to crane his neck to look up at his face. As soon as he did, he wished he hadn't. Scarred and pockmarked, it sent a chill down his spine. He just hoped Kate didn't look at him.

The man said nothing for so long Roman began to wonder if he just planned to kill them outright and not even bother to ask any questions. In all reality, they likely didn't need to ask them much. They had Jonas's laptop and jump drive, and those contained all the information they'd need about what he and Kate had been up to.

Finally, the ugly man said in a deep voice that

matched his giant size perfectly, "Why were you at the governor's headquarters?"

Behind him, he heard Kate's sharp intake of breath and knew she must be terrified. He needed to make her think everything would be fine.

"I'm not talking to you or anyone else until your boss gets here."

The man's eyes flew open wide in rage, and a moment later, his large, bulbous fist came flying down and crashed into the side of Roman's face. His head ricocheted back and then came forward to hang as blood began to leak from his mouth.

"Once more, smartass. Why were you at the governor's headquarters?"

Roman pressed his lips closed, tasting the metallic tang of blood as it pooled on his tongue. He wasn't going to tell this bastard anything. If he planned on beating him to death, he was going to do it if he answered or not.

Kate sobbed behind him, whimpering, "Roman, are you okay? Are you hurt?"

He opened his mouth to answer her and blood poured out onto his chest. She asked him again if he was okay, and that set the big lug off. But instead of hitting Roman again, this time he punched Kate. She cried out in pain, and in his mind, Roman swore to God once he got loose from his ropes, he'd kill that motherfucker for what he did to her.

"Your girlfriend doesn't take a punch as well as you do," the man said with a hearty chuckle, taunting him.

"Nice. Hitting women. What's next? Kicking babies? You're a real man," Kate said behind him.

"Kate!" Roman barked, hoping she'd understand she needed to keep her mouth shut.

He looked up to see the man cocking his arm back and watched in horror knowing he couldn't do anything to stop him. He'd been tugging at the ropes since he woke up, but he was nowhere close to getting free in time to stop this thug from beating on Kate for what she'd said.

Better for him to take the hit than her.

"I know her mouth makes you want to hit her, but I'm the one who thinks you're a Grade A asshole. We'd see if you're as big a pussy as I think if I wasn't tied up and unable to hit back. My guess is you'd still be a candy ass with an ugly face to boot."

That did it. The man's attention returned to Roman, and a few seconds later, he took out his rage on his face with a series of punches that left him dazed and with blood pouring out of his mouth and nose and some nasty kicks to his ribs that made him feel like he'd throw up at any second. His eye began to swell shut, so he could only see from the left side, but Kate had been spared.

At least for the moment.

The sound of another set of footsteps walking across the concrete floor toward them made him look up, but he couldn't see who had come over. "Kate, if it's another one like this guy, don't speak."

"It's not," she said with tears in her words.

"Who is it?"

She hesitated at first and then said in a terrified voice, "It's the governor."

Roman lifted his head and through his one eye that hadn't swelled shut, he saw a man standing there next to them. Tall and thin, his jet black hair sat slicked back and shiny on his head. His long face looked tight, the cheekbones straining against the skin to give him a painful, angular appearance. Everything about this man reminded Roman of a snake.

Ice cold and slick.

"So these are the two found snooping around my campaign office," he said in a flinty tone, an implicit threat hanging off each syllable.

Roman sat silently and hoped Kate would remain quiet too. Now was the time to listen.

"Your boss and that whistleblower didn't know when to stop. It seems you two don't either. I do want to thank you for the laptop and drive, though. One last loose thread that I don't have to worry about anymore. Once Melvin gets his hands on you two, you'll be taken care of too."

All while he spoke, Roman worked to keep the governor's focus on his face while he twisted and turned his wrists to loosen the ropes holding him. He stared into the man's eyes and saw pure evil, but he refused to look away, hoping to distract him long enough to let him get free.

The governor turned his head and looked down at Kate. "All I want to know is who got you into my New Orleans office. Answer that and I promise you and your friend will go quickly."

Roman closed his eyes and listened to hear what Kate would say, but she stayed quiet, for once. The governor then asked Roman the same thing and made the same promise to him, but he simply shook his head. If he was going to die, he sure as hell wasn't going to do it on some poor soul's back.

Their refusal to tell him what he wanted to know infuriated him, and he stormed away to go find Melvin. Roman knew this was their last chance to get free.

He whispered to Kate, "Don't worry. I won't let them kill you."

"You aren't going to be able to stop them. They're going to kill both of us, Roman," she sobbed.

He continued to fumble around with the ropes tying his wrists until they were as loose as he could get them. "Trust me. I'm going to get us out of this."

Curling up into a ball, he pulled his hands down behind his legs and around his feet. Now he just needed to find something to cut the ropes so he could be free. Quickly scanning the area around him, he saw a screw coming out of a pole a few feet away. Inching over on his stomach, he frantically rubbed the ropes over the screw as he watched for that big guy to return. He tore through the rope enough to tug his hands free and then freed his ankles.

"How? Roman, tell me. Where did you go?"

Hurrying back to where he'd sat on the floor, he whispered to Kate, "I won't let them kill us. I just need you to trust me."

Two men came walking toward them and announced that they were going to be moved. Taking what he saw as the only chance to get free, Roman jumped up, picked up a nearby chair and hit the one of them closer to him with it, knocking him out. He grabbed the man's gun, but Melvin pointed his gun at Kate.

Roman took aim and shot him, but before he went down, he got off one shot. Roman watched as Kate contracted on the floor in the lifeless heap. Rushing over to her, he saw the gunshot wound to her shoulder. She needed help right now. Untying her wrists and ankles, he kissed her as his mind raced with how he'd save her. He needed to get her out of that place. He grabbed one of the men's phones from his pocket and then lifted her into his arms to carry her out of the hangar.

Calling the Project Artemis compound, he said quickly into the phone, "I need assistance. The client is down. Kate has been shot."

Nick asked, "Where?"

Roman looked around and saw a sign that said Lafayette. "We're at a hangar, but I don't think we're still in New Orleans. I see a sign with the word Lafayette. Find out if there's a local airport near there. It's definitely small, Nick."

Nick told him, "Okay, we'll find you. We'll have someone there in less than thirty minutes. Hang tight. We're coming."

Roman set her down on the ground and saw blood coming from her shoulder. Bending over, he kissed her lips and whispered against them, "Stay with me, Kate. You're going to be okay. I'm right here with you."

She looked up at him and gave him a tiny smile. "I'm sorry, Roman. You were right. I'm sorry."

He kissed her again and pulled her to him. "No apologies needed. We're going to be fine. Don't leave me, Kate. I love you. I can't let you leave me."

Her eyes began to close as she mumbled,

"Always telling me what to do. I think I've grown to love that."

She stopped talking and her head dropped onto his chest. Panic rushed through him as the reality that Nick might not get someone there in time to save her settled into his head. She couldn't die. She couldn't.

"Kate! Don't leave me, Kate!"

He watched for her to react, but her eyes remained closed. He couldn't lose her now. Not now that he finally found her and wanted to spend the rest of his life with her.

Chapter Twenty-Two

KATE SLOWLY OPENED her eyes, still groggy from sleeping and unsure if she'd just had the most vivid nightmare ever. Had she been beaten? Slowly, she came alive again, and the details began to get hazy.

Looking around the room, she instantly knew she didn't recognize it. Her bedroom in her apartment had blue walls. She knew this because she remembered how much time she'd taken picking out that pale blue color at the home improvement store. She painted those walls herself on a long Fourth of July holiday weekend after her last breakup made her decide to completely change the room to rid herself of every last remnant of that boyfriend.

The walls surrounding her now were beige. No, this was definitely not her bedroom at home. Bits and pieces of other rooms she thought she knew flitted through her mind. A dive motel room with a hideous green and brown bedspread. When had she been there? A much nicer hotel room and a bed she didn't fear sleeping in. A million dollar home out by the lake.

Scenes began forming in her head, like parts of a story she should know. Then the heartbreaking truth came rushing forward into her consciousness. Jonas was dead. Samuel Darnell, his client he refused to tell her about, was also dead. How? Who had done that?

She didn't have the answers, but she needed to find them.

A twinge in her shoulder made her wince, but she knew her body always ached when she spent too long in bed and she had no idea how long she'd been asleep in this strange place. She needed to get up and figure out where the hell she was. Sitting up, she felt the twinge instantly grow to a red-hot shot of pain that stabbed through her shoulder and took her breath away.

"Ohhhh," she groaned as she eased back down onto the bed.

"Kate? Are you awake?" a familiar voice asked from beside her.

She turned her head to see who had spoken and saw Roman. A jolt of recognition at seeing his face brought everything back to her, and she nearly became overwhelmed by the reality of what had happened.

"Where am I? Did I get shot? What happened, Roman?" she asked as she reached out for the comfort of his hand.

His dark eyes filled with happiness, and he smiled as he took her hand in his. Standing, he hurried to her side and sat down on the edge of the bed with her.

"I'm so happy you're okay. The doctor said he got the bullet out, so now you just need to take it easy and rest. Whatever you need, just tell me and I'll get it for you so you don't have to move out of this bed."

He sounded so happy and so hopeful that she hated having to bring him down to earth with her questions, but she needed to know the answers. "Where am I, Roman?"

"We're at the place where I live. We brought you here after you were shot."

"Where is the place you live?" she asked, sure only that he didn't mean anywhere in New Orleans.

"Virginia. We're at the Project Artemis estate. Specifically, we're in the hospital wing of the estate," he said with a tender smile.

"Where you live has a hospital wing?" Kate asked in amazement.

He'd told her a little about the group he worked with, but he hadn't mentioned it had enough money to own an estate and one with a hospital wing. Who had that kind of money? Did he work for some reclusive billionaire or something? Images of masked superheroes floated through her mind, making her smile.

"Yes. Persephone and Nick, the two people who run Project Artemis, found out we needed one after a few of us came back from assignments pretty banged up," Roman explained casually, as if every workplace needed a hospital on site to fix up their employees.

"What kind of people do you work for, Roman?"

He brought her hand to his lips to kiss and smiled. "The best kind. They rushed you to a hospital and then when you were safe to transport, they brought you here so you can recuperate in somewhere nicer than a hospital ward. As soon as you're well enough, they told me we could use one of the outer houses on the estate for as long as we want."

Kate glanced over at her shoulder and saw it bandaged up. Wincing, she remembered the pain she felt right before she passed out. "I remember getting shot but nothing after that until I woke up here."

"Don't think about it. You're safe now."

Whatever else she felt, she knew he'd keep his word. He always had from the moment he walked into that motel room at the Bayou. Now, as she slowly pieced everything together, she couldn't believe that out of everything, he'd stayed true to her in all he'd promised.

Out of the corner of her eye, Kate saw the bedroom door open and a gorgeous woman with long brown hair and big brown eyes came into the room. Roman stood, still holding her hand, and introduced the woman.

"Kate, this is Persephone Gilmore, the owner of Project Artemis and the estate. Persephone, this is Kate Sheridan."

So this was the reclusive billionaire. Kate had imagined her as a man and more imposing. Instead, Persephone Gilmore physically wasn't much more than a slip of a thing with model looks who carried herself like she'd had money every day of her life.

Not that Kate held that against her. She just knew old money when she saw it standing in front of her.

"How are you doing, Kate? You gave Roman here a good scare back there in that hangar. I'm just glad that we were able to get you the help you needed and here so you can be comfortable as you recuperate. Is there anything you need?" Persephone asked as she walked over to the dresser to pick up the remote control for the TV.

"I don't think so," Kate answered as she watched her move around to the side of the bed where Roman sat next to her.

"Well, anything you need, anything at all,

please don't hesitate to ask."

Persephone turned on the TV, and as the picture came into focus, she said, "I thought you two would like to see this."

Kate glanced over at Roman for some explanation, but he shook his head, clearly not having any information about what Persephone meant. Holding hands, they watched as Governor Williams was led out of the state capitol at Baton Rouge by federal marshalls. Reporters swarmed as he was escorted down the stairs and into a waiting black sedan that sped away as the newscaster explained he would be indicted on an array of charges, including corruption, fraud, conspiracy to commit murder, and attempted murder. In addition, the news reported, other charges may be pending upon completion of the investigation into crimes the governor's office had been committing for years.

Not exactly shocked, still Kate couldn't believe that finally the truth had started to come out. She turned to look at Roman and sighed, happy to know they'd helped reveal the governor's crimes.

"So Jonas was right all along? He just didn't have all the details," she said sadly, hating the governor for what he'd done to Jonas and Samuel.

Persephone nodded as she switched off the TV. "He was closer than he even knew. I suspect when Governor Williams realized he figured out enough of the story to endanger the governor's future, which was rumored might involve a run for president someday, he had him and his client killed."

Shaking his head, Roman asked, "So all of this revolved around a whistleblower thinking the state police were crooked because of Williams?"

"Oh, no. It's far more than that."

"What do you mean?" Kate asked, confused. If Jonas had been right all along, how was this not a case of police corruption involving the governor?

Persephone walked to the foot of Kate's bed and set the remote back on the dresser as she began to explain the whole sordid tale. "In 2007, two years after Hurricane Katrina, a twenty-five year old woman named Diana Preston died in a Lafayette, Louisiana apartment in a building rebuilt with federal money given to the owner of the building, a man named Joseph Battier. This Joseph Battier was a friend of the mayor of Lafayette at that time, Charles Williams, who helped him get the federal money. In 2008, Charles Williams ran for state senate and won. But when he was mayor of Lafayette, he and a few of his friends, including Joseph Battier, took federal money to rebuild properties while they cut corners, which led to Diana Preston's death. He continued to funnel money to his cronies even after he went to Baton Rouge."

"Did he and Battier know the shoddy work on the apartment had been responsible for the woman's death?" Roman asked.

"From all Xavier has been able to find out, yes, they did. In 2012, Williams was elected governor, and as Governor Williams, he helped his friends in Lafayette when Diana Preston's estate sued Joseph Battier. He sent the state police to intimidate people involved in the case, including Diana's neighbor who witnessed the shoddy construction in her apartment and moved out right after her death and her friend who had been staying with her at the time of her death. Those initials you found in your boss's files were those of the officers involved. That neighbor was your boss's client, Kate, Samuel Darnell. It seems when he first approached Jonas Flynn, he thought it was a police harassment case. It was only when Jonas began doing some digging that he found out that the state police intimidation was just the tip of the iceberg."

Kate stared at Persephone in stunned amazement. Never in her wildest dreams did she believe Jonas had stumbled up a conspiracy like the one she'd just heard. He was just a local personal injury attorney, and he'd succeeded in scaring the governor himself so much that he had him and Samuel killed. She hung her head as tears filled her eyes, sad that they'd paid the ultimate price simply because Jonas had wanted to know the truth.

"I want you to know I think you're a very brave woman, Kate. Roman's told me all about what you two did, and while I never like to see any client of ours get hurt, I'm honored to meet you."

Lifting her head, Kate dried her eyes. "Thanks. I don't feel brave. I just wanted to find out who had killed Jonas and Samuel and try not to die in the process. All the bravery belonged to Roman."

"Your boss may have started all of this, but it's because of you and Roman that the governor's corruption has been uncovered. I made sure to let the lieutenant governor know that when I presented him with what we found."

Roman added, "And Xavier. Don't forget him."

Persephone smiled. "I'm sure he won't let me. Well, rest up and don't worry about a thing."

Before she left, Persephone looked over at Roman, and Kate noticed how her expression changed from the happy one she'd worn just a moment ago to one that seemed to show worry when she looked at him. He'd done his job, so why would she not be happy with him?

Alone with Roman, she said, "It looks like you

fulfilled your mission, I guess. Thank you for everything you did. You saved my life."

He kissed her softly on the lips and leaned back to look at her. "I didn't have a choice, and it wasn't because of the mission."

"It wasn't?"

He shook his head. "No. I love you, Kate."

Before she told him how she felt about him, she needed to know about his relationship with Persephone. "That woman is your boss? She didn't look too happy with you. Why? Does she blame you for my getting shot? Because I'm more than happy to tell her how much you did for me. Unless it's something else."

"I think it might be. I think she knows how I feel about you."

"Is there a problem with that?" Kate asked, worried he was unhappy about Persephone knowing how he felt about her. Was there something between Roman and his boss?

"Not with me."

Kate searched Roman's dark eyes desperate for the answer she wanted to hear. "Are you sure? I mean, if there's something I should know, tell me. Don't feel like you have to lie to me to save my feelings because I was shot. I'd rather know the truth, Roman."

For a moment, he seemed confused and then he smiled broadly, shaking his head. "Oh, you think Persephone and I are together? No way. She and Nick started all this together after something similar to what happened to you happened to her. There's nothing between us except she's my boss."

"Oh."

Roman kissed her again and whispered against her lips, "Let's try that again. I love you, Kate."

"I love you, Roman," she answered back, happy but unsure what the future held. "So what happens now?"

He pressed his forehead to hers and smiled. "I don't know, but whatever happens, it's going to be the two of us together."

CHAPTER TWENTY-THREE

ROMAN WALKED INTO the very room where he'd first met Nick and Persephone and the rest of the men who would join Project Artemis with him. He'd attended weekly meetings in that room whenever he wasn't out on assignment, but today's meeting would be different from those others because his part in the group was about to change.

The rest of the group, except for Dax and Marius who were out on assignments, walked in and took their usual seats on the couches and chairs while he remained standing near the window where he always positioned himself whenever they got together. He'd never truly become friends with any of the others, preferring to keep to himself. But like every one of them, he remained committed to the cause he'd signed up for that night when Persephone told them what she wanted Project Artemis to be.

Nick walked in alone and made his way over to where Roman stood. They shook hands as they did each time they met. Nick was that kind of guy.

"So Persephone tells me Kate is doing well. I would have stopped over at the carriage house, but I didn't want to interrupt anything," he said with a sly grin.

"She's up and around again, so feel free to stop over," Roman said with a chuckle. "We'd love to have you and Persephone over for dinner some night."

His eyes lit up at the offer. "Sounds good! Persephone and I never go out much anymore. I should be able to pry her away from her desk to at least get her to cross the grounds to do dinner with friends."

Roman contained his surprise at Nick's use of the word friends since he'd always kept so much to himself that he didn't think he had any real friends at the estate. Acquaintances, sure. But not friends.

"You know, Roman, we do think of you as a friend. I know you've been an employee, but Persephone and I consider each and every one of you more than that. You signed on to something that had never existed in this form before. You took a chance and believed in what we were trying to do here. We've never forgotten that."

"Thanks, Nick. That means a lot to me. You guys have been incredible letting Kate and me stay out at the carriage house. We really appreciate it."

Just then, Persephone walked into the room. Nick patted Roman on the shoulder and smiled. "Time to get to work. I think she has some announcement to make today."

He walked away, and Roman moved a step into the center of the room to hear what she had to say. The rest of the men stopped talking and turned their attention to the lone woman who stood behind the chair at the opposite side of the room.

"Today's meeting will be short and sweet. When you all started with Project Artemis, you signed an agreement saying you would be retired from the company if at any point you were no longer unattached. Nick and I initially thought that was for the best, but I've had second thoughts about that recently. So from today onward, you may choose to remain with us even if you find yourself personally involved. Each situation will be handled on a case by case basis, so it might mean your position in the company changes, but you will no longer be retired because of personal issues. Thank you."

Xavier raised his hand and waited for Persephone to call on him. "This isn't school, X. You can just ask me whatever you need to."

Grinning, he looked over at Roman and then back at her. "Yeah. Is this because Roman finally decided being alone sucked and now has a girlfriend? Inquiring minds want to know."

The rest of the group laughed and glanced at Roman as Persephone rolled her eyes and Nick stifled his own chuckle at Xavier's complete lack of tact. As much as Roman wanted to slug him, he had helped solve his case, so he hung back. He'd get him later.

"At least we'll never have to worry about losing you, X," Persephone said with a wink. "Roman, when you can, please come see me," she added before turning on her heels and walking out.

As Xavier tried to convince everyone in the room that he did fine with the ladies and any woman would be happy to be with him, Roman followed Nick to the office he shared with her and sat down in front of her desk.

"You wanted to see me?"

She smiled as she sat down in her chair and nudged it up to her desk. "I didn't expect you to come see me now. I figured you'd want to get back to Kate. She's still improving?"

He nodded, happy to report the good news. "Yeah, she's doing great. She's already fighting me on everything I suggest, which is typical Kate."

"Good. Well, you heard my announcement. As much as X likes to be a joker, it was in response to your situation with Kate. Nick and I have talked about your position here, and we don't want to lose you."

Roman looked across the desk at her in confusion. "I'm not sure I can still do the job you hired me for, Persephone. I wouldn't feel right leaving Kate to go protect other women."

"I understand. I wouldn't be comfortable with Nick doing that for another woman. That's why we'd like you to stay on and work with us here. You wouldn't have to leave on assignments, and if you chose to, you could continue living in the carriage house. Project Artemis means the world to me, and I want the best people working on what we do for women who need our help. You've been committed from the day you signed on with us. I just want to give you the chance to keep working on a cause you believe in."

Roman couldn't deny he cared about what they did at Project Artemis. His life had been dedicated to protecting people, and the women he and his fellow members of the group helped in each case needed them. He didn't know if he was ready to walk away from that, even though he now had someone he loved and cared for at home for the first time.

"Can I think about it? I want to speak to Kate about this before I make any decisions."

Persephone smiled. "I thought you would, so take your time and talk it over with her. When you're ready to make a decision, let us know. We'll be here."

ROMAN FOUND KATE making the bed one handed, her other arm still in a sling after her surgery weeks before. Sneaking up on her, he wrapped his arms around her waist and nuzzled his lips against her neck.

"I got some interesting news at the meeting today."

She giggled from the feel of his new beard growth against her skin and turned in his hold. Smiling up at him, she kissed him on the lips.

"Oh yeah? What's that?"

As soon as she finished saying that, the smile slid from her face. "Wait, did they fire you because of me?"

"No, no. The opposite actually. They offered to let me stay on and keep working for Project Artemis but not in my old job. I'd be working with Nick and Persephone here on the estate."

Kate's eyes opened wide. "Really? Are you going to do it?"

He pulled her into his arms and kissed her long and deep, loving the feel of her body against his. For so long, he'd been alone and thought he'd been happy that way. Now he had Kate in his life, and he couldn't imagine a day without her.

Whatever he ended up doing about his job,

they'd decide it together.

"That's for us to figure out. Until then, we can stay here or we can go wherever you want. I've saved up enough money to last three lifetimes. Whatever you want to do, we can do it."

Kate tilted her head back to look up at him and smiled. "I know what I want to do right now."

Roman swept her into his arms, careful not to hurt her shoulder still healing from the gunshot, and lay her down on the bed to kiss her. "Sorry you just made it, but I promise to make it after we're done."

"Promise?"

He smiled and nodded before kissing her again. He'd never broken a promise he made her yet, and he didn't plan on beginning the rest of their life together by starting now. As for when they'd get out of bed for him to make it, he couldn't say.

A day. Or two. Or whenever.

They'd figure that out together too, just like everything else between them.

LOOK FOR BEHIND THE SCENES, THE NEXT PROJECT ARTEMIS NOVEL, COMING SPRING 2018!

Alexis Marchand is one of the biggest movie stars in the world, loved by millions of fans around the globe. Her meteoric rise to fame has come with its fair share of heartache, but she's remained strong, thanks to those closest to her and their unfailing support. Life as a movie star is good.

Until one day a simple letter arrives and turns her world upside down. Now she lives in terror, afraid of that one fan who has taken it too far.

Hunter McKary knows something of movie stars because of his time as a LAPD detective. He thought he left those days behind him, but when he's sent to find out who's stalking the beautiful blond actress the world adores, he grudgingly goes to New York, expecting to find a typical spoiled diva like those he met so many times before back in LA.

The woman he finds isn't anything like he expected, and a job he dreaded becomes something else entirely. But someone out there has different plans for Alexis.

ABOUT THE AUTHORS

K.M. Scott writes contemporary romance stories of sexy, intense, and unforgettable love. A New York Times and USA Today bestselling author, she's been in love with romance since reading her first romance novel in junior high (she was a very curious girl!). Under her Gabrielle Bisset name, she writes erotic paranormal and historical romance. She lives in Pennsylvania with a herd of animals and when she's not writing can be found reading or feeding her TV addiction.

Anina Collins has always loved a good mystery. From Agatha Christie's Hercule Poirot to Sir Arthur Conan Doyle's famous detective Sherlock Holmes to Dan Brown's intrepid Professor Robert Langdon, she's spent some of her favorite reading times with mystery novels. When she's not writing her favorite mystery couple, she can be found watching entirely too much Supernatural and dreaming about the beach.

Be sure to visit K.M.'s Facebook page at **facebook.com/kmscottauthor** for all the latest on her books, along with giveaways and other goodies! And to hear all the news on K.M. Scott books first, sign up for her newsletter today and be sure to visit her website at **www. kmscottbooks.com**

Visit Anina's Facebook page at **facebook.com/ Anina-Collins-429334270597293** for news about her books, along with giveaways and other fun stuff! Sign up for her newsletter today for exclusive news first! Visit her website at **aninacollins.com** for more details.

Books by K.M. Scott writing as Gabrielle Bisset:

Vampire Dreams Revamped (A Sons of Navarus Prequel)
Blood Avenged (Sons of Navarus #1)
Blood Betrayed (Sons of Navarus #2)
Longing (A Sons of Navarus Short Story)
Blood Spirit (Sons of Navarus #3)
The Deepest Cut (A Sons of Navarus Short Story)
Blood Prophecy (Sons of Navarus #4)
Blood Craving (Sons of Navarus #5)
Blood Eclipse (Sons of Navarus #6)
The Sons of Navarus Box Set #1
The Sons of Navarus Box Set #2

Stolen Destiny (Destined Ones Duology #1)
Destiny Redeemed (Destined Ones Duology #2)

Love's Master
Masquerade
The Victorian Erotic Romance Trilogy

Books by Anina Collins:

The Eleventh Hour (Poppy McGuire Mysteries #1)
After Hours (Poppy McGuire Mysteries #2)
Top of the Hour (Poppy McGuire Mysteries #3)
The Darkest Hour (Poppy McGuire Mysteries #4)
Happy Hour (Poppy McGuire Mysteries #5)
The Witching Hour (Poppy McGuire Mysteries #6)
The Finest Hour (Poppy McGuire Mysteries #7)